South of the Pier

A Murder Mystery

By

Janet Elizabeth Lynn

Print Edition

ISBN 978-1-53481630-5

1

Books by Janet Elizabeth Lynn

Murder Mysteries

South of the Pier

West of the Pier

East of the Pier

North of the Pier – *Winter 2013*

Cozy Mysteries

Eggnog

Crepes Suzettes

Charlotte Russe – *Summer 2013*

Dedication

To my wonderful husband, Bill, who has supported me throughout my many endeavors.

And to the wonderful people I have met on my travels.

Introduction

Welcome to <u>South of the Pier</u>. I got the idea for this book after a visit to Guatemala. This beautiful country of warm, loving people was riddled with illegal activity that preyed on their own indigenous people. What fueled the story was a chance encounter with an Interpol agent, and a charming man from Brussels who accompanied me on my trip home from a previous trip to Russia.

This is the first novel in a series of four murder mysteries. All the books are centered around the fictitious community of Hacienda Beach and branch out to far reaching areas.

I hope you enjoy this journey as much as I enjoyed writing it.

Author's Note

Additional background stories for each chapter will be marked with an § and can be found at the end of each chapter.

CHAPTER ONE

Palmer Railton peered out the small, wrought iron window of his front door. A familiar face greeted him as he opened the door.

"Well, this is a surpri..."

Two gunshots terminated his sentence. Palmer's eyes grew wide as the bullets burned into his chest. He grabbed for a potted tree and dragged it to the floor. He rolled onto his back choking on blood, gasping for air, desperate for some way to stay alive. Not tonight.

As Palmer's lifeless eyes stared up, the shooter pocketed the still smoking, nine millimeter automatic and paused for a moment flicking an empty ring box off the table before taking one last look at his face.

Hurried footsteps echoed against the flagstone surface of the courtyard. Faces appeared in the windows facing Palmer's open door as the shadow rushed past the burbling fountain into the night.

CRIME SCENE

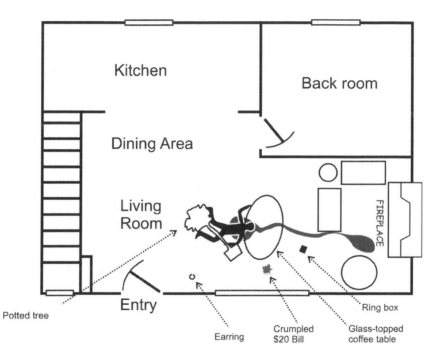

Kitchen

Back room

Dining Area

Living Room

FIREPLACE

Entry

Potted tree

Earring

Crumpled $20 Bill

Glass-topped coffee table

Ring box

CHAPTER TWO

The moon was rising in the east. Detective Marcello Prado got out of his unmarked Mercury Marauder. The sweet ocean air filled his head. A crowd of onlookers had already gathered around the stark crime scene tape that encircled the Spanish style apartment building. He ducked under the tape and walked up the steps through the tropical plants and trees that crowded the courtyard. The Police floodlights and a trickling fountain made the front door of apartment THREE look like a Hollywood premiere.

"Whatcha got, Jim?"

"Well, he's still warm."

The body of a man dressed in a yellow polo shirt and dark brown slacks laid face up on the parquet floor. Vacant black eyes stared at him through the glass top coffee table. Marcello scanned the room. He noticed a potted fichus tree on the floor across the man's legs. Blood had pooled under the table and flowed along the floor.

"Someone was in a hurry to get out of here." Marcello spun around as a petite brunette popped up from behind a chair. "Hello, Detective."

"Don't just pop up like that, you startled me. Who are you?"

"Sorry. I'm CS Investigator Kyra Dennis. I found a footprint in the blood by the fireplace."

"From the looks of things," Jim continued, "the shooting must've happened about two to three hours ago. Two shots to the chest, front entry. One probably in the center of his heart. No blood trail, so it happened here."

"Looks like Mr. Railton was a silent movie buff."

Jim stood, "Are you kidding? Those are movie posters of the greats from the Golden Age. That one is "Breaking the News", 1938 starring Maurice Chevalier and June Knight. I was in love with June from the first time I saw her on the screen. That one, "Escape in the Fog", 1945. Ah, Nina Foch another big screen sweetheart. Great mystery! And that one, "Christmas Holiday" 1944, first time I heard Irving Berlin's, "Always." We had it played at our wedding."

"So you're an old movie buff too?" Kyra added.

"They just don't make them like they use to. Jim crossed the room to examine a double poster display. "If these two posters are original, they are worth a small fortune at best. Metropolis, 1927, the movie all science fictions are based on. Look, 2001: A Space Odyssey, and Blade Runner too."

Marcello was listening carefully, "Can't be a motive for robbery, they're still here."

"If, in fact, they are originals," Jim added. "It could be."

"I'll check on it." Kyra held out the dead man's wallet. Detective Prado pulled an evidence bag out of his pocket.

She nodded toward the body, "The victim is a Palmer Railton - looks like he was ready to leave on a trip. Luggage and airline tickets to D.C. are on the sofa."

Marcello figured her for a newbie with the crime lab. She was too precise and enthusiastic for a seasoned investigator.

"Someone didn't want him to leave." Marcello looked at the body. "Can you do something with his eyes, Jim? I'm getting creeped out."

"Looks like a nine millimeter," Jim held up an empty shell casing. "I would have thought you'd be used to stuff like this, Prado."

"Sorry to disappoint you, but I never get used to people hurting each other."

Kyra went back to take photos of items scattered across the floor. There was a crumpled twenty dollar bill, an empty velvet ring box and one gaudy cloisonné earring.

"A woman was definitely here." She shook her head as she examined the earring and placed it into its own evidence envelope. "Whoever it was, they have awful taste. I hope I can get some DNA. Clip-ons aren't as easy to get DNA as pierced earrings. But maybe I can lift a print."

"Why do you women hang stuff from their ears in the first place?" Marcello asked. "I mean, whose idea was that?"

Kyra looked up from the viewfinder in her camera, "Probably some man. The same guy who came up with stilettos." She smiled, "Actually earrings are intended to frame a woman's face - y'know, to take a guy's attention away from our chest."

"Detective," their exchange was disturbed by a uniformed officer, accompanied by a beautiful brunette with sad eyes.

"This lady has something to say you may want to hear."

"I'm Lisa. I was a friend of Palmer." Tears rolled down her face. "I can't believe someone would do this."

Marcello turned his attention to Lisa, "Were you two dating?"

"Who me? Oh no. I live two doors down. He has a lady friend, Camille Brewster." She pointed through the doorway to a framed photograph on Palmer's mantle. "She was here yesterday. They're very close. I don't believe he had any relatives except for Camille and her family. She's my friend, too. Her son and mine have play dates. I have her phone number. I just know she'll be devastated, so please go easy on her."

9

"Here's her address. She lives in L.A." Lisa glanced over his shoulder and saw someone she knew.

"There's a guy standing behind you across the courtyard. I think you should talk to him. His name's Ricky, and he was real tight with Palmer."

Ricky saw them looking at him and turned to leave.

"Hey, stop right there." An officer grabbed his arm.

Ricky glared back at Lisa as he was escorted to Detective Prado. "You live around here?"

"Interesting you think someone like me could afford a place like this," avoiding eye contact with Marcello.

Marcello stared at him.

"No, I do not live here."

"People say otherwise. I'll ask you again, do you live around here?"

"Now Detective, my man, you didn't ask me if I live around here. You asked...

The officer slapped him in the back of his head. "Answer the Detective."

"Very well. I was just walking down the street and saw the crowd."

"You know Mr. Railton?"

"I do." His hands were quivering and his eyes bloodshot. "In fact, I was talking to a fine gentleman just before your people grabbed me and he feels this was premeditated. Can you imagine? In a high class place like this."

"We need to take you downtown for a few questions and a drug test," Marcello nodded to the officer.

Ricky yelled as the officer took him in the police car. "Oh I see. You have nothing to do but harass innocent people out of a quiet evening stroll on this lovely night..."

"I'm going to need to see the autopsy report before we contact..." he glanced at his scribbled note, "Ms Brewster."

"Detective," Kyra interrupted, "Why should we wait? If it were me, I'd want to know ASAP. Besides, what if she bails?"

"Just follow procedures," he snapped. Kyra turned and walked out dialing her cell phone. Marcello figured she was calling her supervisor, probably to complain about him.

Sprawled on her bed, Connie gazed out her bedroom window. Actually, it was the living room window. Her tiny, nine by nine bedroom couldn't hold her double bed. But the living room, complete with fireplace and a picture window that framed the ocean, was perfect. Monday evenings were the night to enjoy her beach cottage in Hacienda Beach. Her home cooked meal deliveries were done and she was on her own until the next delivery on Thursday. This night was especially beautiful as the full moon reflected off the sparkling Pacific. Her place on the "edge of the world," as her Aunt Dolly called it.

Her cell phone rang. "Midnight. This can't be good," she muttered.

"Hey. He did it," her twin sister, cried, "He actually did it, and I got my ring."

Camille's bigwig boyfriend, Palmer Railton, a hotshot Washington D.C. lobbyist did something he promised he'd do for months. He asked her to marry him.

"Wait, don't say another word," Connie propped the cell under her chin, pulled on a pair of shorts, grabbed her

11

purse and sandals.

"I want to hear every detail from start to finish, Camille."

Connie started her engine and headed for Camille's high-rise condo in Los Angeles while Camille sobbed into the phone, making little sense. She always was a romantic.

"Okay, I'm here." Connie shut off her phone and pulled into the parking garage. Camille was waiting by the elevator.

"Let's go upstairs and get Aunt Dolly on the phone."

Connie pressed her speed-dial button and winked at her sister while they waited for the connection to Catalina Island. She noticed how comedic her high fashion sister looked with matted hair, rumpled clothes and long dark streaks of mascara running down both cheeks.

She held her hand over the receiver, "This is supposed to be a happy occasion, kiddo." It was one in the morning, but Dolly wouldn't want to miss this.

Camille nodded and fingered the huge rubies that sat proudly on her finger. She didn't care what she looked like right then. She got what she wanted, a proposal and a ring, in one night.

"Hi Aunt Dolly." Connie chirped, "Let me put you on the speaker so we can all hear each other. "Hello my beautifuls," Dolly squawked on the speaker. She sounded wide awake. "Now, don't tell me anything until I get this old arthritic body in my easy chair." Camille rolled her eyes at Connie while they listened to their aunt rustle around.

"You're up late." Camille was nervous.

"I couldn't sleep, so I was vacuuming. Now girls, take one step at a time and take it slow. Is this good news?"

"It happened, Aunt Dolly! Palmer proposed to me... I only expected a cheesy airport gift from... well, from wherever he was." Camille took a deep breath and slowed down. "But he ushered me to his couch and took my hand in his. He got down on his knee and presented me with a dozen long stemmed red roses".

Dolly had been quiet until this moment. "What did he say, Honey? How did he say it?"

Camille sobbed, "He said, 'Will you make me the happiest man in the world by being the love of my life? Will you marry me?'"

Connie opened a new box of tissues for both of them. Dolly was weeping on the other end of the phone.

"Aunt Dolly, you should see the ring. It's three huge rubics." Connie volunteered, "I'll send a picture of it to you in a minute."

"Wait, you guys, I'm not done," Camille wiped her eyes and looked at the rich red stones on her hand. "He slipped it on my finger."

"...and?" Aunt Dolly persisted.

"He whispered softly, 'You haven't given me an answer yet.'" Camille wiped her eyes again, "I was so excited, I forgot to answer him. Can you imagine?"

"So what did you say?" Dolly screamed.

"Yes! Of course! What else would I say?"

They all cried and laughed at the same time. Connie had predicted last weekend that a proposal was coming. Aunt Dolly tried to help things along by soaking some mustard blossoms in vinegar to cast a spell on Palmer while Camille just hoped.§

As soon as they hung up, Connie sent a photo of Camille's ring from her cell phone to Aunt Dolly. Then a picture of themselves smiling and crying, and included a text

13

message, "For your scrapbook."

Dolly called Connie back, "Camille, you must have the wedding here. How about fall? What do you think? We're in April now. That gives us six months to put it together for October."

"Let's ask the bride-to-be," Connie looked at her twin for approval. Without waiting for an answer, Dolly decided that they should have two bridal showers, one in L.A. and another on Catalina. "I think a Tuscan theme would be wonderful," Connie announced, "in Aunt Dolly's back yard, what do you think?" Her aunt agreed with everything, but still waited for Camille's approval.

"I don't care. I just want Palmer. That's all I ever wanted." She blew her nose, "And to be a family, a whole family."

Connie put her arm around Camille. She knew full well what Camille meant, a family with two full-time parents for her son, Bradley. Her son's time had been split between Camille and his father for the past four years. Connie had seen the effect of this arrangement on Camille and Bradley. It wasn't good.

"Your mom and dad would be so very happy to see you looking forward to a good future. I'm so very proud of you both," Aunt Dolly always made sure to tell her charges she loved them and how proud she was of them.

Connie turned to Camille, "Well we should celebrate tonight at my place. Let's do a big party on the beach. What do you say? A Moonrise party!"

Camille sighed, "Palmer's on his way to D.C. He flew out earlier. But, we made plans to celebrate when he gets back and you two are invited."

Camille didn't seem to care. Palmer made a commitment and that was all that mattered to her. Well, that and the big rocks that sparkled under the track lights of her living room.

"Well," Dolly added, "we certainly can't have an engagement party without the future groom. So let's have a Moonrise party anyway. I'll get the phone tree going. Be here in Avalon by six o'clock tomorrow...er... tonight, my two lovelies. I love you both," She gave them a big noisy kiss over the phone.

Camille didn't think she had any tears left and the new box of tissues was running low. It was three in the morning and both of them were wide awake.

"You look like Hell, Camille. Go clean up, and I'll take you for an early breakfast."

Connie took a deep breath, happy for Camille. She picked up one of the roses, smelled it's sweet fragrance and fluffed the ribbon cascading down the vase.

Ricky sat up straight in the hard chair, drumming his fingers on the wooden table top.

"You seemed very anxious to leave, back there. Something make you nervous?"

He stopped drumming and glared up at Marcello. "Now, my man, when have you ever known anyone with fingers elegantly strumming on the table who didn't need a nicotine fix? Ha? When?"

The detective tossed his note pad on the table across from Ricky and sat down.

"You can have a smoke right after you answer a few questions about why you were hanging around Palmer Railton's place. You don't live in the complex."

Ricky started drumming his fingers faster.

"Now, I know you police are downsized and overworked, and I really feel for you. Really I do. But I got to tell you

15

Detective, I'm a bit worried about your memory. Just a few minutes ago."He looked at his watch, "Exactly thirty minutes ago, I was very specific on what I did while the victim was busy dying. I was just walking by and saw all the lights from your cars and stuff. And don't forget about the charming gentleman who gave me his attention for a few minutes to explain that he..."

"Enough," Marcello held up one finger, "Think carefully before you say anything else. We have witnesses who say you're always coming and going from the victim's place."

Ricky dropped his eyes and stopped drumming his fingers.

———————————

When Camille stepped out of the bathroom, she wasn't the wreck her sister saw when she arrived. "They are lovely," Connie said as she carefully replaced the rose.

"Yep, first time for roses, too."

"Come on," Connie took her by the arm, "I'm hungry. We can stare at your ring over breakfast."

Camille opened the door and found a man and woman in business suits. "May I help you?" she asked.

The man flashed a Police ID while the woman pulled a photograph out of her notebook. She looked at the sisters, "Are one of you Camille Brewster?"

Camille was silent. Connie, on the other hand, looked at her sister, "This is my sister Camille." The two detectives looked at each other while the twins did the same. "What's this regarding?"

The woman detective shook her head. "Do you know a Mr. Palmer Railton?" Connie's glance now became a gaze into Camille's face.

"Palmer? Why yes." She held out her hand to display the

16

big ruby ring. "He just asked me to marry him."

The male detective responded, "I'm very sorry, Mr. Palmer Railton was shot to death sometime during the night." Camille slumped back against the wall.

"I just saw him. He asked me to marry him." Camille took a deep breath, "This can't be happening. Are you sure it's him?"

Connie put her arms around her sister, "What do you want us to do?"

The woman said, "I know this is a difficult time, but you need to come to the station...in Hacienda Beach."

As they stepped out of the elevator in the Lobby, Connie looked toward the large glass doors, "At least you came in an unmarked car. I have very gossipy neighbors."

Camille stared out the window all the way to the Police Station.

Marcello was patiently pulling information out of Ricky.

"Y'know, I have a copy of your police record here. I must say it's rather unimpressive - Doesn't look like you ever spent more than 30 days in here for the crap on this list. You still dealing?"

"No way. You think I'd have stayed around Palmer's place with the police all over if I was holding? I haven't sold anything for almost a year, let alone use any."

"We can be here all night or you can convince me what your relationship with Mr. Railton was."

"We were friends, that's all. We both liked old flicks"

"You expect me to believe a piece of crap like you was the

17

friend of a high powered political figure like Mr. Railton."

"We met a few years ago at a bar. I told the gentleman my aspirations to be a political animal. He agreed to train me and show me the ropes of success in politics when I was ready. I wasn't ready...it was that simple."

"You're too young to know old movies."

"Ah, my mother lived to watch old, romantic movies on TV. And I, of course, joined her."

The two detectives sat Connie and Camille in the lobby and disappeared down the hallway.

"Do you think they're going to make me look at his body, like on TV? If they do I'll probably throw up." Connie patted her on the knee, "They just want to establish your relationship with him and then we can get something to eat."

Camille rubbed her wrists and fingered her ring. "How are we getting back to my place? Both our cars are there."

Camille glanced up just as Marcello turned Ricky over to a uniformed officer. The Officer escorted him toward the door while Detective Prado turned his attention to the twins.

"I take it you two are sisters."

Camille stopped rubbing her wrists and rolled her eyes at Connie.

He motioned to the two women to follow him. They held hands as he lead them to an interrogation room. Memories of walking these halls when she was a uniformed officer came flooding back to Connie as she passed her old office that now had "Lester March – Captain" lettered on the door.

"I'm detective Marcello Prado"

18

Connie looked closely at him, "I thought I recognized you," she handed him her ID.

"Connie Cane," Marcello matched the photo to her. " I didn't recognize you. You've changed."

He took Camille's drivers license and held it next to her face. "Hmm, twins."

Camille interrupted, "That man who just left. You talked to him, right? Because Ricky was always hanging around with Palmer. I think he's a drug dealer. A lot of the guys who hang around where Palmer lives, er... are pretty flaky. You aren't going to make me look at his dead body are you? I love him dearly, but dead people creep me out."

Detective Prado stifled a chuckle, "We know it's Palmer Railton, but there were photos of one of you all over the place. This Ricky and the neighbors say it's you Camille."

She held up her hand. "He just asked me to marry him last night," she sobbed. "Who could've done this? Did that jerk Ricky kill my Palmer?"

"We're looking into all possibilities right now." He pulled up a chair and sat down facing Camille. "I'm very sorry for your loss, Ms Brewster. We'll figure this out. Since you were so close, maybe you can help us."

He stood, pulled a DVD from his coat pocket and put it into the wall mounted playback monitor.

"Camille, did you know Palmer had hidden a video surveillance camera in his apartment?"

"In the bedroom?"

He shook his head, then turned around and pushed the play button on the remote. An image of Palmer's living room appeared on the screen. They watched as a man walked in and had an animated conversation with Palmer. "Oh my

19

God," Camille and Connie said in unison, "That's Dale." Camille put her hand over her mouth while her eyes grew wide.

"Did he kill Palmer?" Connie asked.

"I guess that means you both know this person."

"He's my freaking ex-husband," Camille responded. "Why would he do that?"

Detective Prado turned off the video. "This was not recorded at the time of the murder. Did he give you the DVD, to commemorate his proposal?"

Camille straightened up and glared, "How would he give me a DVD when I didn't even know about the video camera?"

"Anything else Detective? My sister is very upset."

"Now that he's gone, I wish he had recorded the proposal. Or maybe he did? Do you have it? Do you?" Connie could hear hope in Camille's voice.

"We have several boxes of discs we need to go through. Some are missing, last night's, for one. So whoever did this knew about the video setup?

Marcello placed his hand over Camille's. "Don't worry. We'll find out who did this to him and to you."

Connie stood up, "Are we done here or do you want to upset her more while she's mourning the loss of her finance?"

Drawing back, Marcello countered, "I was just trying to ease her pain. I imagine this is a terrible shock."

Connie didn't like the message Marcello was sending or the way he seemed to be putting the moves on Camille at her weakest moment.

"Hey guys," Camille stood between them. "Don't talk about

me like I'm not here."

"I'm hungry." Connie turned back to Marcello, "We need a ride back. Now!"

§ Chapter Two

Background Information

On a boat ride back from Aunt Dolly's house in Catalina, Camille and Connie relaxed by the window of the hovercraft as it flew over the waves to Hacienda Beach.

"Why are you trying so hard with Palmer? I know you want to marry again and make a home for Bradley and you, but why him? He's a nice guy, but if he doesn't want to marry you, he'll only break your heart."

"Oh, I'll change his mind," She gave her mischievous smile. "I'll make it happen."

"But why him?"

Camille was quiet for some time, which didn't happen very often.

"You don't understand, Connie"

"Hey, I'm your twin sister. Try me".

"After Mom and Dad, died I thought for sure we wouldn't be kept together. But we were raised by a wonderful aunt and uncle. They treated us as their own. I mean, how could two eight year olds take care of themselves? We owe a lot to them. More than Aunt Dolly will ever know. When Uncle Henry died, our little family was minus one. That's when I decided to marry Dale. I wanted a family, a real family. I wanted to have people to send Mother's day and Father's day cards, graduations cards, birthdays, and anniversaries. I need to belong."

"Camille you've got me and Aunt Dolly. Most of all, you'll have me... for a very long time." Connie put her arm on Camille's shoulder and they gave each other a long, cozy hug.

"Palmer's a wonderful guy. He's good to me. I wouldn't trade him for the world. But he can only be a father to Bradley and a husband to me. Not uncles, grandfathers or cousins..." She could tell by Connie's confused look she obviously was not getting it.

"Do you remember how painful it was to sit in Girl Scouts and hear everyone talk about their cousins, aunts, uncles, grandparents? All we had were our uncle and auntie and an occasional neighbor for holidays and celebrations. We never had extended family growing up. We had no idea what it was like to sit at a table with two turkeys and a room full of people. Or what it's like to get with the ladies afterwards, to do dishes and chat. I need an extended family for me and my son."

Connie remembered the loneliness she felt when her parents were alive and it was just the four of them. She wanted an extended family too, but didn't know Camille was as affected by it as well. Then it was Uncle, Auntie, just the four of them again. She remembered the wonderful stories her classmates would tell about their family gatherings and wished she had tales to tell, too.

"I hate to see you disappointed if it doesn't work out."

"That's the chance I'm willing to take. If I knew I did all I could and it didn't work, so be it. At least I know I tried and gave it my all. You know, the good old college try."

"But if Palmer isn't ready, he's not ready. Why force the issue? Why waste your time? There are others you can marry."

Camille leaned forward, "I know it will work. He loves me, he loves Bradley and it will work. Mark my words."

That was a year ago. Watching the two of them together, Connie saw the changes in Palmer. Though he hadn't made a commitment, Connie saw how deeply he cared for Camille and Bradley.

CHAPTER THREE

Camille's attention was riveted on the television over the coffee shop counter. Palmer's death had already made the four o'clock morning news with photos of them smiling together. "I have no idea which function that picture was taken," she mumbled.

The waitress recognized Camille. "You poor thing," and topped off her coffee. "That's your guy, isn't it? I hope this wasn't the way you learned about this."

Camille stared at her plate, tears dripped onto her eggs. Connie looked up at the round cheeked lady with the ruffled apron, "Thank you. The police told her about it earlier. We've been up all night...it's just awful."

"I remember him. He came here often for breakfast. Nice guy, always dressed really nice. What a shame."

"Camille, maybe you should come stay with me for a while." Connie offered. "Once the media learns you two were engaged, it won't be long before reporters and weirdos are camped-out at your apartment building."

Camille looked around the restaurant. Every face that met hers showed sorrow or turned away and whispered across the table.

"You don't mind? I know your place is tiny, but I'd like that. And I can be close to the Police if they need me."

Camille tossed a few things in an overnight case and followed Connie to her bungalow in the old part of Hacienda Beach, just a block from the water.

"I should call Detective Prado and let him know where I am."

"Why?" Connie asked, "He has your cell number."

"I'm just trying to help in any way I can." As soon as she finished her sentence her cell rang. It was Detective Prado. "Have you seen the news? Someone leaked the information about your relationship with Palmer and now your picture is all over the television."

"I'm staying at my sister's house."

"You need to come to the police station. I'll send a car and explain what we need to do when you get here."

"I'm going with you," Connie threw a few things in a backpack. They stood by the picture window, lights out, waiting for the police car.

In the morning darkness, the police station lawn was packed with gay activists, animal rights and pro-life people wandering around, holding candles and singing for Palmer Railton. He had a way of helping these people. They were his pet projects. He made things happen for them that others couldn't or wouldn't. Reporters, cameras and lights lined the sidewalk of the station.

They stared out the car window at the flickering candles. Mournful songs drifted into the car. Connie held her sister's hand. Everyone wanted to hear Palmer's fiancé say something. It was Connie who broke the silence.

"They miss him terribly and you're their only link to him. They feel for you, and you need to tell them that everything will be all right."

"I'm not going to do a news conference. Who knows what the reporters will do with what I say. No way."

As they exited the car, the media rushed toward them with microphones in hand, TV lights and flashes blinded them. The police surrounded the pair and escorted them through the gauntlet. "Camille Brewster" was yelled from different directions. Connie put her jacket over her sister's head and pulled her by the arm, "Don't look their way," she whispered.

Once inside the Police Station, Detective Prado rubbed his chin, now showing overnight stubble. He motioned for them to follow him to an interview room. On the way, he asked, "So Connie, how have you been?"

Connie knew what he was really asking. How did I survive the mess at the station last year? Do I need to give him information? She asked herself. "Besides this, fine. And you?" she politely responded.

"I hear you have a gourmet chef business now."

He opened the door and showed Camille in. Connie squeezed Marcello's arm and whispered, "My sister is priority now. Do both of us favor and don't feign interest in me."

He looked a Camille, "Have a seat. I'll be back in a second."

They sat in the stark, cold room away from the madness outside. Connie reflected on yesterday before the news broke. Her routine life was just that. She let her mind drift to her clients and knew they were all sct. She was shocked how this day was way different. Her senses were numb from the range of emotions that she'd experienced in the last four hours. She put her head down with her face in her hands and tried to breathe. "God, I hope they find his killer. I can't take much more of this."

"You? How do you think this is going to affect my high-security job?" Camille continued "..and how is Bradley going to take all this?" She couldn't stand being out of the spotlight.

Connie's affluent clientele for whom she prepares meals certainly wouldn't want the notoriety or any connection with a murder case. If the media found out, her clients would be hounded until they gave a statement. Fortunately, it was Tuesday morning and all the meals were cooked and delivered, so nothing needed to be done until Thursday evening. She mentally went through her schedule while searching for her Blackberry.

As long as the food was ready for the oven, stove top or microwave when they got home, everyone was happy. Connie always left a plate of fresh baked cookies in their homes as a thank you to her customers. The aroma of the cookies was a real treat for them and they appreciated it. "I hope I have time to stop by the medical supply store for more plastic gloves and face shields before Thursday." Connie muttered to herself.

"What are you mumbling about?" Camille was furious that Connie wasn't listening to her.

"You know I'm allergic to onions and I need to protect my face and hands when I cook, otherwise my..."

"I know, your lungs will shrivel up and you'll die and your face will fall off. I'm pouring my heart out to you and as usual I'm talking to a wall."

It's not Camille's fault Palmer got shot, Connie reminded herself. I hope I don't have to clean up this mess, but she's my sister. A gut wrenching pain ran through her. She was always there to pick up the "Camille pieces".

"So, you're just going to sit there like a dumbass while my heart is ripped to shreds?"

What was Connie supposed to do? Camille stormed out of the room just as Marcello walked in.

He sat at the large table that dominated the room and looked at Connie. "Tell me about Dale, your sister's ex."

"Why don't you ask her?" Connie snapped. "She was married to him."

"I'd like to get your take on him. Most wives, especially ex-wives, aren't exactly objective when it comes to information

28

on a spouse."

"If you think he was jealous of Palmer, you're wrong. Dale has custody of their son. He's remarried and could care less about Camille."

"Why do you think Dale would be on this DVD?"

"I know you're just doing your job, Detective, but do we have to do this now? Camille needs to be with her family and deal with her grief in private." Connie brushed back her hair, "I'm afraid she'll fall apart any time now. She can't go home, and the media now knows I'm her sister, they're sure to find her at my place. So I can't go home, either."

Marcello sat back in his chair. "We're just trying to get to the bottom of her fiancé's murder. You know the more information I have the faster we'll find the person who did this."

A uniformed lieutenant came into the room and whispered to Marcello. He looked back at Connie and excused himself.

Alone again, frustration hit her hard.

She left the room and found Camille pacing around the lobby. "Camille, I..." Before she could finish, Camille's cell phone rang. Her end of the conversation was full of "Yes... I understand. When? Why? Thank you very much, I appreciate it... Sure," and hung up.

"Okay Connie, you're in for the surprise of your life. Be thankful you have Camille Brewster as your sister," the twinkle in her eye was illuminating. Connie questioned her but Camille held up one finger and looked at her watch.

Marcello and Captain March approached them, "There is a helicopter on its way for you. We need to get you both to the roof now," and motioned them to the elevator.

Camille called Aunt Dolly on her cell and told her to meet them at the helipad in Avalon. Aunt Dolly's burst of excitement rang in Camille's ear.

The Captain led the way up the stairs. Camille gave Connie thumbs up as she held the door open for her.

Marcello whispered to Connie, "Apparently, your sister's pretty well connected with the big guys in Sacramento. She made a phone call and now we're flying you both to Catalina by helicopter."

The captain raised an eyebrow, "I don't know who you know, but you must've called in one Hell of a favor." He pushed open the door to the rooftop helipad just as a Jet Ranger touched down.

"She's a long time court reporter for LA County and now the state supreme court. I guess you meet people that way," Connie muttered to the captain, too shocked to say any more.

"You're going along to make sure they get there safely." The captain shouted to Marcello over the deafening noise of the whirling copter engine.

"What? I'm in the middle of this investigation. How did I get stuck babysitting these two?"

The captain shrugged, "Those were the orders I got."

Well, what the hell. A free helicopter to Catalina, Marcello thought, "Cool."

"Hey, Prado!" The captain added, "They're your responsibility. And make sure you bring them back here to the station this evening."

Camille climbed into the front seat. The pilot handed her a headset and motioned her to put it on. Connie climbed into the back, battling the wind. Once in, she looked out the window at the city just lit by the dawn light. Marcello tapped her on the shoulder and motioned for her to don her headset as well. With the four belted in, the decibel level of the copter's gas turbine engine rose to the roar of a jet taking off. Camille peered out the window at her feet and watched as the ground shrank away.

Connie and Camille jabbered back and forth over their headsets during the fifteen-minute flight to Catalina. Just outside of L. A. Harbor the pilot hushed everyone and listened intently to his own headset. All Camille heard was, "Roger. Will do. I can be on scene in fifteen."

As they touched down, the morning sun was peeking above the horizon, under a layer of dark clouds. Connie glanced out the side window and saw Aunt Dolly wrapped in a down jacket, waiting in her golf cart.

Camille jerked her headset off and ran to Aunt Dolly. "Somebody killed my Palmer."

Connie joined her. Detective Prado watched from the helicopter while the three embraced. Marcello told the pilot he had orders to return Connie and Camille to Hacienda Beach that evening.

"No can do detective," was his reply. "I just got a call from L.A. County to assist in a rescue out near Barstow. I don't think I'll be back until tomorrow morning."

"I guess we can take the boat back." Marcello was confused about what to do.

"Maybe not. I got the weather report that a storm will be in here this afternoon. You might be stuck 'til tomorrow anyway." With that comment, he wound up the engine and lifted off again, leaving Marcello stranded on the island with the three women.

"This is Detective Prado" Connie explained. "He's the one working Palmer's case."

"Well," Dolly remarked, "Since you delivered my precious children to me, you'll stay with us at my place, just around the bend. I insist on it. I have plenty of room."

Marcello called the captain, who growled back, "I'm trying to get the media to ignore the murder for a while so we can get a hold on it. Keeping them out of the news for twenty-four hours may help. I want them back early A.M. Got

31

it? I'll set it up with Air Support...And don't hold up the chopper," he yelled and slammed the phone down.

Camille overheard Marcello's call. "I guess we're not leaving until tomorrow."

"Besides," Dolly winked at the twins, "You're going to want to keep an eye on these two, aren't you?"

The cart putted through Avalon and up the winding road toward the house. Rain began to fall in large drops pelting the fiberglass roof of the carts. Dolly called back, "How are you doing back there?" A flash of lightning streaked across the sky. Marcello gave thumbs up just as a deafening clap of thunder shook everyone to the bone. "Guess the storm's coming in sooner," Dolly added.

A cold wind blew rain inside the cart, drenching everyone. Dolly's house appeared over a rise. The lights glowed warmly in the windows.

Another flash and crash of thunder, and the house went dark. Now the house on the hill reminded Marcello of the Bates house in Psycho.

Running through puddles, they made a dash for the door. Dolly went to the kitchen and returned with lit candles.

"We're in for a big blow," as the clouds darkened the early morning. "I'll get some more candles lit so we'll have some light in here."

Camille picked up the telephone by the front door, "The phones are out, too."

"No problem." Marcello pulled out his cell.

"Forget that," Connie offered, "There's no cell service on this side of the island."

"Come in the living room." Connie added, "I lit the gas fireplace."

Chilly and wet, Marcello settled into the overstuffed sofa.

"We haven't been to bed yet." Connie moaned. Marcello's eyes were at half mast.

"Before you get too comfortable, let me show you where you'll be sleeping."

Dolly led the detective upstairs to a cozy bedroom. He looked the room over.

"There's a robe and some dry clothes in the closet, if you don't mind wearing them. They were my late husband's. When you've settled in, come on down to the kitchen for tea and snacks." Marcello first declined, but hunger pains took over. He hadn't eaten since lunch and it was almost ten in the morning. He hesitated, then replied, "I'll be down shortly."

He opened the closet door and noticed it didn't reek of mothballs as he expected. Inside, he found a robe that fit him. His wet jacket, pants and shirt came off and he spread them over a chair to dry He found a pair of green sweat pants and white cotton socks. He looked in the mirror. The white terrycloth robe, pale green sweats and white socks made him look like a clown!

His footsteps made the stairs creak as he followed the warm glow of the candlelight into the kitchen. The table was set with candelabras and small candles along the counters. The ladies sat around the table in sweats sipping tea and eating muffins.

Dolly waved him to her chair and set a hot cup of coffee down in front of him. "I pegged you for a caffeine kind a guy. I have tea if you prefer. The muffins are pumpkin raisin. Help yourself."

"You pegged me right and I like pumpkin, too. You're a real mind reader."

Connie told Dolly about the last time she saw Palmer alive.

Marcello observed Camille half-heartedly stirred her hot tea and picked at her muffin. Between sobs and sips of tea, Camille repeated Palmer's romantic proposal. The roses and how he slipped the ring on her finger. Connie put her arm around her sister, "Last weekend, the three of us were in Palm Springs. I remember our last evening there. Palmer asked Camille to come to his place because he had a surprise for her. I just knew he was going to propose." §

Dolly interrupted, "Well I always thought Palmer was a real gentleman. I remember when you first brought him to meet me. I waited with Connie on the dock for the boat to come in. We were so excited to meet this man that swept you off your feet. More and more people got off until the boat looked pretty empty. We thought maybe he chickened out. Then we saw you and waved. This tall, good looking guy with a mop of black hair waved back carrying a huge basket. I wondered why a man would pack his clothes in a laundry basket. How odd! As he came closer we noticed the basket had a yellow gingham cloth over it."

Camille giggled and nudged Connie at Aunt Dolly's impressions.

"So I thought maybe it was for a picnic. I was so surprised when he put it down in front of me and shook my hand, 'Aunt Dolly,' he said to me, 'It's a pleasure to meet you. I'm Palmer Railton,'" Dolly wiped her eyes which had filled with tears. "He pulled off the cloth and there was a small sapling tree! A tree! I still remember his words, 'Camille said you were from Virginia, so I looked it up and the state tree is a Flowering Dogwood. So I brought you one.'"

Camille giggled, "I remember how we tried to get the basket in the cart and held onto it through the curves." Marcello listened as they laughed together. He'd seen this kind of tragedy before and knew it would take this family a long time to get over Palmer's death. He was grateful he wasn't the one who had to get them through it. His job would be over as soon as he delivered them back to the police station tomorrow.

He heard a knock at the front door. The women were having so much fun, they didn't hear it. He opened it and found the chopper pilot had come back! It was noon!

"The Captain changed his mind," the pilot shrugged. "And the storm let up."

Marcello hoped they could just take the twins back to the mainland. He worried that his dog would be running out of food. But the pilot was starving and the aroma of the baked goodies was too much to resist, so he sat down. They watched as he chowed down on a pumpkin raisin muffin. Marcello changed into his own clothes.

"Tell me Detective," Dolly asked as she poured the pilot a cup of coffee, "How do you feel about help with your investigation, I mean from the community?"

"We always appreciate leads, no matter what or where they come from. We have a policy to follow up on all leads." He noticed the twins, smirking at each other as he straightened his damp shirt.

"Detective, I have decided to help with the investigation." Camille announced as she fidgeted with her engagement ring. "I knew Palmer better than anyone and I know I can provide information for your files that no one else knows. I want the killer of my fiancé caught and brought to justice."

Detective Prado cleared his throat, "Fine, as long as you don't interfere with the investigation and do as we ask. Leave the dangerous police work to us. We'd be more than happy with any information you may have."

"You see, Detective, that's what I'm afraid of," Dolly insisted. "Camille can get rather rambunctious about things and I dare say she may forget to leave the 'dangerous stuff' alone." Dolly made quotes in the air, "I would much prefer that Camille not be involved and just kept abreast of the investigation."

"Auntie, I'll be fine. Don't worry about me." Camille excused herself to change for the trip to the police station.

"Connie, I need you to watch over your little sister."

"Little sister, I thought you were twins?" the pilot asked.

Connie rolled her eyes, "Yeah, I'm a whole three minutes older."

"Connie may be only three minutes older, but she's emotionally years older than Camille." Dolly leaned over to Detective Prado, "They think I don't know, but Camille is constantly getting into trouble and Connie is always there to pull her butt out of the fire."

———————————————

"I wish you could be with me during this time, Aunt Dolly." Camille yelled over the helicopter noise.

"I'll take the first boat to the mainland." Dolly shouted back, "I'll meet you there around three." Camille gave her a big hug and kiss.

Detective Prado put his hand on Camille's shoulder, "We have to go now."

Dolly kept her good-byes short. She packed up some muffins for Marcello and the pilot.

With everyone on board, Dolly's nieces waved to her as the helicopter lifted off and made a beeline toward Hacienda Beach. No sooner had the chopper crested the top of the island than Marcello received a radio transmission from police headquarters.

"Where the Hell are you? It's after one o'clock." The Captain's voice boomed in his ear. "Not that you care, but we've located Palmer's grandmother."

"Terrific." Marcello replied, "I'll get over there and pick her up."

"Not so fast, Amigo." The Captain interrupted, "She lives in Georgia. She's flying out to make arrangements for shipping his body to Savannah."

"At least we don't have to bring her in. Maybe she can shed some light on this deal."

"She wants to meet the fiancé. Maybe we can get these two together and learn more about this guy."

Marcello switched his headset to communicate with Camille and Connie.

"We found Palmer's grandmother, Camille. She wants to meet you."

The twins looked at each other. Camille shook her head at her sister, "I can't."

Connie spoke into her headset, "Why not Camille? We have to do whatever we can to find his killer."

"Do you think it'll help? I mean talking to someone I don't know about someone I lost."

"I'll be there for you and so will Aunt Dolly. Please do it."

Camille looked down as they descended toward the police station. The reporters had gone and the crowds of people were gone. All that remained was the old brick building in bad need of repair. Camille thought it ironic that someone like Palmer, sophisticated and concerned with appearances, would be kept on "ice" in a place so old and run-down.

The three of them walked down the staircase they had run up in the early morning hours to escape the media chaos. They were then ushered to a waiting patrol car for the hospital morgue.

"Your Aunt should be here about the same time as Palmer's grandmother," Detective Prado explained, "Then we can take her down to the morgue for a positive I.D."

The place gave the twins the creeps, especially Camille.

As Marcello ushered them into a conference room, "I can't identify the body. He was my fiancé, but I can't look at him. Not like this."

"That's perfectly understandable, but we need a family member for this when one is available. His grandmother can do it now."

Neither one of the twins had the slightest idea of what to expect when Palmer's grandmother arrived. She might be an angry old dowager and blame Camille for everything, or a gold digging fortune hunter waiting to cleanup on someone else's tragedy. After what seemed like forever, but was only ninety minutes, Dolly stepped into the room and took a seat beside her girls. Shortly after, Marcello brought in a tall, frail African American lady. She had a head full of curly gray hair and swollen, red eyes. All their imagined worries were instantly rinsed away.

"Ladies," Marcello began," This is Palmer Railton's grandmother, Earlene Railton." He pulled a chair out for her, "I'd like you to meet Palmer's fiancée, Camille Brewster, her sister Connie Cane and their aunt, Dolly Moorhead."

Earlene scanned Camille's eyes, then shifted her attention to Connie and finally to Dolly. A tear appeared in the corner of her eye and slowly crept down her cheek when her gaze fell back to Camille.

Marcello broke the silence, "I wish I had words to tell you how badly the entire community of Hacienda Beach feels over the passing of your grandson. He was respected by so many in the community for his work to making laws protecting the rights of others."

Earlene wiped away the tear with a small, lace edged handkerchief. Then in a charming southern accent, she politely thanked Detective Prado for his sentiment.

Dolly cleared her throat, "Pardon us for appearing rude, we weren't prepared for..."

"Prepared for what?" Earlene interrupted with her southern drawl, "The fact that I'm black? The fact that my grandson was African American? What exactly were you not prepared for?"

"Please," Dolly stepped around the table and approached Earlene, "Please, sit with us. We'd like to talk to you about your wonderful grandson."

Camille and Connie made no move, but kept staring at Earlene.

"You know, Earlene. May I call you Earlene?" She nodded to Dolly. "Palmer's passing left a terrible void in our family. In the short time I knew him, I grew to love your grandson and we were all looking forward to him joining the family." Earlene looked Dolly in the eyes as she spoke, calculating the sincerity of her words. Then she looked at the twins.

"I'm Connie, and I was excited about Palmer becoming my brother-in-law."

Camille was very uncomfortable with Earlene's piercing gaze. She cleared her throat and in an unsteady voice said, "Yes, I'm Palmer's fiancée. We had planned to announce our engagement after he returned from his trip to Washington DC. Earlene, you were on the top of the list of people he, we were going to call."

"Come here child," Earlene encouraged. Camille looked at Dolly not sure what to do. Dolly nodded and Camille slowly rose from her seat, rounded the table and pulled out the chair next to Dolly.

"No, my dear." Earlene motioned to the chair on her left, "Come here child," Earlene encouraged. "Come and sit here beside me," She looked deeply into Camille's beautifully marbled green eyes and gently pushed her long golden hair back to the side of head, "Palmer loved green eyes. When he was in high school he tried green contact lenses. They hurt, so he stopped wearing them. I'm not surprised he'd pick a lovely lady as yourself with such stunning eyes." Slowly, a blush gathered along Camille's softly freckled face.

"I'm sorry, but I need to go," Detective Prado interrupted. "If you'd like to continue this meeting, there are a couple of coffee shops close by that are usually quiet this time of day." He held the door open for them, "Ladies?"

Dolly took Earlene's arm and ushered her along with her nieces to the nearest coffee shop. Camille sat across from Earlene. "Apparently, there was a whole lot I didn't know about Palmer. I figured that in two years I would've learned more about him."

"Yes, could you please tell us a little more about him?" Dolly added, "After all, he was soon going to be partly mine, too. You see, I never had children. But I do have two lovely nieces I raised and I was rather looking forward to sharing a son."

Earlene took a sip of her coffee, "One evening my daughter Daisy, Palmer's mother, showed up on my doorstep eight and a half months pregnant."

Dolly and the twins leaned in to listen. "She was in a mess of trouble so I took her to the hospital for a checkup. The doctors were concerned because she'd had no prenatal care. In a couple of weeks she delivered normally and little Palmer was healthy as could be."

"Honestly, I don't know what came over that girl. Daisy had been wild since she was fifteen. She left the hospital the day after she delivered and we never saw her again. We didn't know she took off until the hospital called us."

Connie sniffled into her napkin, "That's awful. How could she leave a little baby like that?"

"My late husband and I took him home, adopted him and raised him as our own. We'd already been blessed with a daughter, but we always wanted a son." Earlene beamed with joy, "As a child, Palmer was a model student. We did everything we could to get him the education and social experiences he needed to do well in life. And since he was half white and looked very mixed, we felt his best bet was to learn how to mingle with both races. My husband died of a massive heart attack and he left the house...and Palmer to me."

"You did a wonderful job," Dolly commented, "He seemed to get along with everyone."

"You have children in your life, Ms Moorhead,"

"Please call me Dolly."

"So I'm sure you understand how young ones are. After Palmer won a scholarship to Jamestown University and left Savannah, he never came back. Oh, he sent money quite often. But never with a return address and always cashier's checks. How I wanted to be a part of his life, but I guessed I was an embarrassment to him because of my paint job. All I could do was follow his career in the newspapers and occasionally get a glimpse of him on the TV. We never spoke again. Tears poured from her eyes. Dolly hugged her while Connie put her hand on Earlene's shoulder.

Camille said nothing and avoided eye contact with Earlene. Connie understood that Camille was sad, but didn't know why she was being so cold to Earlene, the woman who raised her fiancé. She kicked Camille under the table several times and finally succeeded in getting in a polite glance toward Earlene.

When they parted, Earlene told them that the Police wouldn't release the body yet. She promised to let them know the funeral plans.

§ Chapter Three

Background Information

Connie, and Camille spent Palmer's last weekend in Palm Springs. Connie recounts her sister's romantic evening with Palmer.

Palmer invited Connie and Camille for dinner at a restaurant in the desert, The CASBAH. It was a romantic, Middle Eastern restaurant that specialized in 40's & 50's ballroom music and dancing.

Since it is in the desert, late April is the perfect time to enjoy an evening dining and dancing under the stars. The decor is right out of Lawrence of Arabia with pillows, ornate brass and hanging lights. The stars glowed in the warm desert breeze.

Dinner was magnificent. They lingered over mint tea and a basket of fruit and dates while listening to music. Though Connie was the "third wheel," Palmer made her feel welcome and comfortable. Even so, Camille couldn't care less. Both recalled Auntie and Uncle always dancing to this music in the living room.

Connie and Palmer danced several times and the conversation was always about the movie or the background of the song being played. The last dance was accompanied by, "A kiss to build a dream on."

"My favorite! It's from the movie, 'The Strip,' 1952." Palmer closed his eyes and smiled, "Louie Armstrong made it popular." He looked at Camille, helped her from her chair, then guided her to the dance floor.

Connie couldn't help but admire them as they danced, so much in love. The words floated through her mind, "Give me a kiss to build a dream on, and my imagination will thrive upon that kiss. Sweetheart I ask no more than this, a kiss to build a dream on."

The couple snuggled as they glided along. Slowly, other couples moved to the side, leaving Palmer and Camille the only couple in the middle of the floor.

They strolled back to the table, holding hands and smiling at each other.

As he was leaving the next day, he told Camille to come by his place. He had something to talk to her about. Connie felt sure a ring and proposal was imminent.

Janet Elizabeth Lynn

CHAPTER FOUR

The medical report showed what Marcello already knew. The victim had two gun shots to the chest, one pierced his heart. Also, two strands of blonde hair from a wig were found on the body. As Marcello poured over the crime scene reports, he noted there were fingerprints belonging to several individuals. One belonged to a former teacher who lived in LA. Detective Prado brought him in for an interview.

"Tony Dillon, former high school art teacher, I see."

"Yes former...What's this all about?"

"You know that Palmer Railton is dead."

"Yes. I know. I saw it all over the news. I knew him. We were friends."

"Your fingerprints were all over the ground floor of the apartment. When was the last time you saw him?"

Tony fidgeted, eyeing the two way mirror facing him. He'd seen CSI shows, so he knew he couldn't deny what was found at the scene of the crime.

"About three days ago. We had dinner at his place."

"Where were you on April fourteenth about eight p.m.?"

"At a singles bar. Check it out. People saw me there. The Platinum Fox on Fifth Street."

"We will...that's a gay bar." Marcello wasn't sure if he should have said that right out.

"Yeah, so what. You got a problem with that?"

"What was your relationship with Railton?"

"I said we were friends. Gay people do have friends, you know. We're not all florists and hairdressers. We even have straight friends."

Marcello got up and opened the door, "We may need to talk to you again in the near future Mr. Dillon, don't leave town anytime soon."

———————————

Dolly and the girls spent the night at Connie's with a full bottle of wine. After breakfast they took Dolly to the boat terminal for her trip home to Catalina and kissed her good-bye.

When they got back to Connie's place, they went for a walk along the beach. Camille kicked the sand along the way.

"How're you feeling about all this, Camille?"

"I can't believe Palmer was half black. I just can't believe it. Our kids would have been part black. Why didn't he tell me?"

"Would it have made a difference? Would you have loved him less? If you had kids, would you have loved them less?"

Camille thought hard, "No, I loved him very much. I guess maybe that's one of the things he wanted to talk to me about when he got back. As far as kids go, I'd love them just as much as I love Bradley. It's just that, I wasn't prepared to deal with those issues." Camille squinted up at the sun. "Do you mind if we go in? I didn't put on sun block."

They walked back to the house. Camille sat by the living room window and watched the ocean waves while Connie made a couple of sandwiches for lunch. She brought them out and slid one in front of her brooding sister.

Camille picked at the lettuce, "I need to be part of this investigation. How can I not get involved?"

"Why don't you let the police do their job? Detective Prado is competent and genuinely interested in your case."

"I want his murderer in jail. Whoever it was, they stole a dream from me. They need to be punished. I can't let this go."

"The best thing to do is to leave the investigation to the professionals. They deal with this all the time. You'd only get in the way or even jeopardize the investigation."

"No, it won't feel right unless I'm involved. I want to be a part of this. If you don't want to join me, I'll do it myself."

"You could get hurt, Camille. You have to think of your son. What if something happens to you? Do you know who'll have your son, permanently? Dale. Is that what you want?"

Connie was right when she predicted Camille's ex-husband would sue for full custody and win. Camille was left with only two weekend visits a month. She had planned to sue for joint custody, but that was when she owned a house and had money in the bank. No judge would award her joint custody while she lived in a singles only condo, her ex would make sure of that. Camille wiped a tear from her cheek, "It doesn't matter, I have to do this."

"Camille," Connie yelled, "All my life I've had to rescue you, fix your screw ups and get you out of trouble. I'm sick of this. I need to live my own life and for once. I need to do what I need for me and right now, I need to have peace. Your life keeps me from living mine. You know, Aunt Dolly worries about you constantly."

Camille stared at the floor.

"For once, little sister, please, do the right thing. For once, stay out of trouble. Aunt Dolly is old, she can't take all the stress you've been giving her anymore."

"Sometimes, Connie, it's hard to believe you're my sister, or even that you were a cop once."

Camille grabbed her purse and drove to Lisa's house. Bradley and Mickey were playing war in the courtyard. He ran up to her, "Mommy, you're here."

"Hey sweetheart. I missed you." She bent down for a hug. He put his arms around her neck and squeezed hard. That was his signal that he missed her. "I'm just visiting Lisa, Honey. This is not my day to be with you, but I'll be sure to say good bye before I leave."

He made her promise with a boy scout sign that she'd see him before she left, then went back to his friend. Camille heard his friend Mickey ask, "Hey, how come you still hug your mom? Only babies do that."

"I'm not a baby. You see your mom all the time, I don't. I like hugging my mom, she smells nice." Camille knew then she still had his heart.

She pressed the doorbell and watched her son go off to play. Lisa greeted Camille with a big smile, "Hey!"

Lisa watched Bradley after school until Dale picked him up after work, or when it was Camille's turn to have him. Dale and Camille were ordered by the court not to meet unless a medical emergency or school issue was involved. Lisa was good to Bradley and Camille liked her for that. They'd become friends and took their sons for play dates at the beach in the summer.

"I'm so sorry about Palmer, he was a good man. Everyone in the apartment complex loved him."

Lisa took Camille by the arm and escorted her to the sofa. "I'm not sure if you know," Camille confided, "Palmer proposed to me the night he was...shot." She held her hand out to show off the ring.

"I'm so sorry, Camille. I am so, so sorry," and hugged her again.

"I've decided to help the police with their investigation. I don't think they've told me everything that happened that night. Do you know if anybody saw anything that can help me...us in the investigation. I think the police said they talked to you, didn't they?"

Lisa told Camille how people saw a man run from the apartment just after the shooting.

Camille was confused, "A man? The police didn't tell me that. A man? Who? What did he look like?"

"Nobody particular, I guess. Someone called 9-1-1. I stayed in the apartment with the boys until the police came. I didn't want them to be involved with the awful business. I heard it was pretty bloody."

"A man?" she repeated still confused, "Lisa, I can't just sit and do nothing. Is there anything else you can remember?"

Lisa went over it all in her mind, "Oh, I pointed out the young man that hung around Palmer's place all the time. You know, the skinny, dark haired boy. I believe his name is Ricky. He was at the scene with rest of the crowd. I believe the police took him in for questioning."

Camille thought back, there was a young kid that hung around the courtyard when she came to visit Palmer. "That young guy? That's interesting, I always assumed he lived here. Who is he?" Lisa shrugged, then invited Camille to stay for dinner until Dale's wife picked up Bradley. Camille thanked her but declined, and went outside to find Bradley. When he saw her by the car, he came running up and gave her a hug. "I'll see you on Friday, sweetheart." She gave him a warm kiss on the cheek and told him to be good.

When she got back to her condo, she put her keys on the glass table. She ordered a pizza, pulled on her jogging shoes, set the treadmill speed to four and got on.

As she got up to speed, she gazed out her picture window over the city and glanced at her roses. "They saw a man running from the apartment?" She wondered, and upped the speed of the treadmill to six thinking of all the men she knew that Palmer associated with. Deep in thought, she didn't hear the doorbell ring. She was finally pulled out of her zone by the loud pounding at her front door. There was Detective Prado in his brown suit, wrinkled from the day's work.

"May I come in? I have a few things to review with you."

He sat with her on the couch and went over what they knew so far; a man running from the apartment, the velvet ring box, a large clip-on earring, a crumpled twenty dollar bill thrown on the body, hair from a blonde wig and Tony's fingerprints.

Camille vaguely remembered Tony as a friend of Palmer's, but they didn't seem to be more than associates or colleagues.

When the pizza arrived, she flipped back the box. "You want some? What's your pleasure Detective or may I call you Marcello?"

"Call me whatever you want. Just water for me. I'm still on the clock."

Camille walked back from the kitchen with a glass of red wine in one hand and a glass of ice water in the other.

He couldn't resist the smell of hot pizza. "On second thought...". He took a big slice of the cheese pizza, "You seem to be handling your fiancé's death well."

Camille nibbled the pointy end of her pizza and took a sip of wine, "Crying fits, wailing, and screaming aren't my style. It's stupid to make a spectacle of oneself. Besides, we all handle grief in different ways. I plan to channel my energy in a more constructive way. I'm going to help you guys get the asshole who stole my dreams."

The front door opened and in walked Connie. She stopped in her tracks when she saw Marcello and Camille on the sofa eating pizza.

"Hi Connie." Camille waved her sister in, "Come join us, we

still have some pizza left,"

"Do you have keys to each other's place?" Marcello asked Camille.

Camille took another sip of wine, "Sure. We've never had secrets from each other. We're sisters."

Connie went to the kitchen got a glass of water. She sat quietly and nibbled on a piece of pizza, trying not to be conspicuous. Camille went back over what she knew while Marcello checked his notes.

"I should go now. Thank you ladies," Marcello stood to leave.

Connie took another bite of her pizza. "I just came by to see how you were doing. I need to go, too. Love ya," she kissed Camille on the cheek and left with Marcello.

They walked to the elevators and rode down to the lobby. Once outside, Connie grabbed Marcello's arm. "Do you mind telling me what you think you're doing with my sister?"

"Excuse me? I simply wanted to review a few things about the case.

"Over a pizza?"

Marcello could see how inappropriate it looked and assured her it was strictly business. "With pizza?!" Connie yelled.

"Please, I didn't mean this to seem inappropriate, really. It was strictly business."

"I'm warning you, don't hit on Camille. Am I clear?" She poked her finger into his chest. "You want to keep your job?"

Marcello looked into her clear green eyes noticing the difference in their eye color. "Don't worry, Ms Cane, there's no romance between us. I will be more careful in dealing with both of you." With that statement he nodded and walked away.

Lisa walked into the police station and shook Detective Prado's hand. "Why did I have to come down here? I already spoke to your people the night of Palmer's death."

"You'll be home for the boys when they come home from school." He pulled a straight-backed chair from the wall for her.

Lisa sat down and looked at Marcello noticing the large mirrored wall behind him.

"We have a few more questions to ask you about the night of the murder."

"I told you all I remembered."

"What's your relationship with Ricky Row?"

She thought for a minute, "Who?"

Marcello showed her a photo of Ricky. "Oh. Is that his full name? He's the short, skinny boy who hung out with Palmer. I pointed him out to you the night of the murder."

"Did you see him leaving the apartment the night of the murder?"

"Actually, I didn't see a thing. I gathered the boys and stayed with them in the living room until the police came. I didn't want them to see anything that would give them nightmares.

"Do you know a Dale Brewster?"

"Yes, you know I do. He's the father of the boy I baby sit."

Marcello flipped open the laptop on the desk, pushed some buttons and turned it around so Lisa could see the screen. "I want you to watch this."

Lisa watched as a surveillance video flashed onto the screen. She saw a man, Dale, appearing to shout, waving his arms around. Palmer stood there looking at him.

On the screen, Lisa watched Dale storm out the door, slamming it behind him. Palmer turned, looked up at the camera and walked out of the frame.

"Now, I ask you again, what's your relationship to Dale Brewster?"

Lisa looked at the mirror and then looked at Marcello. "Like I said, Dale is the father of Bradley Brewster. I babysit him for Dale and his wife after school. Bradley and my son are playmates." She stopped for a minute. "Dale and I...are friends. That's all that there is between us. I took Bradley to the hospital last year when he fell and hurt his knee. I called Dale. He met me at the hospital. Camille was out of town, so I stayed with Bradley. Dale and I had lunch together while Bradley was in the hospital, but that was it."

"Where are Dale Brewster and his wife now?"

"All I remember is that he's out of town on business, with his wife. I have his cell number in case of an emergency, but I don't know where they went. If you would like his number, I can provide that for you."

Marcello pushed a piece of paper toward her. She pulled out her cell phone and wrote his number down. "I expect him back tomorrow."

He looked at the number, "Call him."

"Now?" Marcello nodded. Lisa called the number. She got his voice mail, so she pushed the page button.

They waited in silence. Suddenly her cell rang. It was Dale. She told him the police wanted to see him and asked when he would be back. She handed the phone to Marcello. He waved the phone away and told her to tell him to come to the police station when he gets in town. She did and hung

53

up. "He said tomorrow afternoon."

Marcello made a note, thanked her and asked her to keep in touch. "Here's my card. Call me if you remember anything else or if he tells you anything you think might help us."

"Detective," Lisa said as she stood up. "I believe this interview could have been done at my place. Next time you take me away from my home. and work, it really needs to be important."

Marcello looked at his notes, "That's right. I see you do work at home. You create crossword puzzles for the newspaper. I just can't get into those things... Sorry, I'll be more mindful of your situation."

"That's interesting," Lisa commented "I thought a good cop would love crossword puzzles." He got the insult.

In the hallway, the Captain watched as an irate Lisa walked down the hall.

"You see the whole thing, Captain?"

"Yeah. Listen Prado, if you want to have cooperation from the suspects, you need to get them on your side. Quit the intimidation act. If they don't think you're on their side, why would they call you with information? You could've showed this woman the video on your laptop at her house. You didn't need to bring her down here. She's been cooperative since day one. Don't blow it with her".

Marcello put his hands in his pockets and nodded in agreement. "I got a call from the CSI supervisor. You allegedly harassed a CSI named Kyra Dennis. I managed to talk her out of filing charges. For now."

"How could asking questions be considered harassment?"

"Listen, you wanted a second chance," the Captain held up one finger, "I gave you one. Don't blow it. Got it?"

Camille's conversation with Lisa was looming in her head as she made her way to Connie's. She longed for her weekend with Bradley.§

On the way to dinner, she told Connie about her recollection of Ricky. Connie also remembered seeing a young boy hanging around the apartments a lot.

"I can't believe Ricky was more that an acquaintance of Palmer. What in the world would Palmer be doing with a shaggy kid like him?"

Just then Camille pointed out Ricky standing on the corner, "There's Ricky Boy. I'm pulling over."

Camille pulled up and yelled, "Hey Ricky, remember me?"

He shrugged and leaned into the car window.

"I'm Palmer's fiancée. We met several times. This is my sister Connie.

"Duh yea, like I couldn't figure that out!"

"Interesting," Connie muttered, "how the younger ones usually respond with that statement."

"We're on our way to dinner," Camille mentioned, "Want to come?"

After Ricky ordered a large plate dinner off the menu, he focused on Camille, "I can't thank you enough for the meal, and having dinner with such lovely ladies is a bonus." His dimpled smile and pearly white teeth glistened under a young weathered face. "So what's the catch? You know what they say, 'there's no such thing as a free lunch'. What's this going to cost me, dare I ask?"

"I'm helping the police with Palmer's murder." Camille replied.

"Helping? You?" Looking side to side, "I'm sorry, which one is who?"

Camille ignored the question and continued, "Lisa said you were friends with Palmer."

"Oh did she? Rather observant of her," he squinted until a vein poked out of his neck.

"Now, hold on. the police brought you in. I saw you at the police station. They know that you know Palmer. So what more can you tell me?"

He shrugged, maintaining a steady gaze.

"What more can you tell me about Lisa and Palmer?"

"I know that Lisa and Palmer were very good friends. You know, tight, if you know what I mean."

Connie noticed Camille's face reddening, not a good sign.

"They were together a lot, always doing stuff together." Ricky continued, "Palmer really liked the boys, Mickey, and I believe the other's name is Bradley." Ricky pointed, "I also saw them with you. Or was it you? Anyway, he liked kids. He even hung out with Lisa while the boys were in school, and the boys after school."

Camille snapped out of her chair and headed for the bathroom. Connie knew exactly what her sister was thinking. Good thing she didn't try to kill the messenger.

"Ricky, you're on thin ice here. A lot of people could get hurt. Were Lisa and Palmer having an affair?"

He scowled, "Lisa and Palmer? Oh no, not at all. He didn't like brunettes. Only real blondes or dark Hispanic women. They were just friends. He called her one of his best buds."

Connie excused herself and headed to the restroom. Camille was bent over the sink squeezing the sides, staring into the mirror, "That Palmer, how dare he..."

"Hold it, you're getting worked up over nothing. Ricky clarified that they were just friends. Calm down."

Camille straightened up and looked at her.

"Had you bothered to continue questioning Ricky instead of jumping to conclusions, you would have gotten all the information you need."

"How do I know he's not lying?"

"You speak English, so does Ricky. Just talk to him. You're acting like a third grader in need of a candy fix."

Ricky was chewing down his hamburger and gulping his Coke. After watching for a minute, Connie said, "So, what else was Palmer up to besides playing games with the boys and hanging out with Lisa?

Ricky dabbed his mouth with his napkin, "Palmer was moonlighting at a security service in Carrington Beach to make extra money."

Camille knew better. Palmer had plenty of money. He had more than he'd ever need, even supporting his Grandmother.

Camille patiently waited for his next gulp of Coke, hoping he'd elaborate.

"What else can I answer for you?" he held up both hands. "Is dessert on the way?"

"Tell me about this security company."

Ricky ignored her, hailed the waitress and ordered a Hot Fudge Sundae.

"If you're looking for an affair, I'd look at Anna Lopez, the owner. Now she's a hot Latina woman." He gestured for nice breasts.

Connie saw Camille's face redden again, so she kicked her under the table.

"So where can I find this Anna person?" Camille forced through her teeth. "The one with the big boobs."

"Would you like me to take you there?"

"How much is that going to cost me?"

"I see you've heard the same saying about a free lunch, too."

They agreed to meet in thirty minutes for two hundred dollars, "I like to savor my sundae."

Connie and Camille drove to the bank. "Don't do this, "Connie pleaded, "call Marcello. Let him handle it."

Camille offered to take her home. Connie knew she had to be with Camille to hold her back from hurting the woman.

They met Ricky on the street, Camille slipped him a pile of twenties. They drove to a dumpy strip mall on a dirt road in Carrington Beach, surrounded by weeds near the oil wells. Ricky directed them to what looked like an abandoned storefront. She turned off the ignition.

"There she is. You want the one and only, Anna Lopez," he whispered into Camille's ear from the back seat. "Just slither through the doors and you'll find her."

"Are you sure you want to go through with this Camille?" Connie warned. "Maybe we should call Marcello. The place looks..."

"Get out Ricky," Camille opened her door, "If you want to stay in the car Connie, just wait here."

Connie hesitated, thinking of all the possible scenarios. She pulled out her cell phone to call Marcello, but to tell him what? What could he do? Arrest Camille? For what? Connie wasn't going to let her sister go in alone, not in her mental state.

When they got to the front door Ricky quickly walked away.

"Where are you going?" Camille called after him. "Hey, I paid you two hundred bucks!"

"You paid me to show you where Anna Lopez was. You said nothing about an introduction or holding your hand. Good luck." He kept walking down the dirt road, never once looking back.

"We better not go in," Connie reached for her cell phone. "I'll call Marcello."

Camille grabbed the cell phone out of her hand, "No! I'm going in. You stay here if you want."

Connie looked back as Ricky slowly walking down the dirt street, his silhouette getting smaller by the second.

Tony Dillon continued to squint at Anna Lopez, "You had the means, the people and the guts to kill Palmer or have him killed. If you didn't then who did?"

Anna slammed her lipstick red, finger nailed hands on the table and stood up, "You are intolerable. If you want to believe I killed a trusted employee, that's up to you. I was devastated when I heard he was killed, and so close to our next event. I had nothing to do with his death."

Tony thought for a minute. She's right, they were supposed to leave tomorrow for Guatemala.

"I have been good to both of you with your contract. Maybe the last time I couldn't pay you, but I made it right with collateral. And this is how you reciprocate and respect me?"

"So, who is my partner this time..."You?"

Anna was about to face off with him when her intercom suddenly screeched, indicating trouble up front. Anna held up one finger.

Connie and Camille opened the heavy glass door and walked into a brightly painted reception area with copies of Jackson Pollack paintings exploding on the walls. For the 10 foot by 10 foot room, five pictures were way too many. A pretty freckled faced, redhead matching dress and scarf was sitting at the desk and looked up at them in surprise.

Anna switched on the video camera covering the reception room. Two pretty blondes were standing at the front desk, one waving her arms in threats. "I want to see Anna Lopez, NOW!" The women sounded desperate and not the kind to give up easily. Connie was about to grab her cell phone back from Camille and call Marcello when a door opened. Out walked a lovely dark haired woman with copper complexion, with long, wavy hair cascading past her shoulders. A picture of elegance dressed in bright red.

"Ladies, I'm Anna Lopez." She extended her hand to Connie. Three heavy set Hispanic men in brown suits gathered behind her. "Bodyguards," Connie whispered. They shook her hand and introduced themselves.

"What can I do for you, ladies?"

Camille began to talk but Connie nudged her and asked, "May we speak to you privately, please?"

With a wave of her red nails, the men and the receptionist filed out.

"Please ladies," she motioned to the couch. Anna sat like a queen, ankles crossed and her hands laid on her lap in folds of red silk. A slight upturned smile lit up her entire face. "Now, what can I do for you?"

Camille explained Palmer's death and the help she is giving the police in the investigation.

"I was saddened by the news of his death. I knew him at Jamestown University and political events in D.C. You see, we moved in many of the same circles."

"Did he work for you?" Connie asked.

"Why yes, he did. He helped me make government connections for my security company," motioning around the room.

"Were you having an affair with him?" Camille demanded. Connie elbowed her.

"Heavens no," Anna's response was sudden and immediate. Her face changed as Camille explained her theory of a jealous lover who may have killed him when they found out about his engagement to her.

Anna listened silently, watching Camille intently. "Believe me, no one is more disconcerted than I with the cold blooded killing of my dear friend."

It took a minute for Connie to translate what Anna meant. Camille simply ignored the words she didn't understand and focused on Anna's saddened face.

Convinced nothing inappropriate occurred between Palmer and Anna, Camille thanked Anna for taking her time to speak to them.

Anna saw them to the door and gave her condolences before locking the door behind them.

Pensive, Anna walked to her office and noticed her back door was ajar. Tony was gone. "That fool," she muttered to herself. She closed the door and sat down at her desk. "Tony sent those two here. How else would those two *putas* know to show up at this time." She summoned all her goons. "Eliminate Tony and make it clean," pointing to three of her men. "And you two, I want you to get Camille Brewster and bring her here. Don't harm her, just get her here by noon tomorrow."

§ Chapter Four

Background Information

Camille secured a job with the court after she received her divorce settlement and finished court reporting classes. She scored highest in her class for her state boards. Slowly she charmed her way up the ladder, aligning herself carefully with movers and shakers.

She slept with those who could advance her career and threatened to blackmail them if they didn't help her.

She played this cunning, game until she made it to the State Supreme Court. Along with her experience and top notch reporting skills, she quickly went from lead reporter to supervisor. Camille loved her job and made her career top priority.

She'd given up on men since her divorce and saw them more as stepping stones. That is, until she met Palmer at a retirement party. It was love at first sight for both of them. But, she wasn't ready to share her life, and neither was he.

Eventually, she wanted a family, a whole family. She wanted it for her son, Bradley. He got along famously with Palmer so why not try marriage again?

When the time was right Palmer, would be ready and willing. She just had to wait it out.

He constantly evaded questions regarding his family, only saying that they were gone. He had quite a few close friends from all walks of life. He considered them his family. His philosophy was, "You can't pick your family, but you can pick your friends." And these friends were who he planned to make his extended family.

Palmer got along with Connie and loved Dolly. Aunt Dolly laughed each time he called her "Ms Dolly." He was always good to Camille, unbiased toward anyone and always ready to please. Camille loved that about him. That's why so many people loved him.

Janet Elizabeth Lynn

CHAPTER FIVE

"This is exactly the kind of situation that scares me, Camille. Those bodyguards of hers were large."

"Nah, they were short little thugs." Camille tried to maintain a cool air, but her insides felt like jello. "I could have taken them. I towered over a couple of those guys."

"Oh, come on. Your boots have three-inch heels."

"Did you forget I took a self defense class last year?"

"Camille, your instructor stressed it was strictly to get out of a situation and get help."

"Did you forget your cop training already? You've only been off the police force a year."

"Okay, cool your jets, Miss Muscle Beach. We need to tell Marcello. The police need to follow up on what you've learned."

"I'm not calling him yet."

"What? Camille, you promised..."

"What am I going to tell him? Palmer didn't have a lover? Like that would make a difference with the investigation."

"Camille, don't you see? Palmer worked for her. You have no idea what shady dealings they were involved in. Please let the police take care of this."

"Are we really sisters?" Camille was irate. "Because you're a full blown wuss, you know that? I will decide what and when to tell the police, not you. He was my fiancé, not yours."

Connie conceded that working for the police was not the best choice she ever made in her life. She learned that last year.

"These are bad people. It's beginning to look like Palmer wasn't what he appeared to be. Please Camille, get out before you get hurt."

"Lighten up. So what are those goons going to do, lurk in the shadows and kill me? Why? If it makes you feel better, I'll stay out of the shadows."

"Camille, be serious..."

"Just stay home Connie and leave the investigating to me. I can take care of myself."

They pulled up in front of Connie's house. Camille left the engine running and stared straight ahead.

"For God's sake Camille, don't be stupid. You have your son to think about."

"Find your own fiancé and quit living your life through me. You're jealous because I've had two engagements and one marriage. You've had zero. That's what this is all about, isn't it?"

"That's ridiculous! Yes, I liked Palmer, but only as a friend and brother-in-law," Connie shot back. "Nothing else. And now I'm glad I didn't get close to him, the guy is turning out to be a real piece of work."

"Get out of my car!"

"Fine." Connie opened the door and got out. "Remember what I said. I'm not picking up after you anymore." She slammed the door shut. Camille screeched away from the curb. As pissed off as Connie was at her sister, she still feared the trouble Camille would probably get into.

She got a beer and sat on her patio trying to understand her sister. That's when the guilt set in. Camille would get into so much trouble without her. Maybe even get hurt, bad. If she didn't look out for her, no one else would. Maybe, even put Bradley in danger since she's his mother. She waited an hour to calm down, then threw together a quick sandwich and headed for Camille's condo.

Connie fumbled for her key to the security gate at Camille's building and wondered how pissed off her sister would still be at her. They've had their disagreements before, but never over something like a murder. "Actually," Connie muttered, "I should be pissed off at her and should let her get out of her own mess this time to teach her a lesson." She saw Camille's car in the parking garage. She took a deep breath and braced herself for what was sure to be an unpleasant encounter. Connie pressed the doorbell. Nothing. She pressed it again and listened for the ring on the other side of the door. The bell worked. Camille either wasn't inside, or she saw her coming and wasn't answering. On her way back to the parking garage, she spotted Camille sitting by the edge of the whirlpool, dangling her legs in the water. She was talking on her cell phone. Connie sat down next to her and waited. Camille continued talking as she glanced over at a familiar pair of legs. She looked at Connie and rolled her eyes.

Camille finished her call and flipped her phone shut. "They're giving me three weeks off for vacation. I've been saving the time for something, here it is. I need to go in and sign the forms. So what do you want, oh great and good one?"

Connie began slowly and deliberately, "You know I don't like the way you're handling this helping the police thing."

Camille opened her mouth to respond, but Connie held up her hand.

"I love you. You're my sister, for God's sake. I'll support anything you want to do. Just be careful. You don't want Dale to be Bradley's only parent, do you?"

"Relax kiddo, I'm not stupid. I just want Palmer's killer caught and put to justice. No one is going to take away my dream and not pay for it."

"Ah, sweet revenge. It looks good on you." Both women looked up to see Ricky standing behind them. "So how did it go? One can only wonder how the spider woman handles such gorgeous creatures as yourself."

"If you didn't run off like a little weasel, you'd know." Camille snapped. "Don't worry, nothing happened for you to get your cute little shorts in a wad!"

Connie looked up. "You sure do get around. Hey, how did you get past the security gate?"

"I have my personal resources," like he was some hotshot cat burglar.

"So did you manage to meet the wondrous Anna Lopez?" He pulled the tab on his beer can, and gulped down a swallow. "And wondrous she is".

"So where'd you steal that beer from?"

"Like I said, I have my resources. So what's next? What will the gorgeous, vixen twins do next?"

"Well, Ricky Boy," Camille said, "I don't know about you, I'm going to the police and see what they have. I'll bet you can't do that."

"Why are you so interested in all this? What's in it for you?" Connie added.

He took a couple more gulps, and smirked, "One never knows what path they must follow in life especially on unfamiliar paths." He paused, "Or something like that." He turned on his heels and left.

"That was deep," she yelled after him. "Let's see you get out of here without running into trouble." Camille quipped. "Our security guard doesn't like intruders."

It was Connie's turn to roll her eyes. "Be careful. I know firsthand that it's a big, scary, and very dangerous world out there." She held her sister's hand, "There are people who'll kill you as easily as you'd squish a bug." With that warning, Connie added, "I gotta go," and kissed her sister on the forehead.

Connie was at the Catalina terminal boarding the catamaran for her weekly trip to check on Dolly. She actually needed some alone time with her aunt. All the way from Hacienda Beach to the house on the hill, she prayed Camille wasn't getting herself in over her head, even though she knew better.

Dolly greeted Connie with their usual hugging dance in the front yard. As long as Connie could remember, this little dance was something she looked forward to at every meeting. Their standard exchange has always been, "How's my favorite twin? I hope you're doing well because I'm doing just fine." Then they hug and dance a little more.

"Come on in and tell me how your sister is doing. I could never tell when she was just painting a big happy picture of her life for me.

"We were just here yesterday."

"I know. I made pancakes for us", as she poured the tea. Camille said she's helping the police with the investigation and is working closely with that nice young detective that came with you two."

Connie nodded and cut her pancake, "She is!"

"Now Connie, I can always tell how well you two are getting along on the mainland because both of you refer to each other as "her" or "she" when you are having trouble. So what happened this time?"

Connie hesitated telling Aunt Dolly about their adventures. "Camille learned about a woman from a creepy guy that hung around Palmer's place. It seems Palmer worked for her in some way."

"Well, what does this woman do for a living?"

"That's what bothers me. We aren't quite sure what kind of business she's in. She has some very large and scary bodyguards and there's no sign on her office door."

Dolly's sweet, smiley face dropped, and her jaw tightened, "Connie, you have to help Camille. You have to protect her. She's in danger alone, my lands. Who knows the trouble she may get into?" She hesitated for a moment, "Oh no..."

"We both know Camille's history," Connie interrupted. "That woman doesn't know when to quit."

"That woman? Now Connie be nice to your sister. Please, humor me Connie and keep an eye on your sister. She's going to get into trouble, I just know it. Please protect her." Connie lowered her eyes and nodded. She didn't like to see her aunt in distress. But she wondered why no one ever watched out for her? "You've been with the police department," she added, "you know how to protect yourself. She doesn't."

Marcello stepped across the hot beach sand in the afternoon sun with his shiny, dress shoes and ducked under the stark yellow crime scene tape. Something was wrong with this picture. "Why am I in a suit?"

He loosened his tie and scanned the CSIs who were milling around until he found Kyra Dennis. He nodded to her. He thought maybe he should apologize. He already had to sit through a lecture from his captain about respecting CSIs and harassment.

70

"Hey, Marcello." He redirected his stride to the Medical Examiner.

"Whatcha you got, Jim?"

The man in the overalls lifted the white sheet, revealing a small lump on the white sand, a chalk grey lump. He kneeled on one knee to get a better look.

"I'd say the little guy is close to newborn," Jim surmised. "The umbilical cord is still attached. I guess maybe one day old before drowning. Prolonged time in the water, some head trauma. But I'm not sure yet if it happened before, during or after the drowning."

While Jim may have sounded cold and clinical, Marcello noted Jim's quivering voice, "Heart wrenching, isn't it?"

"Who would do this?" A trembling, young voice came from the side. It was Kyra.

"I'll get him to the lab." Jim wrapped the little bundle and gently lifted it in his arms. With the reverence of a funeral, he placed the tiny body in the back of the coroner's truck.

Kyra whispered. "Joggers found the body this morning. He must have washed up from the sea."

It was difficult to keep the tears from coming as they watched the Coroner's van pull away. The rest of the team stopped for a minute of silence.

The heat from the sun beat down on Marcello. The heat of anger in his chest was stifling. He ignored the ring of his cell phone.

Connie went for a jog along the beach as the evening began to cool. She was trying to sort out the events of last night's murder. Long ago, she'd buried the bad memories of her house arrest when she was put on leave with the police department. Her pride in her accomplishments came to a crashing end when not one of the men who worked under her, or above her, had backed her. Good thing she had filed documentation. She was let off with a luke warm apology and an offer for a demotion. That only seeded her mistrust issues with men. "Focus Connie," she whined as she pounded the sand, "Get back in the present."

Her attention was diverted by what looked like a dark brown blanket lumped on the sand. It wasn't flapping in the breeze. What is that? A person? A man! She was about to jog past when she recognized Detective Prado. Maybe this would be a good time to fill him in on their escapades, knowing it would piss off Camille.

"Hey, what are you doing here?" she yelled as she approached the wrinkled brown heap with sunglasses and a crew cut. "Why are you wearing a suit on the beach?"

He looked the other way, but Connie's bouncing ponytail, firm body and sleek legs were not something most men could ignore.

She called again, "It's me Connie Cane..."

Without looking up he replied, "I know who you are."

Connie jogged in place, "You're in a bit of a sour mood. What happened? Can't find enough yellow tape to make you happy?"

"Real cute. If you really want to know why I'm down here, we found the body of an infant...drowned. It was over there," he pointed toward the tide line. Connie stopped jogging and sat next to him, "I've been a cop for years. This isn't supposed to bother me, but I can never get used to adults doing things like this to children." He stopped and looked away. His quivering voice gave away his feelings.

"It's never easy when a baby dies, regardless of whose it is."

Marcello shrugged, his eyes followed a seagull flying by.

She touched his shoulder, "Look, if you need to talk, I'm here."

It had been a long time since Marcello felt the gentle hand of a woman. He wanted to talk now and get it out.

"I was married once," he confessed, "and I had a son. They were killed in a drive by shooting. He was just a little guy. My wife was so young and beautiful," his voice choked.

Connie could feel his pain and anguish as she gently rubbed his upper arm. "How long ago did this happen?"

"Four years ago. The shooters were never found. Neither was the hit and run coward that killed my sister the year before."§

Connie connected immediately. "I lost both my parents in a fire. It could have been prevented, too, but the landlord got off. That was the end of two lives and caused the breakup of my family." She was quiet, "And the guy never apologized. What I would have given for just an acknowledgment...". She stopped and looked at the sky. This was about Marcello and not her.

She turned to the ocean, and watched the rhythm of the blue and white foam going and coming from the vast turquoise sea. The sun was setting, the sky had turned vibrant with color while the distant skyline faded into a silhouette.

"Hey, you want to get some coffee or something?" Connie asked.

"Thanks but no, I need to go," as he stood up he held his hand out to Connie. He was surprised how light she felt when she pulled herself off the sand.

He enjoyed watching Connie brush the sand off her legs, "Listen, that history of mine, it doesn't need to go any further."

"Oh, I see," Connie was surprised at his sudden shyness. "That was all just a moment of weakness when the great Detective became human for a moment? Shame on him."

He had a hurt puppy look, something she hadn't seen before. "I'm sorry, I didn't mean it. It must hurt terribly. I know, I went through that hurt for a long time with my parents. I was the weak one, cried all the time. Camille was the strong one, 'Hard as nails,' Aunt Dolly use to call her."

He looked at the ocean, "Interesting how life makes many turns. Some turns you plan on, some come out of the blue and others smack you up the side of the head. Life's just plain unpredictable."

Connie half listened to Marcello's philosophy watching the orange sky turn dark blue. "Life is how you play your cards. You either play the hand or you don't." She was shocked that she'd said that. It was a direct quote from her father. She hadn't thought of that in years and always swore that the day she started quoting her parents, she would be declared officially old.

"Love sucks," she added. Again surprised she said that.

"Care to elaborate?" Marcello perked up.

"Anyway," she returned to business, "Camille and I will be coming to see you, probably tomorrow, or maybe the next day. We have some information we found out about Palmer. It's probably not important, but it's something we found on our own."

"It'll be dark by time you get back. Can I give you a ride? I know it's a police car but it's better than nothing."

They walked arm and arm across the sand. The traffic noise increased as they got to the parking lot. They were silent until they got to her place. Marcello could have used a soft place to fall for the evening.

"Never assume what's important and what isn't. Let me be the judge of that."

She opened the car door and waited a few seconds for Marcello to say something. Nothing.

"You're welcome, Mr. Detective."

"For what?"

"Oh, listening to you, maybe."

"Yea. Right. Thanks," he said. Connie sensed his smirk in the darkened car.

§ Chapter Five
# Background Information

Marcello's father split when he was eight years old. His mother had to work to support him and his crippled six year old sister, Lupe. Marcello became the man of the house/ He took care of his sister, making sure she had all the help she needed at school and at, physical therapy. He often made lunches for both them. They were close, perhaps closer than most siblings. They often had similar thoughts.

As he hit puberty, he became an angry young man. Having to be father figure to his sister before he was ready and taking care of the house was too much for a young boy. The church didn't assist them, maybe because they never asked for help. He hated to see his mother exhausted after being on her feet all day waiting tables and on her feet when she got home taking care of them.

He got his anger out on the football field. The only thing he could do, was to pounce on others during a game and not get in trouble for it.

He met and fell in love with Maria. They married at eighteen after high school graduation. His mother soon died of cancer, leaving him to care of his sister. She had become a bright young woman with a scholarship to college. A few months, later a hit and run killed her. He went gunning for the guy he thought drove the car until he found out he and his lovely wife were going to have a baby.

Rather than look for a guy he didn't know or run the chance of going to jail, he focused on being a father. He took a job at a hospital as a maintenance worker, then moved on to become an orderly.

His son, Matthew was born. He was the second love of his life, next to this beautiful wife. The plans he had for his son filled his mind every day. He was determined to be the best dad in the world, teach him football, soccer, how to hammer nails... Marcello had it all figured out.

The universe moves in strange ways. The loss of his sister was replaced by his beautiful little boy. His life was one nice little package and he aimed to keep it on track. He would never abandon his son or his wife. Never.

Matthew was two years old when his wife and son were killed in a senseless drive-by shooting. The dreams he had for his little family were gone in a flash.

After the double funeral, he lashed out at his house in a drunken brawl, breaking anything he could with a baseball bat he had bought for his son. Police were called and he was put on a 5150 hold for his safety.

Several days in a psych ward made him realize the only way he was going to get even was to join the police force. After all, the police were not doing their job and he was going to solve both crimes.

He passed the psych evaluation five years ago then joined the police force. He never found the driver or the shooter that took his beloved family.

Janet Elizabeth Lynn

CHAPTER SIX

Lisa was greeted with a face full of fragrant, yellow carnations when she opened her door. The damp, cold blooms tickled her nose.

"Hey," Dale Brewster's face popped up from behind the flowers, "These are for you," he said with a big smile and dimples a mile deep.

The two dozen carnations weighed heavily in her arms, but not as heavily as the weight of what she was about to divulge to him.

"Did you hear?" She blurted, "Palmer Railton was murdered in his apartment."

Dale smirked, "About time that ass got what they deserved," as he walked past her and into the living room. "Where's my boy? I miss him."

"Dale listen, the police have a video showing you threatening Palmer. Have you been to the police? You said you'd go."

"I've been at the convention, I told you. I'll go tomorrow... wait a minute... Do they think I killed him?"

"I don't know what they think. But you have to go to the police now and explain where you've been or they just might think you're hiding from them."

"Wait, wait. What video? When did this happen?"

"Apparently, Palmer had hidden a video camera in his place and kept it focused on his front door. He recorded everyone who came into his apartment. "I've seen it. It's obvious you were really angry, and threatening."

79

Dale slumped into a chair while Lisa went through the events of the murder. She told him how the police questioned her and about Bradley's sadness. She went step by step and left nothing out. "You need to do the right thing. Go talk to them before they come for you."

"That's ridiculous," he fiddled with his keys. "I can prove were I was. Plenty of people saw me in Riverside, including my wife."

"Then go to the police and tell them. Do you want your own son to see you handcuffed and taken away in a police car? And in front of all the neighbors? Go. Do it before Bradley gets home from soccer."

Dale shook his head and stared at the floor, veins sticking out the side of his neck, "And good ol' Kinky Camille, what's she doing with all this?"

"She's pretty broken up and helping the police. She came here and talked to me about my relationship with Palmer."

He walked over to the window that faced the fountain. "You didn't succumb to his ... I guess they call it Metro charm too, did you?"

"He was my good friend, you know that. Don't change the subject. If you didn't kill him, go to the police."

He whipped around and stalked toward her. "What do you mean, 'If I didn't kill him,'" That was the sign of a full blown tantrum to come.

Lisa embraced him, and whispered, "Go to the police, straighten this out."

Her sweet voice and soft touch immediately calmed him like a cuddly down pillow.

"I'm concerned for Bradley." Lisa cautioned, "He can't see you being taken away by the police. Even if it's only a misunderstanding, the image of you being arrested would be burned in his memory for the rest of his life".

"I do love being with you Lisa, you know that. The whole time I was at the convention, I thought of you."

"And your wife? Did you think about her too?"

He put his arms all away around her. "What do you think?"

"Please," she gently pushed him away, "go to the police, now."

"Okay, I'll go... for you. And just so you know, I hated the guy, but I didn't kill him. I'm glad someone finally got that trash off the planet."

"Shhh," she put her hand over his mouth, "Go," and pushed him toward the door.

Distracted and intent on stopping at home to find his business receipts for proof of his trip, Dale rounded the fountain and stepped on a plant that was just watered, getting his Birkenstocks wet, "Shit, man."

"You never could control your mouth or your temper for that matter."

He looked up from his wet shoes to see Camille. Her arms were folded, sunglasses dangling from the neck of her t-shirt.

"What the hell do you want? I got a court order that says you can't come any closer than fifteen feet unless we have a witness," Dale reminded her.

"Oh yeah, we both know about court orders. Perhaps Palmer should have taken one out on you, you big asshole."

He pointed his finger straight at her, "You listen here." His voice echoed throughout the courtyard. "I didn't kill your fucking ass boyfriend and you can't prove that I did."

"I don't have to," Camille smugly lowered her voice. "You set yourself up. I just have to sit back and enjoy the show."

81

"Don't threaten me you slut!" Now his face was inches from hers. Camille stood her ground. She knew Dale would only get more aggressive if she said nothing. Since this was a public place, it was exactly the situation she needed to get custody of Bradley back. His tirade was loud enough and continued long enough for neighbors to call the police on this normally quiet Wednesday morning.

Police sirens grew louder until they abruptly stopped right outside on the street. Two uniformed police officers approached the feuding couple. Breathing heavily and red faced, Dale shut up immediately, though his veins were standing out.

They escorted him away from Camille and took him to Lisa's apartment. When Marcello arrived, Camille pleaded innocence to the yelling encounter. He calmed her down and took her out to the street.

"You have no idea what he is capable of when he gets into these rages, but I do. I was married to him for four years."

"We'll have a little chat with him. You stay out of his way... like your court order says."

"You know about that?"

"Of course, police record."

Camille rubbed her wrists, nodded and sat on a bench by the fountain. "I'll wait here for my son." It was not her day for visitation, but she wanted to see him.

When Marcello entered Lisa's apartment, he found her and Dale sipping water at the dining room table while two uniformed officers kept an eye on them.

Dale looked up at Detective Prado, "Well, what do you want?"

"My department has been waiting for you to..."

"I've been out of town on business," Dale interrupted, his

nostrils flared in anger.

"Mr. Brewster. If you're cooperative, we can collect the information from you now and be done with this. OR... we can take you down to police headquarters right now and do it there. It's your call."

Lisa stroked his arm, "Please cooperate Dale.

"I was in Riverside at a convention for the past three days. Millions of people saw me. I presented three seminars. You can check on it."

"Where were you three nights ago?"

"I said I was in Riverside, You deaf?"

After a long silence, Dale looked up at Marcello and the two uniformed officers, "Sit down, I don't like looking up at people. Especially not cops."

"Officers, cuff him and take him downtown."

Dale stood up and lunged toward Marcello, "You lying Bastard." The officers wrestled the big man to the floor, put a knee between his shoulder blades and handcuffed him. When they stood him up, blood trickled from his nose. "This is police brutality. Lisa, get a camera for God's sakes."

Lisa stood in the corner with her hands cupped over her mouth. He turned his head to look at her, his face now distorted with rage like a Halloween mask, "Dammit Lisa get the fucking camera!"

As they shoved him out the door, he stumbled over the threshold. "I fucking want my attorney, you sons of bitches! Nobody pushes me around." His threats and curses continued across the courtyard until they were finally muted when the door of the patrol car slammed shut with him inside.

Marcello followed behind, but stopped at the door, "You okay, Ma'am?" He waited for an answer. Lisa nodded, "I'll wait here for the boys. They should be home any time.

Dale stared out of the patrol car window and saw Camille by the fountain with her arm around Bradley. He'd seen the whole thing. Dale closed his eyes and rested his head on the glass. His chest filled with tightness. Tears ran down his face. He looked up and yelled, "It's all a mistake son. I'll be back in a little bit to take you home." Bradley stared back at the strange creature mouthing something from inside the police car. He snuggled his face in Camille's sweater and began to cry.

Dale's face pressed against the car window. He couldn't wave with his hands cuffed behind him. He calmed down until he saw a faint smile on Camille's lips. "Dammit! You little shit of a bitch!"§

"You okay?" Marcello asked Camille, squatting down to Bradley's level. "Everything will be all right son. We are just taking your Dad to the police station to ask him some questions. He's not under arrest. It's more like a 'time-out'. You stay with Lisa for a little bit."

Bradley nodded, wiped his eyes, looked up at his mother and hugged her.

"Marcello, can I get a copy of the police report?" Camille asked.

"Is it your time to have Bradley?" Detective Prado asked.

"No." Camille said sheepishly, "Actually, I came by to drop off his soccer uniform. I ordered another one for him before this all came down. You aren't going to take him from me are you? Not now. Not with all this going on."

"I have to follow the court order. Your son needs to stay with his guardian or his stepmother. You can visit him, but only with supervision on your off days."

Camille wanted to protest, but held her temper. "I'd like to stay with him and Lisa for a few...just so I know he will be all right."

Lisa had her arm around her own son and was standing behind Camille. She looked at Camille and Bradley, then nodded to Marcello.

Dale waited in the interview room for the detective to return. They'd left him there to cool off after they fingerprinted him and took a DNA sample. All the while, he knew the glass window he faced was two way. Anyone, even Camille could be watching on the other side.

Marcello walked into the interview room carrying his laptop. and followed by two uniformed officers.

"You calmed down yet?"

Dale rolled his eyes, "Let's get this over with I want to see my son."

"Okay, where were you last Thursday?"

"I've already told you. Now, let's see this video Lisa said you have."

Detective Prado flipped open the laptop and eyed Dale while the computer booted up.

When Marcello played the DVD, Dale watched with a stone cold stare. He realized he was in big trouble with Palmer's murder.

"All right Mr. Brewster, we both know you two weren't rehearsing for a school play. Tell me what happened."

Dale leaned forward and mopped his brow with his sleeve. "That was about a month ago...."

"The date stamp says three weeks ago."

"Like I said, about a month ago." He shook his head in frustration. "You should really write some of this stuff down. Then you wouldn't have to ask the same damn questions over and over."

"I'm waiting."

Dale sat back in his chair and took a deep breath, "I went over to give him a piece of my mind and yes, I did threaten him. But I didn't kill him. Look, the ass has been hanging around my ex-wife, my girlfriend and my son. Actually, I don't care about my ex. That bitch can do whatever she wants. But I don't want that ass hanging around my son, y'know, influencing him."

Marcello noticed Dale's wrist had a narrow white line around it. He pointed at it with his pen. "Where's your watch?"

"It's in my car. My wife gave it to me for our anniversary, so naturally I had to wear it while she was with me on the trip. We were outdoors a lot."

"What is your relationship with Lisa Lowell?"

"She's my girlfriend and my son's babysitter." He realized what he just said was not good for him or Lisa.

"She's a damn good person. Bradley loves her."

"She said you two were just friends."

He nodded and shrugged.

"Which is it?"

"I guess I'd like to be more than friends, but she's not there yet."

"You're a pretty lucky guy, a wife and a girlfriend. Tell me more about your argument with Palmer Railton."

Dale looked down at the table, shrugged and rubbed his wrist, "Nothing more to say. I told him to stay away from my son and my girlfriend or I'd..." He stopped and looked up at Marcello who had sat back in his chair and crossed his arms like he was waiting for the big lie.

"Look detective, all I did was threaten to expose his secret life to Camille. I know my ex. She would've dropped him like a dead rat. Frankly, those two deserved each other. I should've just let her marry the twit. She would've found out about him soon enough. Actually, it would've been fun to watch them crash and burn. But I want him to stay the Hell away from my son and Lisa. So I told him I'd out him if he didn't."

"Out him?" Marcello repeated.

"He's bisexual."

Marcello sat quietly.

"I saw him hanging around that fag bar on Fifth Street. I naturally assumed he was. I didn't kill him. Hey, I got receipts and credit card slips to prove where I was all weekend. You can even ask my wife."

"We plan on checking them all, believe me. We'll check every minute. See, most guys with a girlfriend and a wife think they're experts in covering their tracks." Marcello could tell he had Dale worried, "Riverside is only a forty-five minutes drive away from the crime scene. That's not even as long as a lunch break. A lot can happen. Don't even think about leaving town."

Dale lingered, "Detective," he humbled himself a bit. "Please leave Lisa out of this. She's a good person and loves my son. She's a good honest person. She just doesn't want a romantic relationship with me. That's probably why she told you we're just friends because right now, we are...only friends."

§ Chapter Six

Background Information

Camille knew something was wrong with Dale before she married him. But as a nineties pregnant women, she planned to raise her son with her sister and aunt. Dale would have nothing of it. He pursued her mercilessly until she agreed to marry him. Dolly was totally against the wedding, but agreed to hold it at her house for her niece's sake.

Dale had no family. They disowned him years ago and turned their backs on him. He was the "bad kid." He convinced Camille not to have any family at all anywhere near the ceremony and held it in a park. This broke Dolly's heart and Camille knew it. Connie didn't like Dale, but hated Camille for agreeing to Dale's demands, for what it did to Aunt Dolly.

Their marriage was tumultuous, but Camille held her own with Dale even when he refused to back down. Police were called constantly because of the fighting. By court order, they went to marriage counseling. The therapist called the police during two sessions because of their aggressive behavior.

When Bradley was born, Dale finally had the family he always wanted. He calmed down the first time little Bradley squeezed his finger. That was it, he was little Bradley's father and he set out to be the best father he could.

Camille saw through the façade and knew Dale was working desperately to keep a lid on it. While nursing Bradley, she found an article on Bipolar Syndrome that matched Dale's behavior perfectly. She convinced him to see a Psychiatrist. He was diagnosed with Bipolar disorder. After trying three different medications, he found one that worked well without many side effects. Finally, he became a model husband

and father. A true soul mate. Unfortunately, this bored Camille. She missed the crazy excitement of fighting and the mind blowing sex that followed.

She began to substitute Dale's medication with sugar by emptying the capsules and replacing the powdered medication with sugar and salt. Slowly his behavior changed, and once again she enjoyed the fights and sex. When she tired of fighting, she left his medication alone. When boredom with motherhood and wifehood would hit, she'd substitute his medication again.

She got caught in the act one day when Dale and a police buddy of his came home early for a beer. The cop arrested Camille. She not only lost custody of Bradley, but a restraining order from Dale was issued. In addition, visitation with Bradley with one hundred percent supervision was ordered by the court. She was devastated.

CHAPTER SEVEN

"Time to get to work." Because of Connie's violent allergy to onions, she donned a yellow surgical gown, purple latex gloves, a respirator and a face mask with a clear a plastic shield. Dolly called it her "hazmat suit". Even the vapors from fresh onions badly irritated Connie's lungs. She is prone to severe asthma attacks, needing steroids to breathe. Last Sunday, a small piece of chopped onion landed on her arm and caused a bleeding ulcer. It took four days to heal. That's when she got the long sleeved surgical gown.

"A cook who is allergic to onions is pathetic," she muttered while tying on her face shield. Once she cut her finger because she couldn't see out of her mask. She has since learned to breathe so not to fog it up.

Aunt Dolly gave up trying to convince her to find another line of work. Connie insisted she would not be defeated by little onions.

With her respirator tucked under her mask, she balanced eighteen shiny dishes and lids, and carried them to the counter. She figured she'd be done by midnight. That left six hours for sleep, six hours of delivery and she'd be finished until Sunday. It was close to sunset when she saw a ball come flying into her yard. Two little hands appeared on the top of the fence. A mop headed neighborhood boy looked over and screamed when he saw Connie. A second pair of hands appeared. Another head, then more screams. She understood the screams only after she caught a glimpse of her reflection in the glass of her French doors. The eerie glow of the street lights were shining on her and she almost scared herself. She thought she heard them scream "alien!" They ran away.

"Last delivery," looking at her watch, "A good morning's work." She opened the front door of the eight bedrooms Tudor on the hill, and went directly to the kitchen. She punched in three hundred degrees on the oven to cook the fresh baked cookies she leaves each visit. Connie unwrapped the sugar cookie dough, wacked off twelve cookies, put them on the cookie sheet, shoved them in the oven, and set the timer for thirteen minutes.

While they baked she unpacked the frozen food and put it in their freezer. She set the casserole for tonight's dinner in the refrigerator.

After positioning the menu prominently on the dining room table, she pocketed her check.

The cookies had a few more minutes, which allowed her time to enjoy the fantastic view from the dining room window. Connie saw a picture of their family on the wall and thought how lucky for them.

Before leaving, she artfully arranged the cookies on a plate and looked at the time. "Good, it's, noon. I'm all done." She then set out for lunch with her sister at Camille's favorite Chinese restaurant.

———————————

Meanwhile, two days had passed since Camille had been to work. When she pulled into the parking structure, she felt something familiar, something normal. She felt good. Since her divorce, her job is where she spent most of her time. Her friends were here, people who accepted her for who she was without pretense, they respected her. She was the senior court reporter, a supervisor with a lot of responsibility. she'd made many long time friends. She knew some of them just kissed up to her with gifts and luncheons to get what they wanted, but she felt the five years of tenure was worth every minute. Palmer's murder, the pressure of the investigation, dealing with the police and her sister at times, seemed more than she could bear. But she held it all together. Here, she could depend on her friends in Human Resources to give her some insight. Her name in black and white letters stared at her from her empty parking space. This was home for her car and her. She checked her lipstick and hair. It was the first time since the murder that she even cared how she looked.

She swung open the door, hopped out with the anticipation of hugs and condolences. The garage sounds and smells of tires squirming on the slick surface, car doors opening and alarms chirping were familiar. The parking structure was like the forest in the morning. As she walked toward the elevator, she listened to the familiar clicking of her high heels on the cement. Her pace quickened. Around the concrete wall, the elevator doors would open and whisk her up to her friends.§

As she reached for the up button, a car raced into the parking structure, the tires screeching. Rushed, pounding footsteps coming too close caused her to turn her head just in time to see a brown cloth appear in front of her face. She then felt pressure around her arms and waist, and felt her neck pulled back. A sudden foul stench, then black.

In the lobby, a thin, short redhead with lots of freckles strode in carrying a file folder marked "Dale's Bus. Stuff" in thick black letters. She was met by Marcello and escorted to the interview room where he quickly thumbed through the receipts.

While Detective Prado examined the folder. She watched patiently until he flipped it closed. She asked, "May I see my husband now?"

"In a few minutes, Mrs. Brewster." He slid a few photograph in front of her. "Tell me what you know about Lisa Lowell, Camille Brewster and this man."

"Please, my name is Beverly." She replied. "Mrs. Brewster is my mother-in-law and my husband's ex-wife's name. This is a photo of his first wife Camille Brewster." She smiled politely and put her finger on the edge of another, "This is Lisa." She pushed the last photo back toward Marcello. "She's Bradley's day care provider, a nice lady. She's good to Bradley and he loves her. Mickey, her little boy and Bradley are best friends. They seem to get along well and they're close in age. Why? What's all this about?" She glanced at the time on her cell phone, "It's very inconvenient to be called to the police station in the middle of my workday. I'm very busy."

"How about this man?" He slid the photo of a smiling Palmer in a tuxedo toward her.

"No, never saw him before. Why? Who is he?"

"He was shot to death Monday night." Marcello flatly stated, as if he was reading the evening news.

"And what does this have to do with Dale and myself? I don't know him."

"I understand you were at a business conference with your husband in Riverside all weekend. Was your husband with you every evening?"

She nodded.

"Was he with you for the entire evening, every night?"

Her eyes widened as she carefully placed her cell phone back in her purse and thought for a moment, "I believe Monday night we were together at a mixer, then off to a special fundraising dinner for - Oh, I don't know, something about school supplies, or whatever. Yes, we were side by side until about nine-thirty."

"Then what?"

"Well, let me remember... Dale turned in early. He had a breakfast meeting to conduct the next morning at six. I decided to stay down at the bar until about midnight."

Marcello listened to her story and took notes.

"Hey, it was my vacation, too. I didn't see a need to hang out in the room with him asleep. When he gets to snoring, you can't hear the TV. So watching a movie wasn't an option."

"So, you weren't with him from nine-thirty until midnight?"

"I told you, he was in the room sleeping and snoring."

"Can you verify that? Did you actually see him in bed sleeping during that time?"

She shook her head.

"Did you call the room for any reason? That would show a record of your call to him."

She shook her head again.

Marcello showed her the video of Dale threatening Palmer. She stared at it and sat quietly. When it was finished, he pushed the button and played it again. Afterward, she looked up from the screen and glared at Marcello.

"I know my husband has a temper, I'll grant you that. He's a Neanderthal, as big as a house. But to follow through with his threats? He's too much of a wuss. He doesn't have the balls to kill someone. He'd maybe slap them around, but never any serious violence. He's all bark and no bite."

"So, you've seen his temper before?"

"Sure, but it was never focused at me or his son. I saw him clench his fist at a nursery store manager who refused to take back a garden hose. He threw the punctured hose at him. But never anything to Bradley or me."

Marcello shrugged while he continued looking through the folder of assorted receipts. It was apparent Dale loved his charge cards, since that's what most of the receipts from.

"We'll keep this and go through the rest of these." He glanced toward the door. "You and Dale are free to leave, but stay close by."

Marcello closed the file and handed it to one of the uniformed officers.

Beverly watched the folder exchange hands, "I'll need those receipts back for taxes. When will I get them back?"

"I'll make sure you get a copy of them."

Marcello escorted Beverly down the hall to the lobby where Dale waited. His hands were pushed deep into his pockets. A half smile appeared when he saw Beverly walking toward him. As soon as she got within arm's reach, she punched him in the stomach with her tiny hands several times. Her blows didn't appear to have any effect.

"What the hell is wrong with you? Are you a fucking complete idiot?" She let him know exactly how upset she was. "You dragged me away from work in the middle of the morning. You stupid or something?" She yelled from deep within her diaphragm, "Next time, you get yourself out of the jam." With the chain strap of her purse, she swung back and caught him across the side of his head. Dale staggered back to the wall holding his bloody nose and ear.

Beverly swung her purse back with the other hand for another swipe. Marcello stepped between them and caught her arm.

He ordered her to sit on a bench across the lobby from Dale. All the while, she called Dale names he'd only heard in the lockup from gangbangers. He put a uniformed officer with her and tended to Dale who had blood down his shirt.

"You want to press charges for assault?" he asked Dale.

Beverly shouted across the lobby, "He damn well better not if he knows what's good for him...big dumbass."

She was completely opposite from the polite, restrained person he had just talked to in the interview room.

Dale looked over at her, but she wouldn't acknowledge him. Instead, he shook his head "No", and walked over to her. She stood before he got to her and headed for the door. Dale rushed to catch up and followed her to the parking lot.

"That's interesting," a female officer remarked, "Seeing a guy that big brought down to size by a fiery, five foot two redhead. Who knew?"

Dale tried to match his wife's quick pace to their car. Marcello shrugged, "She must have something on him to keep him in line."

Tony was drinking Mai Tai's - lots of them. He leaned his head against the back of the booth and downed another while he watched the strobe lights and fog machine give the Art Deco Bar a surreal look. He was very drunk.

"Okay, Prince, you've had enough." The floor mother cleared the empty glasses off the table and wiped it down with a clean white bar towel. "I don't care if you drown yourself over Palmer's death or not. But you're gonna have to go now."

"Oh, one more. Just one," Tony groped for his glass.

The floor mother held it out of Tony's reach and gently, but quite firmly took his arm. "Come on Mr. T., time to go home."

"Ha, Pete. I know you," Tony slurred, "even dressed as Mae West, I'd know your voice and strong grip anywhere."

Tony and two other wasted patrons were escorted outside and loaded into a van. The bar had its own designated driver for just such an occasion. If there was one rule to which the gay men of Hacienda Beach held fast, it was no one drives drunk, regardless of their relationships.

After the driver dropped off two other lost souls, Tony and the driver waited and watched until they saluted good night from their front door. He was next. Luckily they lived on the ground floor. After he was deposited at his address, he saluted the driver by his door and watched him drive away. He reached in his pocket for his keys. When out of the corner of his eye, he noticed the rustling of the Lantana bushes to his right.

"Okay cat," Tony searched deeper in his pockets for his keys, "What do you...?"

Someone grabbed his leg and pulled him down behind the large shrubs. They taped his mouth and wrists with electrical tape. In his drunken state, he wasn't sure how many people stood over him, but they beat him mercilessly with something that felt like baseball bats or two by fours. He wasn't sure, but he thought he'd been thrown into a blender with a professional hockey team. Tony grabbed for the roots of the bush and pulled himself under it to protect his head and tucked into a fetal position. His back and legs took the brunt of the attack. The tape over his mouth prevented him from calling for help. The beating continued while he played dead. That was easy since the severe pain had turned to numbness. The attackers then started working his sides. He could hear a rib crack with every kick. Right before he lapsed into unconsciousness, he vaguely remembered the sound of breaking glass and sirens. Tony never expected to die so violently. He'd always imagined that he would be surrounded by loved ones... then blackness.

Connie was worried when Camille didn't show up for their lunch date. This wasn't like Camille. She always called when she was going to bail on her. After forty minute, she stopped by Camille's condo. She found nothing out of place, so she sat down at the breakfast bar and called Camille's cell again. While she listened to it ring for what seemed like forever, she noticed Camille's planner and flipped through to today. She saw that her sister had scheduled a breakfast appointment with some co-workers at the courthouse for nine o'clock, and then an appointment at Human Resources. She kept trying Camille's cell until two p.m., then she called Aunt Dolly.

"Is Camille out there with you?"

"No dear, why?"

"It's nothing. She didn't make our lunch date and she usually calls if she's going to blow me off."

"Well, you know how your sister is. I'm sure there's a simple explanation."

She hung up and called Camille's work. She tried to figure out the "press one and press two thing, but got lost in phone "Hell". Frustrated, she left for the courthouse. No one had seen her. She never showed up.

Connie called Marcello and waited in the Courthouse parking lot. He showed up with several other police officers who canvassed the garage. Camille's Porsche Cayman was found parked in a far corner.

"Open it," Marcello ordered. One of the officers put on a pair of rubber gloves, pulled out a Slim Jim and slid it down between the glass and the door.

Slowly the officer opened the door. With his flashlight, he examined the interior before popping the trunk open. He repeated the systematic search.

"Nothing seems disturbed," Kyra reported. "I'll look at it more carefully at the station." She looked at Connie, "Does your sister always keep her car this spotless?"

"What is wrong with you people, my sister is missing," Connie yelled, "And all you can ask me is if my sister is a neat freak?" She lunged at Marcello and hit him in the chest with her fists, "How could you let this happen? Camille is trying to help with the investigation. You should be taking better care of her."

An officer pulled Connie away from Marcello, "Do you want me to book her for assault?" Marcello straightened up and shook his head. "No, just take her to my office and tow that car to the Station. Get the surveillance video of the garage and send it up to me."

In Detective Prado's office, Connie looked up at Marcello, her eyes swollen from crying. He set a cup of tea in front of her and sat across the table. "Your Aunt Dolly is on her way. We called her to take you home. The helicopter will be landing in less than an hour."

He watched Connie as she sipped the freshly brewed tea.

"We're doing all we can to find Camille, including searching her condo. It was a mess.

"Wait. I was at her condo until two p.m. today and everything looked fine. I didn't notice anything unusual. You saw how neat she kept her car. Everything seemed to be in order."

"You're sure?" Marcello asked as he picked up his cell phone and looked at the photo again. He decided not to show her the photo of how the condo looked at four p.m.

"I thought I was going to die right then and there." Tony told the police officer who took his statement in the emergency room.

The doctor adjusted the brace on Tony's sprained ankle, "Quite frankly, you probably would have died had the beating gone on any longer. You were smart to protect you head. You have several broken ribs, sprained ankles, and severe bruising on your back and buttocks. But, with the exception of a few other bad bruises, your spine appears uninjured."

"What happened?" Tony mumbled, while gingerly touching the bandages on his face.

"For one thing, you have a lot of shallow cuts on your face

probably from the bush you were hugging."

"But why?" he moaned.

"We were hoping you could tell us." One of the officers asked. "What is your name?"

"Tony Dillon. My head hurts really bad. I don't remember much of the attack, just pulling myself under the bushes and somebody beating the crap out of me with something."

The officer took some notes, "Any idea who would do this to you and why?"

"Not a clue." Tony knew full well it was Anna Lopez's goons, but if he told the police and it got out in the media, they'd come by and finish the job.

"So," Tony mumbled, "How did I get here?"

"We got a tip from an anonymous caller. He told us where to find you. We found your front window smashed in. Any idea how that happened?"

"No." Tony slowly faded back into unconsciousness. He heard voices and words in the blackness of his mind, "...chair...earring...witnesses..." then blank.

As the Police helicopter landed on the roof of HBPD head-quarters, Connie waited and watched a figure with a large bun on the back of her head bounce out of the copter and run toward her. They embraced, but without the hugging dance.

"What do the police know about Camille?" Aunt Dolly whispered in her ear.

"Not much. They're waiting for the surveillance video from the garage." Connie took her by the arm, "Everything is so mixed up, I don't know what to think."

Marcello stood by and watched. His heart told him he was falling for Connie, but he didn't want to believe it.

There was nothing they could do at the station, so Dolly and Connie left for her beach house. "After what that nice young detective told me, I don't want to go near Camille's house."

"Whoever it was, made quite a mess of the place."

"The weird thing is that her place was nice and orderly when I left at two p.m. Seems like a hurricane hit it before four o'clock. Do you think someone was hiding there while I was inside?"

"Maybe," Dolly suggested, "and maybe it was done to make it look like a burglary."

"That means they went to a lot of trouble to make it look like one."

They stopped at Tommy's and picked up some burgers.

As they settled into the tiny kitchen, Dolly remarked, "I must be getting old because your place looks even smaller than I remember." Connie looked around and shrugged. "Hmm, nothing's changed since you were last here." With that, they unwrapped their hamburgers, listened to the surf and watched out the window as the luminous waves washed on the beach.

While they finished their makeshift dinner, Connie saw something in the backyard out of Dolly's view. It looked like a figure. She gathered up the wrappings. "I'll be right back, Auntie. If I don't take these out to the trash, we'll be over-run with ants."

Connie went out the back door. After looking both ways, she stepped around the large plastic trash containers and lifted the lid.

"Hey there." Ricky popped up from behind her recycling container.

"Jesus, Ricky," Connie gasped, "you scared the shit out of me". She lowered her voice to a whisper, "What's wrong with you?"

"I'll be brief. I know where Camille is. I saw her being forced into an SUV."

"You have to tell the police, Ricky." She slammed the trash container lid and grabbed his sleeve. "You have to tell them now!"

Ricky cowered behind the container, "Going to the police is not in my best interest. You know that. I just thought you'd like to know that I know where she is. Keep in mind no one else knows but me."

"So what are you going to do with the information?" Connie crossed her arms.

"If you want to know the whereabouts of your sister I have a price, five grand."

"Are you nuts? What makes you think I have five thousand dollars?"

Ricky spread his arms and said, "My dear, you must be joking. Check out your digs. You have to be loaded to live someplace like this. Right on the beach!" He turned his back and scanned the ocean. "This is a million dollar view you have, from your alley, at least."

"Connie?" Dolly's voice chimed from inside the little house, "Is everything all right?"

"I have to deal with a little garbage problem," she glared at Ricky. "I'll be there as soon as I get rid of it." Connie turned back to her uninvited guest, "Even if I did have the money, how do I know you didn't make up a story for the money and split after I pay you. I think you're lying to me."

"Suit yourself, my dear. It's not MY sister who's in danger."

They stared at each other for a moment.

"Can you live with her death if you don't tell what you know?" Connie was getting impatient. "Could you live with two deaths on your conscience, Camille and Palmer's?"

"Damn it, I didn't kill Palmer," he yelled. "I'd never do anything like that to him."

Connie shushed him and whispered, "Okay, I didn't mean that."

"I tell you I didn't kill anyone. Now, am I getting my five grand or what?"

"Go to hell." She reached for her cell phone and called Marcello before she went back inside with Dolly.

Connie waited for Detective Prado on the beach by the lighted bike path. When Marcello arrived, Connie ran up to him. "My sister may have been kidnapped."

"Where's your aunt?"

"She's probably asleep now. I told her I was going for a walk."

"Still protecting her, I see."

Marcello's face went serious. After Connie told him everything, Ricky, Palmer, Anna and her goons, he arranged for a backup team to meet them at Anna's storefront. His deep, pensive look worried Connie.

The Patrol cars were already positioned in the parking lot when Marcello and Connie arrived. The other stores in the area were dark.

Marcello turned to Connie and sternly ordered her, "Stay in the car and keep your head down." He went to the trunk for his Kevlar Vest and drew his gun before joining the helmeted police officers with SWAT stenciled in big yellow letters on the backs of their jackets.

A dozen officers armed with automatic weapons covered

every opening. Two more took a large steel ram and with one swift action, bashed the door open. The others poured into the building through the small door. Anxious to see her sister, Connie got out of the car. She stayed low and crept toward the door. She leaned in and peeked around the corner of the opening. Everything was gone, except for some over turned chairs. It was obvious they left in haste.

Connie dodged the SWAT team members as they filed back out of the empty building. She found Marcello and grasped his hand, "I saw them here yesterday, running a full business. People, papers, fax machines, computers, everything." She wandered around aimlessly, staring at the empty space and blank walls. A few investigators milled around the back rooms, but most of the police had left.

"We have an APB out on this Ricky character. If he knows something, we'll make sure he tells us."

Connie broke down and squatted in the corner crying, her face cupped in her hands. "It's my fault," she whined, "I should have come to you as soon as I learned about this, but I did what Camille asked. I was afraid if I went to you first, she'd do something stupid."

Marcello put his cell phone in his pocket and sat next to her on the floor. "You did what you thought you needed to do. It wasn't smart, but it was loyal." He put his hand on her arm, "We'll find her and Ricky."

"I'm really sorry," she sobbed, "I knew better."

He put his arm around her shoulder and pulled her face to his chest, "Okay, let it out. Let it all out," and handed her his handkerchief. It felt soft on her runny nose.

"Where are they?" she whimpered.

"Our people are on the streets looking for Ricky. As for your sister, I don't know."

"Do you know this Anna Lopez?"

"She's been on our watch list for a long time. We lost track of her a year or so ago. I'm surprised she turned up back here." He looked around the empty store, "I actually thought she had better taste than this."

"You should have seen it when we were here. It was beautiful." Connie blew her nose, "But why were you watching her?"

"Sorry, I can't say... it's classified." Marcello murmured.

"What am I going to tell Aunt Dolly?"

"You're aunt is tougher than you give her credit.

———————————

Slowly Camille began to regained consciousness. She smelled something musty with a faint odor of old tomatoes and something else she couldn't recognize. When she tried to cover her nose, she found that her hands were tied behind her. She felt the lump on her left hand. Her ring was still there. Slowly, her eyes adjusted to the light and focused on a big greasy-looking guy who'd just pulled the blindfold off her eyes. When he stepped back, she could see that she was in an empty warehouse with a big, soapy front window. She knew she was in deep trouble. The greasy guy and two other men had their guns pointed at her head. She tried to call out for help, but her mouth was still sealed shut with a wide piece of duct tape.

"If you scream," a familiar female voice said from behind her, "these men will not hesitate to expedite your demise." Camille could recognize her voice pattern anywhere. Anna Lopez stepped into her view. With her blood red fingernails, she ripped the tape from her face, then walked around behind the three men so not to be in the line of fire.

"OW! What's going on?" Her lips felt like the skin came off with the tape. "I'm investigating Palmer Railton's murder, trying to solve it."

"That may be so." Anna commented while she emptied

Camille's purse onto a dirty table and sifted through her belongings, "But right now, you will need to take Palmer's place for a little outing we had planned."

"You won't find much in the way of money in there. I use credit cards, mostly. Take my ring. It's got to be worth something."

"First of all, I am insulted that you think I would stoop so low as to take your money." Anna sneered, "especially the little money you have. Secondly," she pulled out Camille's wallet and took out her driver's license. "Yes, this picture will do well." Anna held it next to Camille's face before handing it over to a fourth man. "We will need to dress you differently though," she motioned to someone behind Camille.

Her thighs tightened. She could feel the tears running down her cheek at the thought of being raped or worse.

"Don't worry, Miss Camille," Anna assured her, "you will not be harmed by any of my boys. Like I said, you and I are taking a little trip. Palmer was supposed to do this, but he has sadly expired. You are the likeliest substitute." Anna stuffed Camille's things back into her purse and tossed it onto her lap. "I didn't plan on going myself, but unfortunately, now I must. I can't afford to have you harmed if you are to make the trip."

"What trip? Where are we going?" Camille sniffled.

"I need you to look like a kind, sweet mother." Anna stepped up to Camille and flipped the shoulder of her sweater. "That sexy chemise you're wearing simply won't do."

All the men left, except for two who kept their guns trained on Camille.

Anna turned toward the door. "I suppose we should feed you so you will look well nourished. You have your choice, pizza or tacos?" Camille looked at the two remaining men, the barrels of their guns still pointed at her head. "Pizza please."

§ Chapter Seven

Background Information

Dolly Elsworth-Moorhead was born in Richmond. She was raised to be a socialite which she embraced whole heartedly. Her life was centered around parties, representing her family at political events and giving money away. At Dartmouth College, she met a farmer, Harold Morehead. He was a shy polite gentleman who planned to use his business degree to work his family farm in Nebraska. One day at a bar, he used his napkin to sketch a device to imprint designs on a piece of paper. He researched the apparatus and patented it. After visiting several companies, he decided to build it himself. That's when he met Dolly. Her family had money. He approached her and her family to finance the first machine.

It worked beautifully.

He and Dolly fell in love and planned to elope. Rich city girl falls in love with a farmer. He couldn't do that to the family who believed in him. So they waited. He sold his first machine, the second and the third. The rest is history and he became a multi-millionaire worthy of marrying an Ellsworth daughter.

Her family gave them a storybook wedding. After three years, it was time to graduate and move to the farm. They moved into the family home just before his father's death.

His father left the farm to Harold's stupid, younger brother. He was a real hot head with no experience. Knowing his brother, Harvey, would ruin the farm, he protested. After days of arguing, their mother stepped in. She acknowledged that Harold was smarter and told them the farm was left to Harvey because he had no other future. Harold was smart enough to follow his own path. She decided to honor their father's wishes and against her better judgment, and to keep peace in the house. She supported Harvey.

Dolly stood by her husband, admiring his tact and diplomacy. They moved to Catalina where they became active in the community. They never had children, but longed for their yearly visit from her sister's children, Connie and Camille. When the girl's parents, died there was never a question where the twins would live.

CHAPTER EIGHT

Ricky waited in the interview room at the police station. It wasn't his favorite place. He'd made it through life by acting the fool, knowing more than he let on and staying out of trouble enough to run the same old act.

Marcello did not appear happy as he flung the door open. "Well, Ricky, it seems you've been withholding evidence." He leaned forward so his face was only about a foot from Ricky's. "You must want to see the inside of a jail cell again real bad."

Ricky played with his fingers, as he switched roles to that of a confused kid. "So, who said I had anything more to say?"

Marcello sat quietly and stared at Ricky.

Ricky mouthed, "Connie" and slammed his palm on the table, "that bitch." He let out a big sigh and leaned back in the chair, "Okay, what do you want to know?"

"Let's start off with your association with Palmer Railton."

"All I know is that Tony and Palmer were good buds, real close. They went everywhere together."

"...Anna Lopez?"

Ricky cleared his throat. Marcello sensed that Ricky was stunned by the change in subject.

"She was Palmer's girlfriend or maybe Tony's. I'm not sure."

Marcello glared at him in the way that made most young men squirm. "Do I have to drag the information out of you? Forget it, maybe a few days in a cell will jog your memory."

Ricky knew Marcello had the power to put him away or cut him loose. Either way, Ricky knew Anna was probably already out of the country.

111

Marcello glanced at the clock on the wall, then glared back at Ricky, "Well? What's it going to be?" Ricky drummed his fingers on the table as if he was listening to some song in his head instead of the detective's questions. Marcello motioned to the officer by the door.

"Okay, okay. Palmer and I were friends, but he was more like a mentor to me. I told him I wanted to be in politics like him some day. He helped me make contacts and I crunched numbers for him, kind of like research for his Lobbying. Tony was usually there whenever I went over to see him."

"Most of his neighbors remember seeing you, but no one we spoke to remembered seeing you with Palmer."

"Oh yeah, well Palmer was uncomfortable being seen with me in public. He had a reputation to keep up. That's what he told me about politics. First impressions and appearances were everything. So we didn't do much together in public. That was Tony's job."

"When we talked to you on the night of the murder, you said you knew nothing about the killing. Did your memory return? Is there anything more you'd like to add to what you told us?"

Ricky drummed his fingers on the edge of the table, then abruptly stopped.

"It was dark. What could I have seen that the others couldn't? But if Palmer was going or coming from somewhere, Tony Dillon was probably close by, and that's a fact."

"Why didn't you say something before?" Marcello tossed his pencil onto the clipboard.

"First of all," Ricky sneered, "you didn't ask. Second, you didn't mention Anna Lopez."

Marcello reached across the table and grabbed Ricky's shirt at the throat, "Where are they, punk? Where's Anna Lopez and her guys?"

Marcello let go of Ricky's shirt and let him fall back onto the chair.

Ricky smoothed his collar, "I don't know, man. You have to talk to Tony Dillon."

"Okay smart guy, where's this Tony? And you better not tell me some bullshit story."

The Captain leaned in the door. "Dillon's in the hospital."

Ricky straightened up and pointed at Marcello, "Did you see him grab me? That's police brutality, you're my witness! He can't treat me like that." He turned to Marcello, "You asshole."

"You're free to go Ricky, but don't go too far. We're watching you." Marcello poked Ricky's chest twice. "I'm serious."

Ricky grinned and pushed himself away from the table. The captain held the door open and watched him slowly walk down the hall.

After the captain shut the door, "Just what the hell do you think you're doing?" he bellowed.

Marcello sat back, loosened his tie, and looked up at his boss. "What?"

"A year ago you almost lost your job and got put in jail for police brutality. Now you're walking a very thin line with what I just witnessed."

"Okay, Okay. Warning duly noted. What's up with this Tony?"

"I'm serious, Prado." Captain took a deep breath and bit this lower lip. "We've got officers posted at Tony's hospital room. He was badly beat up a couple of hours ago. When he was admitted, he was barely conscious but demanded police protection. I'm waiting on a warrant for his car and house."

"Oh really?"

113

"Yeah, that storefront you raided had Tony's fingerprints all over the back doors."

"Maybe we ought to talk to the guy."

They stopped at the nurse's station and asked about the patient. The nurse told them that he was still in bad shape, but not critical. "He could come off the IV and oxygen, but he refused. Pain pills alone would do the trick, but he wants everything. The neck brace will need to stay on for a few weeks. The doctor wanted to send him to a nursing home to recuperate, but he refused to go."

When Marcello and the captain arrived at his room, the officer posted outside Tony's room jumped to his feet.

"Anything new?" the Captain asked.

The officer shook his head "No sir, been real quiet. All he does is sleep. Windows are locked."

In the darkened room Marcello could see the glowing and blinking lights from the machines monitoring Tony's vitals. Marcello followed the tubes from the IV bags to Tony's arms and listened to the constant beeping from the heart monitor. As he neared the bed, he switched on the light. It became evident how badly Tony had been beaten.

The Captain reached past the tubes and wires, and pulled the oxygen mask off of Tony's bandaged face, "Wake up Mr. Dillon." He kicked the bed for emphasis.

"Hey man. What're you doing? Can't you see I'm injured here?"

"Yeah right. I spoke to the nurses. They said you don't need to be hooked up to all this equipment anymore, but you demanded they leave it in place.

"Well, I'm hurt."

"They said you could've checked out and gone to a nursing home, but you refused."

The captain began switching off the monitors and shutting off the IV flows. "Do you think because you asked for Police protection, that the city is going to pay for all this fluff if it's not needed?"

"It's not fluff. I hurt and I told the doctors I need it." Tony grabbed for the IV stand, but Marcello rolled it out of his reach. "What are you guys doing here anyway? I'm a victim. Don't you have bad guys to catch?"

The captain left the room and returned with the nurse. "See, she's changing the IV. Doesn't that tell you I'm bad off?" To Tony's horror, she pulled out the IV instead and stuck an adhesive bandage on his arm.

The captain stood on the other side of the bed from Marcello, "Well, Mr. Dillon. We searched you car and home - and guess what we found?"

Tony's pained look switched to terror. "You searched my home and...Why?"

"What's a good looking man like you using makeup, wigs and gaudy jewelry for? Unless you're an actor. This usually means you're hiding something." Marcello no sooner finished his sentence than the captain pulled the plug for the call light.

"Come on you guys, I'm buzzing the nurse." He reached under the sheet and pushed the call button.

"Oops. Sorry," the captain held up the other end of the call button cable, "Oh! It came unplugged. I may need some glasses soon."

Marcello leaned on Tony's bandaged hand, "YOU tell me the answers to my questions now or we talk inside a cell downtown." Marcello flashed Tony's fake ID that was found in his car. "Or should I say Ms Tonya Jones?"

"Nurse!" Tony screamed. "Nurse!"

"Scream all you like, they won't come." Marcello turned to

the Captain, "I think the boys at the station would get a kick out of him in a hospital gown. The back don't always stay tied. Get my drift?"

Tony closed his eyes and winced. "Okay, okay. Sometimes I'm Tonya Jones."

"Duh, yeah. Why?" Marcello replied "What's your relationship with Palmer Railton? Where is Anna Lopez?"

Tony stared at the ceiling. He didn't budge or say a word. Marcello threw off the covers and let him lay there with his hospital gown crunched up around his thighs until he began to shiver.

"Talk," the captain threatened, "or we go downtown as you are and with some extra jewelry... handcuffs."

"Okay, all right. If I talk can I stay here?"

The captain asked again, "Where is Anna Lopez?"

"Probably in South America by now, which country I don't know."

"Whaddya think detective?" Marcello pulled out his handcuffs.

Through chattering teeth, Tony whined, "I don't know, honest. They could've gone to Guatemala, El Salvador, Costa Rica or Belize for all I know."

"That's Central America," Captain insisted.

"They? Who else is with her? Why would she go there?" Marcello clamped on one handcuff.

"You want more? Get a nurse in here. I want someone to witness this brutality."

Marcello and the Captain jerked Tony up to a sitting position, clamped on the other cuff and pulled him out of bed. With his gown wide opened in back, they sat him on a chair by the wall.

"Anthony Dillon, you're under arrest for the murder of Palmer Railton." The captain opened the door. A uniformed officer walked in followed by a nurse who pulled off the heart monitor patches while they read him his rights.

"Ow." Tony glared at the nurse. "You were so nice last night. Ow!" She pulled off another patch. Tony looked up at Marcello, "Wait. I didn't kill Palmer, I swear. Someone else did."

"You need to keep the neck brace on." The nurse put his belongings in a pink plastic pail while Marcello and the uniformed officer pulled Tony up by the shoulders causing him to scream with pain.

"Just be careful of his left side," The nurse advised, "several ribs were broken." She handed Tony's clothes and belongings to the Police officer.

"Okay." Tony cried, "I'll tell you. Just put me down."

Marcello nodded and the uniformed officer dropped the shivering, bare-butted Tony into the cold vinyl covered chair.

"I was in Palmer's apartment," tears welled up in his eyes. "in a back room when I heard the shots. But when I got to Palmer, he was barely breathing and had no pulse, so I left.

"I guess you never heard of calling 911?"

"Whoever killed Palmer was probably also after me, too and I wasn't going to wait around. I'm sorry Palmer bit the dust, but I have my own survival to worry about."

"Other than being an idiot, why would someone want both you and Palmer dead?"

Tony put his head against the wall and sighed.

"Anna Lopez has a business." He paused and chose his

words carefully, "For a fee, she procures infants from underdeveloped countries in Central and South America for couples in the United States and Canada."

"Legally?" The captain asked.

"You'll have to discuss that with Anna."

"You're saying she runs a baby stealing ring?"

"Palmer and I were in the thick of it. I would pose as a distraught, but hopeful mother-to-be and Palmer would play my supportive and loving husband. Whenever we went to pick up a child, those poor ignorant locals would fall for it, every time," Tony bragged, "That evening, we just got back from Guatemala. I went in the back room to take off my costume when I heard the shots. That's the truth."

"When was this?"

"I got to Palmer's around five. I heard a knock at the door. I ran to the back room and that was it. I have no idea who was at the door. The killer, I suppose."

"What about the security video, did you tamper with it?"

"Security video? I don't know what you're talking about."

"How about Anna Lopez?"

"I told you, I don't know. She's probably the one who sent her goons to kill me. I'm just glad they didn't succeed. No thanks to the wonderful HBPD."

"When's the next escapade scheduled?"

"I don't know. I was supposed to go someplace, but I guess she wanted me dead instead. The next pickup was supposed to be this week."

"Where is Camille Brewster?"

"That bitch?" Tony's face turned red, "She wanted Palmer, but he wanted me. He loved me, not her. If Anna has her, then good riddance. She was a royal pain in the ass."

"She said she was engaged to Palmer." Marcello stated, "Are you saying she's lying?"

"If he wanted to marry her, which he didn't, he would have given her a ring."

"Now you're under arrest for conspiracy, baby stealing and kidnapping, along with the murder of Palmer Railton." The captain turned to the nurse, "Get him dressed. We're taking him downtown."

"Hey, I cooperated. I told you what you wanted to know." Tony yelled as Marcello and the captain walked to the door. "I'm too sick to leave. You promised."

Marcello turned on his heel. "Be grateful we're allowing the nurse to dress you before we take you in."

"Jeez, why do you cops have to make a federal case out of every little thing?"

The Captain stopped and turned around, " Thanks for reminding us. We'll probably call in the FBI because of the kidnapping charge. That's already a Federal offense."

Connie waited patiently at the front desk of the police station to see Marcello. All the while the receptionist had her back turned, yakking with a friend on the phone.

"Hi Camille," a voice began a one-sided conversation behind her. "How are you doing, my dear? Why didn't you come by yesterday? Bradley missed you."

She spun around only to see Lisa approaching her with a nauseating forced smile.

Connie had forgotten about Bradley. So much has gone on

in the last three days. Did Lisa need to know about Camille now?

"What are you doing here?"

"Dale asked me to drop off some papers the police asked for regarding his business trip.

"First of all Lisa, I'm Connie. And for your information, Camille's been kidnapped," the words fell out of her mouth, but they were foreign sounding. They didn't seem like her own words or voice. Never in her life did she think she would be discussing the kidnapping of someone she knew, let alone her sister.

Lisa brought her hand to her lips, "I'm sorry, I mistook you for Camille." She searched Connie's face. "Did you say Camille was kidnapped? By whom?"

Connie was more than used to people confusing her and her sister. She'd tired of it long ago. Normally, her polite response was, "Everybody does, don't worry," but she couldn't get the words out.

Lisa reached for Connie's hand, "Is there anything I can do to help?" Connie was about to respond politely, when Marcello appeared at the desk.

"Detective, Connie just told me. Is it true about Camille? She's been kidnapped? What can I do to help?" Lisa seemed truly concerned.

Marcello glared at Connie.

"I'm sorry, Marcello. It just slipped out," Connie couldn't hold back the tears any longer. She'd put on a tough face for Aunt Dolly but she couldn't hold it back another moment.

He thrust his hands in his pockets then pulled them out and dropped his hands at his side, anything to keep from reaching out to embrace Connie. He guided her and Lisa around the corner. "I've just received a disturbing video from the parking garage. I'll need you to identify a few things. Would you like Lisa to stay for support? Or maybe help you with the information we may need? If not, I can have her view it separately. Keep in mind, time is of the essence."

Connie nodded, "It's okay. Maybe she can recognize something."

As Marcello set up the video, Lisa put her hand over Connie's, "We've got a good police department. They'll do everything possible to find Camille." Her words were comforting.

As the video rolled, Lisa and Connie watched silently. "Okay-it's a parking structure. What exactly are we looking for?" Lisa asked, when the screen abruptly showed a horrific scene of a terrified woman being assaulted and dragged away by three thugs.

They couldn't see Camille's face. As she was grabbed, the men put their hands over her mouth and threw her into a plain white, windowless van that sped out of the picture. It all happened in less than a minute. Marcello replayed it slowly and pointed out details which made Connie's pain last even longer. "I know that's Camille," Lisa started, "I recognized her sweater set with the pearl buttons. Bradley gave it to her as a birthday present."

"Ricky lied. He told me Camille was kidnapped," Connie added. "She was molested!"

"I see your police training has disappeared." Marcello couldn't avoid insulting her. He was angry that she gave confidential information to Lisa.

"Inconsistencies are important," Connie snapped. "How could he know she was kidnapped unless he was there?"

Marcello zoomed in close on Camille's hand. "Check it out. She's trying to pull the guy's hand away from her mouth. She gave them a good fight."

"Look," Connie jumped forward in her chair, "Look at her hand. That's Camille's engagement ring. I'd recognize those rocks anywhere."

Marcello pointed to the time code at the bottom of the screen. "This video was taken at nine-thirty this morning. Any idea why someone would take her?"

Lisa shook her head and looked at Connie, "I have no idea." Marcello sensed something was up between them.

Connie took a deep breath and shook her head, "I don't have a clue. I told her I was afraid something like this was going to happen."

Marcello separated the two women and first took the weeping Connie back to his office. He ordered a uniform to take Lisa's information and send her home.

The Captain appeared in the doorway, "Detective Prado, the Feds are here. They'll be working with you on the Brewster kidnapping. So, look sharp. These folks will be watching your every move. You know how the FBI likes to hijack our cases so they can claim credit for the arrest."

Marcello nodded and glanced at Connie as they followed the Captain into the room. But before he could make introductions, a rather tall man in a plain, dark blue suit stood and extended his hand to Connie, "Special Agent Jerome Smith, Federal Bureau of Investigation. I've been assigned to assist in the investigation of your sister's abduction." Agent Smith, who looked like a college football player, pulled a chair out for Connie before he introduced himself to Detective Prado. She noticed how he carefully straightened his tie with manicured fingers before he picked up a marker from the trough in front of the whiteboard.

"We have reason to believe Camille Brewster is mixed up in illegal baby trafficking from Central America." Agent Smith pronounced while spelling out "Illegal baby trafficking" on the board in large black letters. Do any of you have information regarding this?"

Detective Prado nodded, "We've been piecing things together and it's beginning to look that way."

"Baby trafficking? No." Connie blurted, "Look at the video. She was taken against her will." Connie spun around and took Marcello's arm, "You know Camille well, Marcello. How could you think that?"

"Could this have been going on without your knowledge?" Agent Smith asked the Captain. His glance then shot to Connie, Marcello, then back to the Captain, "It appears Palmer Railton was heavily involved with this ring, along with Tony Dillon. They both were getting paid handsomely." Could Camille have been secretly involved? She could be acting a part. "Look at how they were all framed right in the middle of the camera's view. Staged perhaps?"

Connie's anger turned to confusion. Could her own sister have been a part of this without her knowledge? She gets in a lot of fixes, but how could she do such a thing?

The Captain's voice boomed across the room startling Marcello and Connie. "She may have kept you in the dark to protect you." He looked directly at Connie, "Or maybe you could be covering for your twin sister? You two are pretty tight. Are you trying to save your own hide by acting like you didn't know this was going on?"

He motioned for Marcello to follow him and Agent Smith into the hall. He closed the door behind him. Connie sat alone, mystified.

A few moments later, Marcello and Smith returned. Marcello looked into Connie's eyes "As you can tell, we aren't sure who's playing who. All we know is that we have to act swiftly to save your sister. That is, if she needs saving. And now that the FBI is involved, they have a plan that includes you."

"I don't know if I want to get mixed up in all this." Connie put her hand to her forehead, "All I want is my sister brought back safely. I don't want to put her in any more danger than she's already in."

"The minute I saw that you two were identical twins, I came up with a plan," Agent Smith said. "I need you to act as a decoy when we go down to Guatemala."

"Guatemala? What do you mean you need me to be a decoy?"

"It's dangerous, but the FBI will be there monitoring you the entire time. It looks like it's the only way to save Camille. We believe the next theft of babies will be in Guatemala."

She looked down at her hands. "I really want to help save Camille, but when Bradley was born she made me promise that I would stay close and take care of him if something happened to her." Her eyes drifted up to Marcello's. "If something happens to both me and Camille, he'll be left with that sorry excuse of a father. Having no father is probably better than that. My Aunt Dolly can't take him. She isn't getting any younger."

"I'll explain the whole thing on the flight down." Agent Smith gave a quick peek at his watch. "We have to move fast. Are you willing to help your sister?"

"Only if you wire me. I want you to hear what's going on. I've never done anything like this and I don't speak Spanish."

"You sure you want a wire? These people don't care about human life. If they discover you're wired, they'd kill you without blinking."

Connie closed her eyes, "Okay, I'll do it for my sister. But I still want the wire."

"It will not..." Agent Smith began.

"I don't trust you. Not the way you were talking about my sister, the victim may I remind you. I want recorded proof that I am not involved in this!"

Marcello hesitated but agreed.

He patted his palm on the table and stood up. "All right. Let's get to LAX. The bureau will have a charter flight waiting for us."

"Now? I have to call Aunt Dolly to let her know where I'm going and what I'm..." She fumbled in her purse and pulled out her cell phone. Marcello took it out of her hand and set it on the table.

"Uh uh, Sorry. No can do. We have to go right now and no one can know you are there."

Marcello opened the office door. "We'll stop at your place so you can pack a couple of things, then we have to get to the airport.

"Unless I call Aunt Dolly, I'm not leaving." She folded her arms and planted herself on the floor. "Make a choice Marcello."

The Captain walked in, "So what's holding you guys up?"

"He refused to let me call my family. I have a business that I have to have taken care of for Monday."

"Let her call. I'm sure she knows what not to say."§

Marcello tossed her the cell, threw up his hands and left the room.

Connie simply let Dolly know she'd be away and left instructions for her on what to do Sunday to prepare for meal delivery for Monday. Confused, Dolly took notes and agreed to follow through. "Just follow the plan on the computer. That's all I can say."

"Be careful my Beautiful. I can't bear to lose you."

§ Chapter Eight

Background Information

Connie completed two years of training as a paralegal. She switched to business law at UCLA while working on the BA program.

She wanted to see bad people like the person who killed her parents pay for their neglect. The faulty smoke detector and heater caused their death and she didn't want that to happen again.

Connie joined the police when she got her BA in Business. She rose up the ranks because of her leadership qualities and marksmanship. She also had political savvy. The department said they didn't want to be known for discrimination against women, and she made sure they didn't discriminate with *her* career.

She worked hard to prove herself. After four years of hardcore police work, she was promoted to captain. She was the youngest and only woman to get that high in the force at that time. She felt good that she was blazing the trail for other women.

There was a lot of grumbling when it was announced that she got the position. Others thought she shouldn't have it because she had been on the force for less than five years. There was lots of media coverage because of her advancement.

CHAPTER NINE

Marcello and Connie headed for the briefing knowing full well every wasted minute put Camille in more danger. As they walked down a hallway to the stark cement prep room, a Hispanic FBI agent in the group looked directly at Connie. "Apprehending Anna Lopez has been like trying to catch a fly in mid-air. Since you two are identical twins, I am sure you will confuse them enough to throw them off. I am not saying that all *gringas* looking alike - but the two of you DO look exactly alike."

Marcello sat in the corner of the room, balancing on the back legs of his chair. "Well," he sat up straight, "I'm going on record that I'm opposed to using Connie in this operation. It's too risky. I want the gang broken up just as much as the rest of you do. But not at the cost of Camille and her sister's safety. I'm not sure putting this young woman in danger is the best way."

"It'll work and they will be safe," Agent Smith said scanning Connie's face.

Marcello stood up, letting his chair fall with a bang, "No, it will not be safe for her. You're using Connie just to make your case. You're putting her in danger - and for what? To get yourself promoted? No - she stays here."

The Captain grabbed Marcello by the arm and pulled him into the hall. "What's the matter with you? We need this woman. Are you sleeping with her or what?"

Connie joined them in the hall, "What's going on? We can hear you in there. You sound like you're going to kill each other." Marcello walked back into the room. The Captain walked the other way.

"Are you comfortable being a part of this operation?"

127

another agent asked. She didn't know how to respond. "You will be wired and I will be monitoring you."

It'd been over a year since Connie handled a gun or cuffed someone. But something inside of her was pushing her to do this against her better judgment.

She nodded to the agent, "I'm fine with this. Let's do it," and fumbled with her wrist. She remembered that Camille did that when she was nervous and unsure. "I've got her little mannerisms and idiosyncrasies down. I know this will work."

The five of them boarded the plane chartered from TACA. Once in the air, each agent cleaned and checked their guns. Marcello handed Connie a 9mm Glock Semiautomatic. It was hard, cold and heavier than she remembered. Seeing all the weaponry made her wonder if she made the right decision. An agent appeared from the back of the plane carrying a heavy steel box in each hand. He stopped next to Marcello and set one on the floor next to him. He noticed Connie staring at the box. "Ammo," he whispered, "it never hurts to be prepared." The agent returned with an armload of unmarked bulletproof vests. He handed one to each person, including Connie.

"Like I said," he whispered, "It never hurts to be prepared.

The men looked at Connie's tiny figure and tossed her the smallest vest. She grabbed it and changed in the back of the plane. Everyone napped in the comfortable seats, except Connie. The four hour flight went fast. She was nervous about finding her sister safe, unsure about the sting operation and hoping everyone would get back safely. "I need to sleep or I won't be in any shape to help tomorrow," she thought. Marcello snored, woke himself up several times and warned Connie each time to get some sleep.

The sun was setting as the plane taxied to a gate at the far end of the terminal. "We chartered this to avoid drawing attention from anyone who might be watching for us. We couldn't exactly show up in a black helicopter or some unmarked plane. If we did, we may as well paint 'US Government' in big letters on the side."

They took the stairs to a waiting limousine on the tarmac, as morning broke. Agent Smith nodded toward two men waiting by the doors dressed in shorts and long white shirts. "Our Guatemalan agents." The head Guatemalan agent introduced himself to Agent Diaz and had a short conversation with Smith in Spanish. Smith then turned to Marcello, "They say they've found the warehouse where they believe Señora Camille was taken, but he's not sure if she's still there. They also aren't sure if the babies will be taken to the US by ship or plane, so the police and local agents have been watching both places."

They were escorted to several black sedans and driven through Guatemala City. The Holy week crowds and traffic held them at a dead stop for almost an hour. The noise was deafening. People screaming and yelling words in Spanish. They decided to walk the rest of the way. Agent Smith held Connie's arm and guided her through the chaos. "I can walk by myself, thank you very much," she pulled her arm free.

He took her other arm in his, "I can't run the chance of you getting lost or kidnapped right now."

People were crowded shoulder to shoulder along the crowded streets. They approached what looked like an arena or concert hall and looked through an entrance to what looked like a football stadium with a huge building looming above them. They walked up several flights of stairs.

"What is this place?" Connie whispered to Agent Diaz.

"This is our beautiful concert hall. It was built a few years ago but it is in use only a few weeks out of the year for graduations from the area schools. We don't hold many concerts here. So we are using it as a staging area for the operation. We have found it to be very useful."

Connie held Marcello's sleeve as they hurried through several dark hallways onto the stage where a couple dozen men were assembled. Agent Smith continued, "Lopez has been working with a doctor and his wife who is a nurse. They either steal the babies from the single mothers or they purchase them, or maybe both. The doctor is definitely involved. We can't seem to get him and the gang together to prove it. Our big problem is that he is a big shot in the community, or rather, his wife is. She is the head of the most powerful woman's organization in the city, Las Floras. They carry a lot of influence."

"You see what we have to deal with?" Diaz added. "This is like accusing the Governor's wife in California of some criminal activity without proof. It's a very delicate and dangerous situation."

"They are not the reason why we're here. We need to find the suspect with the babies as well as this woman's sister." Smith added, "You can do what you want with the good doctor and his wife."

One of the Guatemalan agents leaned forward to say something, but his partner pulled him back in his seat and slapped him in the back of his head.

"Is there a problem?" Marcello asked eyeing the agents. They looked at each other."Where are we going now?" one agent asked.

"To stake out the warehouse. We need to move fast. Has everyone been briefed?" Agent Smith looked at Connie and the rest of the team.

"This all depends on if we can surprise them and how these people respond." Connie and Marcello readied their guns. Smith and Diaz wired Connie with a microphone and transmitter. It was old style with thin wires taped to her back. But it did the trick.

"What kind of assault rifle is that?" Connie was watching the Guatemalan police ready their guns.

130

"They're using H&K rifles. Sweet little German jobs." Agent Smith winked. "Ready?"

Camille was tied to a wooden chair, blindfolded and her mouth taped shut. She felt the swaying motion that told her she was not on dry land. The familiar, yet nauseating mix of diesel fuel and stale air made her gag. And now she had the added odor of mildew and rotting fish to fuel her queasiness. The creaking and groaning boat was in motion. She hardly felt her hands, now numb and cold from being taped. As she rocked along with the boat, Camille found it hard to steady her stomach. Her feet were bound at the ankles. It was apparent to her that if the chair went over, so would she. She knew she still had her clothes on, her cotton sweater was snug around her neck. The smell of dead fish continued to assault her senses.

The last thing she remembered was eating a pizza and drinking Seven Up. It must have been drugged. She was still woozy but couldn't let her stomach give in, not with her mouth taped shut. Instead, she thought of Bradley playing on the monkey bars when they were a family of three. Those were the warm, comfortable times of her life. She remembered how in tune she was with her son and his life. His smile helped keep her mind off her dancing stomach.

She was jerked back to the uncertain presence with the sound of a metal door opening, grateful for the blast of fresh air into her nose. She could hear people coming down the stairs. She swallowed, took a deep breath and tensed herself for the unknown.

A women's voice spoke in a language unfamiliar to her. Suddenly the tape was wrenched off her mouth leaving her lips and face on fire. She gulped in a breath of air as soon as her blindfold was yanked off. It caught in her hair as it was pulled up, forcing her eyes open. Camille blinked at the now blinding sunlight streaming through the door. She tried to focus on the three figures in front of her.

131

"Well, Ms Camille," the woman now spoke in English. "Have you recovered?" The voice was Anna Lopez. Camille's eyes focused on the beautiful woman with long dark hair wearing black tights and leather jacket.

"Why are you doing this? Where am I? Why?" was all she could get out. Her lips burned as she moved them. She licked her lips and coughed, "What? Why'd you drug me?"

Two large men in brown suits positioned on either side of Anna stared at Camille. She returned their stare, but they scared her. Their eyes seemed like vultures and she was easy prey. She struggled in her chair, but her bonds were too tight. The men each put a hand on her shoulder and pressed her down.

"Relax, Ms Camille. You are not going anywhere just yet. There is some work you must do for me, the work your beloved, late fiancé was supposed to have completed." Anna made the sign of the cross, "Now you must continue his legacy."

Beloved late fiancés legacy? The words echoed in her head.

"We have clients in the United States waiting for us to bring their babies to them. We cannot afford to disappoint them or we won't be paid. Palmer was to take delivery of the little ones and bring them to the States. A responsibility that is now yours."

Anna's words went by too fast. In Camille's semi-drugged condition, she wasn't sure if she understood the plan. Was Palmer stealing babies?

"I know this is probably too much for you to take in all at once, Ms Camille," Anna lifted her face by the chin, "But the truth is, Palmer was one of my three closest associates. He was paid quite handsomely for his services, which were many and varied". Anna nodded to one of the brown suited men. He stepped in front of Camille and pulled a switchblade knife from his pocket. A smile broke across his face that revealed several gold caps among his yellow teeth. With a press of a button the long blade flicked open. Camille squeezed her eyes shut as the man bent toward her and cut the duct tape binding her wrist and ankles. She got a nose full of his awful breath and sweaty body, but grateful that blood immediately returned to her fingers and toes.

"I'm really very sorry about using drugs on you, but we had no alternative. In a few hours, the dizziness will subside. I don't recommend you put anything in your stomach for the next few hours or you will surely vomit. But, I must warn you, the worst of the dizziness and nausea is yet to come." Anna pointed to a cot with a blanket and stack of pillows.

A large pail sat on the floor next it. "Sit over there. Whatever you do, don't lay flat or you will definitely vomit. My Jorge and Fernando will watch over you."

Camille glared at them and looked back at Anna.

"Don't worry. They are under strict instructions not to harm you in any way," Anna looked knowingly at both of them and with machine gun rapidity, said something in Spanish that caused both of them to look down at the floor. She turned back to Camille, "I'll return in a few hours," and walked up the stairs to the door.

As Jorge and Fernando helped Camille to the cot, Anna warned from the top of the stairs, "You will have a severe headache Ms Camille. But it will pass soon. I highly recommend you breathe deeply to get as much oxygen to your brain as possible. In my experience, I've found that it usually helps."

The men sat her on the cot and propped her up on pillows. They covered her, making sure the pillows were under her head and back.

"Where am I?" she pleaded for an answer. They stared at her and shrugged their shoulders. "*Donde estamos?*" The men looked at each other, then at her. "*No se importante.*"

It was at that moment her headache hit like a mallet to

the top of her head. It was worse than the worst hangover she could ever remember. When she took a deep breath, it only got worse. Her head felt like it was peeling apart. Jorge and Fernando snickered at her pain and pointed. Camille winced with each deep breath, all the while trying to make sense of how Palmer could have been involved in baby stealing. He always said his flights were to Washington DC and Central America. Camille assumed they were for his work as a lobbyist. She knew he did a lot of pro bono work for high-profile cases, gay rights, beach conservation and especially cases involving foster children, who were his passion - But to be a part of stealing babies and smuggling them into the U.S.?

The deep breathing seemed to help, along with the fresh air from the open door. She felt the pain in her temples lessen. Camille thought of the brocade purse Palmer brought back for her from one of his trips and she remembered he said he bought it in Guatemala. He'd presented it to her when he picked her up for a formal dinner party. It was lovely and it went so well with her outfit.
She was too excited to ask him anything more about his trip. But now things seemed clear to her. Palmer was leading a second life that she knew nothing about.

She knew she was in big trouble. Anna probably thought she knew a lot more about what Palmer was doing than she did.

Camille dozed off only to wake up with the return of the same deep headache. Half-awake, she felt a hand lift her head accompanied by the overpowering reek of onions and garlic. She opened her eyes to Jorge's face above hers, a pillow grasped in his other hand. Camille summoned all her energy to jerk her head away, but she had no energy to move. The look of terror on her face caused him to pull back immediately. In broken English Jorge blurted, "Pillow en floor," as he slipped the pillow under her head. Fernando laughed at Camille's reaction to his efforts at kindness, "*Muy hermosa, Sí?*"

134

Jorge glared at his partner, "*Callate! Hijo de cabron!*" He then held up the rumpled blanket. Camille tugged it out of his hands and covered herself. Jorge stepped back and whispered, "el *pelo huele como flores*". Camille had no idea what they said, rolled on her side and slowly drifted off again.

After what felt like hours of sleep, she was startled awake by a loud noise which turned out to be the cabin door being slammed shut. A mustached man in blue slacks and white uniform shirt slowly became clear to Camille. "Are you an officer?"

"You feel better, Ms Camille?" He asked with a pronounced foreign accent.

She nodded and slowly sat up, expecting to be slammed with another headache from the drugging. To her surprise, her headache was gone and her stomach had settled down.

"You can estand?"

Camille nodded again. He extended his hand and helped her to her feet. Again, she couldn't believe how much better she felt. She didn't even feel wobbly.

"Excuse me, *Señor*, but just where the Hell am I?"

He shrugged and escorted her topside up the metal steps. They went down a long passageway and up another set of steps until they were on deck. The air was moist and warm. Camille shaded her eyes from the bright sun with one hand and held tight to a railing with the other. Through the slits of her eyes, she saw an island off the starboard side. It was dotted with small trees and a jumble of tiny houses all crowded along a hill. She was in no condition to dive into the rough sea and swim for the island.

"If circumstances were different," she thought, "this would be one hell of a vacation." The ocean swelled, forming mountains of water topped with white caps that rocked the ship.

A quick glance forward only showed open sea. Camille turned her head and looked toward the stern. From all her trips to Catalina, she could tell this ship was very well maintained, at least on the outside. The white paint gleamed in the sun and all the brass was polished. Her nose told her the teak trim had been recently varnished as she ran her hand along the glossy railing. This boat must've been at least a hundred feet in length, but she couldn't make out its name.

The uniformed man took her arm firmly and led her to an elegant cabin with a table set with silver trimmed china on a white linen tablecloth. The windows glistening along the side brightened the wood paneling and teak wood floors. The wind howled through the open doorway. She allowed him to plop her onto a chair at the table where she watched him go to a small refrigerator across the cabin and pour a glass of some kind of orange drink.

He set it on the table in front of her and said, "Drink."

She shook her head, "I can't. I'll throw up."

"Sí, You drink." he repeated.

Anna Lopez entered the cabin and closed the door behind her. She was dressed in a black and white polka dot dress with a full skirt and black bolero. Her long black hair was pulled back in a pony tail and looked as if she'd stepped out of a 1950's fashion magazine. Camille was amazed to see Anna move so easily on the rocking boat in her two inch heels.

"Gracias, Caesar." She placed her hand on Caesar's shoulder, "I'll take it from here." He bowed and sat along the side railings of the room.

Anna picked up the glass and took a small sip, "It's just an orange drink. There's a lot of sugar in it to help hydrate you and give you energy. Go ahead. We are not going to drug you again or poison you. We need you in optimum health."

136

Camille cautiously sniffed the orange liquid and took a sip. The overpowering sweetness rattled her teeth, but felt good going down.

The drink was like Tang on steroids. Her body reacted to the sugar rush like a volcano trying to blow it's top. She set the glass down. It was too sweet to drink all at once. She looked up at Anna who was standing on the other side of the table with one hand on her hip and the other at her side. "That's a very classic look," Camille said. She'd read someplace that if a captive can makes friends with their captors, they might receive better treatment.

Anna gave a faint sigh, then uncovered a plate of cheese and sliced fruit. "Here, you need to eat." She slid the plate toward Camille. "I'll explain our plan for you as you partake of this fine repast."

Camille's lips were still tender from the duct tape. Gingerly, she ran her fingertips around the edge, feeling for any blisters or scabs. The acid in the orange drink only made them burn more.

"That burning sensation will subside." Anna pointed out. "Your lips are a bit red, probably because of your fair complexion. But, not to worry. It will return to normal."

Camille placed a small cube of white cheese in her mouth and followed it with an apple slice. "What do you want with me?"

"You need to take Palmer's place on our next escapade in Guatemala." Camille's eyebrows popped up.

"Don't look so terrified, I'm not going to dress you in men's clothes. You will play the part of a worried, anxious mother who is finally taking her long awaited baby from the clutches of the government. I will play another mother picking up her baby, hence my current costume."

"I'm surprised Palmer didn't explain more of this to you."

137

"Believe me, Palmer said nothing of this to me. Never mentioned you or the business or your goons. I am completely in the dark about all of this."

"Fine, you've been told all you need to know for now. All my boys are well respected in Guatemala and well paid for their services.

Anna showed Camille a closet full of clothes and accessories. "Get dressed. We leave tonight."

"We just walk in and take a baby? Aren't we going to get arrested?"

Caesar and Anna chuckled, then her smile disappeared. "After you are dressed we'll photograph you for your new passport."

"But how...?"

"Stop asking questions. This is a quick turnaround job. We just get in there, pick up our babies and then we are out of here."

"I don't like it." Camille crossed her arms. "If Palmer was involved in this, that was his problem. What makes you think I'll help you?"

Anna picked up a remote control from the table and pointed it at the wall mounted television. "I will show you an example of what happens to people who don't cooperate. The screen flashed on CNN. In one frame, a video showed a bloodied man being loaded in the back of an ambulance. The camera panned to a pool of blood where the man had laid. Beneath the picture the story scrolled past, "A Southern California man was beaten nearly to death by several assailants and is reported in grave condition."

Camille recognized him as Tony, a friend of Palmer's.

"What happened to him can be easily arranged for your son, your sister, even your beloved Aunt. Yes, my dear, we even know where she lives on Catalina." After Anna read off each address and phone number, she tossed the list on the table and walked around to Camille's chair. Bending down next to her ear, she whispered, "Don't think I won't do it." She was silent for a moment, then straightened up. She walked around the room, occasionally looking out one of the windows.

Caesar sat at the table and unbuttoned one of his shirt pockets. He pulled out a picture of Dolly walking out of a grocery store with an armload of bread and placed it carefully in front of Camille. "Your Tia Dolly is a sweet lady." Caesar commented as if they were having a friendly chat. Camille recognized the Safeway storefront. He pulled another photo from his pocket and tossed it toward Camille. It landed on top of Dolly's photo.

She glanced down and saw the image of Connie walking with Bradley, her hand on his shoulder. Instantly, Camille recognized the plants by Palmer and Lisa's place. "You seester Connie is also very lovely like you. What a pity it would be if something bad were to happen. It would be very sad," Caesar commented.

Anna Lopez strode over to the table and looked down at the picture of Bradley and Connie. Her eyes then focused on Camille, "As you can see, we have studied your life. Either you cooperate, or one by one, something terrible will occur to each of them. If you make a problem of yourself, your loved one's problems could be fatal. Do I make myself clear?" Anna picked up the photograph and caressed the image of Bradley with her fingertips. "I really do love children. He's such a handsome little boy, but much too old for my business. I'm certain one of our customers could use him for other more profitable purposes."

"Why are you doing this?" Tears ran down Camille's cheeks. She never meant to endanger her family. "I've never hurt you or interfered with your business. I'm no threat to you. Why me?"

"Oh, I guess I needed someone to help me and you presented yourself to me, with a ready-made family as collateral.

You must make your decision soon, or your son will be the first to experience an unfortunate fate."

Caesar added, "He will be followed by your dear Tia. And your *hermana* Connie will be last. It is so sad that all three will have such problems because of you."

Camille looked away from her captors and stared out the window. How could she have stepped into this nightmare. It all seemed so unreal.

Camille shook her head, "I can't do this, I can't."

Anna Lopez nodded to Caesar. Immediately, he pushed one button on his cell phone. He said a few words in Spanish then looked at Camille. "Your son Bradley has just been dropped off at the school by your friend Lisa. She is leaving and he is inside putting his coat and lunch in his...cubby? One word from me and he will disappear...poof."

Camille looked at her watch. Caesar was right. In a few minutes Bradley would walk into his classroom. She knew it, Caesar knew it and whoever was watching Bradley knew it. He put the phone to his mouth and said, "*Oye.*"

"Stop! Okay. Just stop." Camille cried and slammed her hand on the table, "I'll do it." She put her head in her hands, "Damn you!"

"What will you do?" Anna asked.

"I said I'll help you. Just leave my family alone... please."

Caesar returned his cell phone to his pocket and rebuttoned it. "That is good for them."

"How do I know Bradley is safe right now? How do I know you haven't done something to him?"

"Oh, you don't trust my word?" Anna Lopez picked up her phone, pulled out a paper and called. "Yes, I am inquiring if Bradley Brewster has arrived at school?" She paused. "No, I'm a friend of the family. Could you hold on I will get his mother?" She handed the cell phone to Camille. Caesar pulled out

140

a gun and put the barrel against her temple.

"Hello?" Camille trembled as Caesar pressed the cold barrel against her skin.

"Hello, this is Sharon, the school secretary."

"Hello Sharon, it's Camille Brewster. I was just checking to see if Bradley got in on time this morning."

"I'm sure he did, but if you'll hold, I'll check with the teacher."

Camille ran her fingers through her hair while she waited. After what seemed like forever, Sharon came back on the line, "Yes he's doing just fine. They're getting ready for the assembly this morning."

A hint of a smile broke across Camille's face followed by a sigh.

"Is there a problem, Ms Brewster?"

Camille wanted to say, "Yeah, a big problem." But with a gun against her head, "No, Sharon, everything is fine," and hung up.

"Your son is at an assembly." Caesar uncocked his gun and put it in his pocket, "It would be a shame for him not to enjoy it."

She gave another sigh and asked with resignation, "So, what am I supposed to do next?

Straightening her white cotton blouse with rolled sleeves, she went topside again and saw only ocean. The island she saw earlier was gone. The sky was blue, dotted with gray clouds. The only things on the horizon, were huge swells and white caps. As she looked up at the sun in relation to the horizon she guessed it was mid-afternoon. "Where am I in this world? Am I still in the western hemisphere? I sure hope so."

141

"As a matter of fact you are," a male voice came from behind. Another man in a ship's officer's uniform. This one had matching pants and no accent.

He looked over the side and pointed, "That's Southern Mexico off that way." He shifted his arm and pointed toward the bow. "If you look carefully, you'll see the silhouette's of volcanoes. That's Guatemala. We'll be pulling in there."

"I'm in Central America?" Camille thought back to images of a map she remembered seeing in sixth grade of the American Hemisphere. "How did I get here?"

"They tell me you came by plane to a small airport in southern Mexico, Tehuantepeo to be exact. Then they brought you to Puerto Angeles." He chuckled, "You were pretty out of it when they brought you aboard."

Her short black skirt was just a little too tight, and just a little too short. Just enough to show off her smooth thighs and shapely legs, the officer couldn't avoid. Her lovely marbled green eyes caught his attention. His soft voice mellowed her fears. She was at home, comfortable at least.

"I don't remember a thing."

"You're probably sore, one of the guys carrying you dropped you on the dock. Ms Lopez had a fit. After seeing the way Anna kicked and slapped him, I felt sorry for guy that dropped you." He stepped closer put his hands gently on her shoulders and massaged her neck. "Does that feel better?"

The release of tension on her neck rippled down her spine.

"Mmm. I guess we were introduced but I don't remember."

"Actually Ma'am," his thumbs in the base of her neck felt like heaven, "We were never formally introduced. "I'm Peter, the ship's captain. I'm here to see to it that you get to your destination on time and safely. That's my job."

"Well Peter, where are we going?" her head and neck were

relaxing more and more.

He steadied her with his other hand around her waist. "My customers give me money to pick up people from one port and deposit them at another, in this case Guatemala. That's all I know and all I want to know. And I get paid at the end of the voyage. Real simple."

"I suppose it doesn't matter to you that I am being held against my will."

He stopped and twirled her around. "You look fine to me, lady. Just fine."

Camille breathed in the salt fresh air and knew he wasn't going to help.

"You must think I'm a coward, or maybe an idiot who can't be trusted. Well, on the contrary, I'm reliable and dependable as long as I agree on a price and a destination. I figure that people get themselves into fixes and it's up to them to get themselves out. Like you, for instance. You must have done, said, or seen something to cause this or you wouldn't be here. You're scared to death and you hope I'll come to your rescue. "Well," he stepped back, "I'm not here to do that. I repeat - I'm no Rambo. Never have been, never will be." He moved her head from side to side, "There, you look more relaxed," he smiled, "and whole lot looser than when I found you." He looked at her for a long time. She wondered what to do next. If she was in her own element, the beach, Los Angeles, Palm Springs, she would've put the moves on this guy. But she wasn't sure what he wanted or what good it would do her. She let him lead the way.

"Shame we met under these circumstances. We could have... I make it a practice not to mess with the cargo." He ran his fingers through her hair. "Good day, Ma'am," nodded, turned and left.

She opened her mouth to say something, but nothing came out. It must've been the drugs, Camille never had difficulty coming up with comebacks. "God." She muttered, "I'm on my way to freaking Guatemala."

When they docked, "Rather bucolic, wouldn't you say?" was Anna's comment. "These gentlemen and I will ensure you don't wander off. We want your visit to be enjoyable. And it will be if you do as you're told."

After Peter stopped the motor, the crew tied up the boat and let down the plank. Camille looked up at the boat's bridge and took one last look at Peter. She still hoping he might rescue her, a knight in shining armor. Instead, he saluted her as the men led her by the arm to a waiting car with darkened windows.

They traveled over a one lane road lined with small villages, through hills and valleys surrounded by tropical plants and trees. Signs appeared as they continued to drive. As the evening darkened, all Camille could see was broken trees and paved road.

As they drove through Guatemala City, the streets became dense with people.

"This is Holy Week. The entire town celebrates the Procession of the Virgin of Assumption. The crowds are huge, so if we have problems we can get lost in the crowd. Do not, under any circumstances, lose or drop the baby. The noise of the crowd will drown out any gunshots I may need to employ." She produced a small chrome plated hand gun with a pearl handle. "Have I made myself clear?"

Camille nodded, but was distracted by the overwhelming number of people in the streets. The car came to a dead stop. The driver argued with Anna, then she threw up her hands. "Okay, we will walk from here." The men held onto each of her arms as they navigated along the streets and alleys. They stayed close to the run down old wooden buildings until they arrived in an old industrial area. Warehouse doors were closed and children were coming and going. Camille peeked in one of the open doors to a lovely courtyard full of plants with a flowing fountain, centered in a circular walkway surround by residual rooms. Children ran from a side room blowing whistles, then out to the street. She looked into a room as the door was opened, revealing a well decorated parlor.

Anna stopped and faced Camille, "We'll be there in a few minutes. Remember, you agreed to cooperate. We can always turn you over to the Guatemalan Police as an illegal visitor. They are, how should I say this, enamored with American blondes. Keep that in mind. If they learn you are in this country illegally, there's no telling what they might do with you." Anna rattled off Spanish to her goons.

They stopped at a large industrial cement building. The men pushed her inside. Actually, it was nice to get away from the deafening street noise. As her eyes adjusted, she saw several people milling around, sorting through piles of clothes. The air inside was hot and heavy, filled with the sounds of crying babies and the odor of dirty diapers. Several women held infants wrapped in blankets, rocking them in their arms.

Camille counted three babies. The women who held them were short with long, thick black hair, tied with ribbons. One of the men in brown, let go of Camille while the other tightened his grip on her elbow. She moved toward one of the women, but the man holding her elbow said, "Alto."

"Just stand still, Ms Camille, Anna cautioned. "If you make a move, he will tear off your arm - literally."

Camille watched her approach the three women. Two of them stood, looking at their children. The third sat on a box cradling her crying baby. Anna handed each of the two women a stack of Guatemalan money. The seated woman wept, kissed her baby then handed it over to a man. Wiping her eyes, she made the sign of the cross and ran out of the building. The other women and man laid the babies side by side on a dusty table and unwrapped the blankets. Anna looked at the babies. A man in a Hawaiian shirt entered the room and pulled a stethoscope out of his pocket. He examined the babies while explaining something to Anna in Spanish. Anna glanced at Camille before turning her attention back to the babies. She handed another stack of money to other the women. She then waved the remaining women away and watched them leave the building, taking one of the crying babies with them. After they'd gone, Anna pulled two baby bottles filled with formula out of a box and jammed them in each of the babies mouths to quiet them.

Camille was escorted to a chair near the table. The man with the stethoscope handed her a baby with the bottle attached to its mouth. *"Tome el bebé"*. She had no idea what he said, although *"bebe"* sounded just like baby. It smelled terrible, like it hadn't been cleaned in a while. At least it wasn't crying. Anna picked up the remaining baby along with its bottle and walked over to Camille. "We're going to a hotel now to clean up and head to the airport. We'll be bringing these to Los Angeles. For the next few hours, you are the baby's mother, so act like it."

At dawn the next day, a large van with the police and FBI decked in riot gear stopped at a field. "The building where I believe the babies are exchanged is about two blocks east. It has a brown door." The head Guatemala Federal policeman looked at Connie and Marcello, "You two stay back behind as we hit the building. Watch your backs and keep an eye on the buildings behind you when you enter the warehouse."

Marcello nodded as he checked Connie's bulletproof vest. "Tell me why she has to be here right now?"

"You'll see," the policeman motioned to his group. Suddenly, several hooded men, dressed in black appeared with their automatic weapons at the ready. They crept down the alley toward the warehouse building.

Marcello moved in front of Connie. They crouched down. Connie kept her hand on his back. Connie looked around at the deserted streets, a far cry from the overcrowded downtown. "Where is everyone?" She whispered, after spotting more armed men on the rooftops.

"Everyone was evacuated earlier this morning," Marcello

put his finger to his lips, "Just follow me." Slowly they inched down the alley, one step at a time.

Marccllo stopped and pulled her to the ground, "Stay."

"No! You stay!"

He squatted in front of her and aimed his Glock down the alley.

She heard a loud bang and suddenly the men in front of her rushed into building across the alley, kicking the door open with their boots. Expecting bullets to come flying everywhere, she cocked her gun. But nothing, no noise, no bullets, no screaming, nothing. Did they have the wrong building?

Connie felt two strong hands lift her off the ground by her arm pits. Marcello led the way with his gun poised for action while Connie was whisked inside the building by two men. It took a while for her eyes to adjust to the darkness. Slowly the images of large pillars appeared in the massive space. Her feet didn't touch the ground as the men moved her to the center of the room. To one side she saw piles of blankets, baby bottles and diapers scattered across the floor. The air was permeated with the awful smell of urine. On the other side, were stacks of light brown boxes with something in Spanish printed on them. The Guatemalan officers had several men lined up on their knees, hands behind their heads. Most of them looked bewildered. The Guatemalan police shouted something in Spanish at the men. They just stared at Connie.

Gunshots prompted the agents to push Connie down onto the dirt floor. Marcello threw himself on her, crushing her under his weight. More gunshots and shouting. The damp smell of dirt filled her nostrils. The shouting slowly lessened, muffled by distance.

Marcello rolled off of her and moved toward the ruckus, while two other agents stayed with her. She listened as the noise moved outside the building and stopped. Everything was quiet. Connie tried to sit up, but the agents kept their hands on her back.

She again felt the strong hands under her arms as she was slowly lifted to her feet. "You okay, Ma'am?" A young agent wiped the dust and dirt from her cheek. She noticed his kind large chocolate brown eyes examining her face. He looked so young, she thought.

Her eyes refocused. She began to feel the effects on her back from Marcello's weight. Several men were laying face down on the ground arms and legs spread out. "Are they dead?" she whispered."

"No, they are hostages." The agents motioned Connie back outside with their guns. "Move."

Anna and Camille were back into the heat and deafening streets where the crowds were chanting. They carried their babies and their bags to a rundown hotel with paint peeling off the walls and roaches everywhere. She was sure she smelled cats. Anna took her to a room with a cracked sink and leaking faucet. Anna laid the baby on the bed and set its diaper bag beside it. The baby drank most of the bottle and was asleep.

"Okay," Anna unloaded her bag, "let's see what we have here."

Two men guarded the door while Anna and Camille busied themselves bathing the babies in the broken sink. They rubbed some cream on the baby's diaper rash and powdered their little bottoms. The rough dirty diapers were replaced with new disposable ones. They finally wrapped them in fresh, clean blankets. Anna had ten bottles full of formula for the trip in her diaper bag.

"Well, little ones," Anna said, "at least you come well supplied."

As Camille washed and dressed her charge, memories of her son came flooding back. She remembered the anticipation of the birth, agony of a breach birth and the miracle of holding her little son at home, all alone, just the two of them. Bathing was always a time she enjoyed with Bradley. Now with clean, sweet smelling babies, Anna looked at her watch, "It's time we left for the airport." She checked around the room, straightened her clothes and then looked Camille up and down. "Fix your hair in a more conservative manner." She took the baby from Camille's arms and nodded toward her diaper bag. "Use the hairpins and bands in the front pocket."

Camille did as she was told. She wet her now dirty hair, pulled it back in a pony tail and secured it with pins. She evaluated herself in the mirror and shook her head. This was not her look. It was way too maternal for her taste, but it would fit the role she had to play.

On the way to the airport, Anna was surprisingly quiet. Camille noticed that she seemed to really enjoy being with the little one, cooing with him and making curls on his forehead with his large locks of hair. "They're about three months old." Anna finally commented, "This one has lots of hair."

Camille was shocked to see this softer, feminine side of Anna. They chatted for a while about how she was forced to raise her younger brothers and act as kind of a surrogate mother when her mother died.§

Camille talked about raising her son alone and the torture she felt of giving him up to her ex-husband because a court order. Then her face changed as she remembered where she was and what she was about to do.

"So, are you going to fill me in on what to do?" Camille asked, "You wouldn't want me to make a mistake, would you?

Anna opened her mouth to answer when her cell phone went off. She spoke in Spanish, constantly saying, "*Que?*

Repitan. Que?" Silently, she folded up her phone and waited.

"What's the matter?" Camille asked. She could see a concerned look on Anna's face.

"It's nothing. I couldn't hear a word they said so, they're texting me".

Anna shielded the phone from Camille's view and read her cell phone. With her thumb flying, she quickly responded. She then slowly turned her head and squinting her eyes, looking at Camille for a few minutes. She opened the diaper bag and pulled out a large tin of diaper pins. Anna flipped open the lid and produced her small pistol and pointed it directly at Camille.

She said something in Spanish to the driver. He made a quick turn and parked on the side of the airport terminal building.

Anna got out, carrying her baby, the gun poking out under the blanket.

"Get out on this side. Be careful not to drop your package." Camille grabbed her diaper bag managed to slide out the door with her baby. "What happened?"

Anna motioned Camille toward the door, keeping the pistol under the baby's blanket pointed at her the whole time.

Two goons held Camille's arms as they negotiated the crowded street. "We have a long walk my dear." Anna came close to her ear and whispered. "Be careful."

§ Chapter Nine

Background Information

Anna Lopez was raised in Texas. Her parents were undocumented farm workers from southern Mexico.

Anna's mother died when she was 12. She was forced to work as a housekeeper, basically taking over the job her mother had. Her father turned to alcohol. He no longer worked and demanded to be waited on by the young Anna. While her brothers went to school, she worked to make money to pay bills and keep house for everyone.

Her heart ached as she watched the other girls in the neighborhood walk to school together. She was lonely and missed her mother. She had no one to talk to.

Exhausted, she poured through her brother's homework and books at night and taught herself to read, write and do math.

At seventeen, she ran away to join the armed services. But since she was undocumented, she had no Social Security Number. She lived on the streets for a while frequenting libraries to work on her education. One rainy day she was reading a magazine and found a story about a socialite in New Orleans whose passion was working with underprivileged children. This Anna Lopez, "real" Anna Lopez, died twenty years ago in a small town in the deep south. She adopted her name and Social Security number, and applied to Jamestown University. She vowed that if she was able to pull this off and finish college, she would dedicate herself to continue Anna Lopez's work. With much hard work, she made it through the prestigious MBA program.

To pay for living expenses and college, she smuggled drugs and guns across the border. Fluent in Spanish, she did well for herself and never looked back.

151

She met Palmer at an International Business seminar for students. They remained good friends through college, but they lost touch after graduation. Palmer went into politics and Anna into "Special International Business" as she put it.

They unexpectedly reconnected in Los Angeles. Palmer didn't need the money, but he worked with Anna out of respect to her and to help babies get a better, healthier life in the U.S.

CHAPTER TEN

Camille held the baby and diaper bag as she walked ahead of Anna into the terminal building. Her warm bundle slept and made the walk comforting. Anna smiled at the security men, she showed them the baby and motioned for Camille to do the same. Camille forced a smile as she looked around for anyone or anything she could do to get help. The officers looked and smiled at each baby making funny cooing sounds to them. They made it through security and headed for the waiting area. "I'm starving, Anna, I need food or I'm going to pass out from low blood sugar."

As they walked toward their boarding gate, they were followed by a cleaning lady who nodded several times. Was she police? Secret service? Anna gave Camille her baby and motioned toward the lady's room with "ALTO" posted on the door. Burdened with two babies and diaper bags, Camille had no choice but to follow orders. Anna reached under the sink. She pulled off a large brown envelope and slipped it into her diaper bag.

Camille then followed Anna to the vending machines. She took her baby back then put coins in the machine, "Take what you want." Camille got a hand full of chocolate bars and bottled water.

"You want anything, Anna?"

"No, I cannot consume anything when I'm traveling." Anna sat on a bench and pointed. "You sit in that chair and eat-quickly . We do not have a great deal of time."

Camille placed the baby on her lap and set the diaper bag on the floor.

"Eat." Anna ordered. Camille obeyed, balancing her baby while she took a long drink of water and unwrapped a

153

chocolate bar. She knew that under Anna's sweet smelling little bundle, a gun was pointed at her.

"Will we stop at a hospital to be sure the babies are healthy?" Camille asked between bites, "Shouldn't we at least be sure they are in good health?"

"I appreciate your concern over their health." Anna looked deeply into the face of Camille's baby, "Every baby deserves a good life, a healthy one, too. These two have been checked out by the doctor in Guatemala. We will have them checked out once again before they are given to their parents in the U.S."

Anna spoke a few Spanish words into her cell phone and hung up. "Take the baby. I'll sit behind while we wait to board. Then I'll change my seat on the plane, so I can watch you across the aisle. I will also be in constant contact with my people in LA. If they hear from me..."

Camille's heart pounded as she took the baby. Anna carefully slipped the gun under the blanket. "Please don't be stupid," and motioned for Camille to move to the waiting area. Camille overheard, "*Mate el Pajaro.*" She recognized the word kill, but not sure what the other word meant. Is Anna ordering them to kill my family? Her chest pounded. No matter what she did, someone was going to get killed. The baby fussed and squirmed. Camille knew he'd probably need a bottle and she'd have to do something soon.

While they headed for the Guatemala City Airport, Connie was briefed by Agent Smith and Marcello.

"Hold it," Connie held one hand up. "Why is everyone treating me like a child? This is insulting. We're a team, I can take care of myself," she looked at Marcello and Agent Smith.§

"We can't afford for you to get hurt or worse. You're an integral part of the operation. We're here to protect you at all cost."

Agent Smith turned to the group, "There was one man hiding behind the boxes. We let him escape, hopefully he headed straight for Anna. Our men managed to follow him to the airport. He seemed to be looking for them when he used his cell phone. He led us back to Anna Lopez and the babies, but a couple more got away and we lost them. We must have missed the baby exchange by a couple of hours. Your sister was seen with Anna. They had the babies in their possession and were on their way to the airport. Probably heading back to the States."

"Now what?" Marcello said, irritated. "You put her in jeopardy only to lose these guys? That makes no sense to me."

"Keep insulting them Marcello, and we'll never get the babies or Camille back." Connie's eyes were on fire. "Just follow their lead."

Some of the police spoke a little English and figured out the insults Marcello was throwing at them. "I want my sister back in one piece." Connie strained to understand the Guatemalan's rapid fire Spanish and guessed they were deciding on a strategy for their next step. Airport signs began to appear on the road. Connie knew the moment of truth was coming.

"Please God," she thought, as tears welled in her eyes. "Please keep my sister safe."

"We will need your help again," the Guatemalan Policeman told Connie. "You need to be cool and calm. Can you do that?"

Before she could answer, they'd arrived in front of security headquarters at the airport.

Marcello whispered, "The Guatemala City police tell me they also staked out the seaport." "But I'm convinced Anna is here at the airport." Inside the Security office, dozens of video monitors covered one wall.

"If the criminals are trying to leave the country through our airport," The airport police supervisor offered, "We will see them." He swept his arm across the wall proudly. "As you see, they cannot escape our eyes."

Most of the cameras were focused on the planes at the gate and the waiting areas. "Our security is normally very tight, but since your New York World Trade Center incident, it is even tighter now. Connie sat looking at all the monitors when she noticed a familiar figure, "That's my sister, sitting there holding the baby."

They zoomed in, "You are sure? I can't get a good view of her face."

"That's her! And look, that's Anna Lopez sitting behind her," Connie put her finger on the screen.

Marcello knew they had to act fast and act now.

"Okay. Listen up everyone. *Escucha me*! Here's the plan. We have to distract Anna long enough to retrieve Camille and replace her with Connie. Everyone agree?" Marcello checked back at the monitor to be sure they were both still there. "I have a doll in my back pack," Connie added."When you snatch Camille, I'll wrap the doll in her blanket and sit in Camille's spot with the doll."

"We must move *muy pronto*!" He pointed at a female police officer and told her to go ask Anna for help her with a map, to block her view of Camille. When I give the okay sign, you grab the baby and run. We'll move in and arrest Anna along with any of her goons that may try to help her."

The team spoke all at once in Spanish, obviously disagreeing with each other. Connie didn't need a translator for that.

"They don't like it, too many people in the terminal. Someone will get hurt," Agent Smith translated, avoiding all eye contact with Marcello and Connie.

"Look," Connie pulled back her hair in a pony tail and

rolled her t-shirt sleeves. "See, I look just like Camille. Let's do this."

She grabbed a small blanket Marcello had his gun wrapped with and rolled it up. "Looks like I'm holding a baby, no?"

The men stared at Connie and simultaneously shook their heads, no. While they argued, Marcello took Connie's arm and shoved two Guatemalan agents toward the door to the waiting area.

Marcello barked, "You help distract Anna and you cover me." He faced Connie, "As soon as you see the okay sign, we'll get Camille out of view and give you her blanket. Then you can change places with her. If we can pull this off smoothly, no one will get hurt." Connie rolled her gun in the blanket with the doll.

"I'd feel a lot better if someone was watching the people in the terminal, but we do what we have to do, right?" The agent popped the safety and cocked his pistol. Marcello did the same.

With heart pounding, she followed the rest of the team toward the gate where Camille and Anna were spotted. It had been a while since she was part of an operation like this. She had to consciously remember to breathe, to calm her pounding chest. They came in view of the waiting area and stopped. "Wait here until I give the sign." Camille was sitting alone while Anna went to the gate, keeping an eye on her. The female agent approached Anna and unfolded her map. Anna glanced up at Camille, then disappeared behind the huge map. The officer decoy pleaded with her for help.

Anna very loudly said, "I'm very sorry, but I don't live here. I can't help you."

The decoy said, "*Ayuda me Señora,*" and pointed to the map.

"*Por favor Señora,*" she pulled out a note scribbled on a scrap of paper. Anna jerked it out of her hand and read it.

157

"We're in luck," Agent Smith said and pulled Connie up close to the action, but still out of sight. Marcello holstered his gun, straightened his shirt and stood in line behind Anna pretending to talk on his cell phone. He wandered in front of Anna, completely blocking her view. Anna tapped him on the shoulder, hoping he would move away. Instead, he turned around and smiled. He looked down at the baby gave it a little wink. "Going to Los Angeles?" he asked while he put away his cell phone. "That's a good looking little boy, how old is he?" Marcello steered Anna around so he could look at the little bundle. She smiled and nodded like a new mother. "He is three months old, thank you. I don't mean to be rude, but I need to talk to the ticket agent." Anna tried to see around him, but she only caught a glimpse of Camille readjusting her baby and tried to keep watch. The decoy agent with the map returned and moved directly into her line of sight. With the baby in her arms, Anna turned to go back to her seat in the waiting area, but Marcello called to her, "Excuse me, but the ticket agent is right over there." He pointed to a gate desk in the opposite direction from where Camille sat. "Let's catch her before she disappears again." He took Anna's arm and led her to the agent. Anna tried to look over her shoulder, but couldn't risk revealing her true purpose. Not now. Not when she was so close to success. Marcello hustled her down the aisle and away from Camille. With his free hand, he gave the sign to go.

Camille reached in her diaper bag for a bottle when a pair of hands appeared from behind, snatched the baby and took her by the elbow. The stranger whispered to her, "FBI, we're getting you out of here." Connie passed her, took the blanket and wrapped her baby doll with it. Camille tried to say something, but everything moved so fast. The baby was whisked away and suddenly Camille was outside on the tarmac. Connie quickly took her seat and pulled the bottle from the diaper bag. She took a deep breath and hoped she wasn't sweating.

Anna finally pulled away from Marcello, "Never mind!" He let her go and watched her march straight back to the seat directly behind Connie. In the excitement, her baby began to fuss. Under her breath, Anna said, "Give me your bottle. Now." Without looking, Connie dropped her arm and passed the bottle to Anna behind her.

"Where did you go?" Connie muttered.

"It was some irritating good Samaritan." Anna complained. "I left him at another gate. Now, don't talk to me." Connie sighed with relief. She knew she'd just passed the first hurdle. Anna didn't see the switch. Occasionally, Connie rocked the doll in her left arm to make it look real. Every second that passed seemed like an hour until Connie spotted Marcello with a magazine standing by the windows, appearing to be reading. He was good at this. He looked like any other guy traveling on business. His tie was messed up and his hair was a little disheveled. He gave subtle thumbs up to Connie. That simple gesture made her smile. She knew her sister and the baby were safe.

The ticket agent returned and announced "Flight 27 to Los Angeles will begin boarding now. Those with small children and the disabled only may board now." It was repeated in Spanish.

Anna leaned forward, "I'll go first." Her cell rang.

Connie listened as Anna said something in Spanish. She then looked at her baby boy, pretending to talk to him, but she was directing her comments at who she thought was Camille. "Remember, you do anything stupid, say anything that makes me nervous and I got the old lady and your boy." How could Connie tell Marcello?

Anna stood up with the baby cradled in her left arm, bottle propped against her chest. She looked around, then pulled Connie's boarding pass out of the diaper bag. She placed the pass in Connie's hand, but held on to it. "Where is your ring?" she frowned.

"Oh, I took it off. It's in with the baby's stuff. It was poking my little bundle."

Anna pulled the pass back, "You're wearing a t-shirt. What's going on?" She dropped the pass and took her gun from under the blanket. Anna held it to her baby's head, and backed up to the wall. Her eyes flitted back and forth as she scanned the area for her men, but all she saw were foreigners and soldiers gathering in the waiting area.

"*Nadie se mueve!*" she yelled cocking the gun by the baby's head. "Everyone Freeze". Connie was in shock not knowing what to do. Aunt Dolly and Bradley were in danger! She backed up stumbling over a chair, dropping the blanket and doll, but steadied her gun with both hands. Anna gasped when she realized it was a doll that fell out of the blanket.

"Don't let her use the cell," Connie yelled to the police. "She's holding two people hostage in LA. She'll have them killed."

The FBI and Police stopped, guns poised while everyone else in the terminal immediately hit the ground crying and screaming.

Marcello was about ten feet from Anna. He could see her Bluetooth earpiece and her phone in a holder on her belt. With a baby in one arm and a gun in the other hand, she couldn't push any buttons without dropping the baby or letting loose of her gun.

"Put the gun down, Anna Lopez, you're surrounded" Agent Smith ordered in English. His words were echoed by the Guatemalan police in Spanish.

Anna appeared calm and self assured. She turned to Marcello, "Move back Mister or I'll kill this baby right now." He put his arms out and stepped back five paces.

"If I don't call my boys," she yelled at Agent Smith, "a person will be dead and Camille's son will never be seen again." She looked directly at Connie, gun poised. "It's your decision."

160

Anna had the baby, Aunt Dolly and Bradley. To Connie, it appeared she had all the negotiating tools she needed. Apparently, the police believed her. "Okay Bobsey twin, drop your gun and move closer to me, slowly." She waved the pistol at Connie.

Connie looked toward Marcello, he nodded. She dropped the gun and began to move half steps toward the baby and Anna.

"You can't win, Anna," Agent Smith yelled across the aisle. "Give up the baby or you're going to be the one who is dead."

"Maybe, maybe not," Anna glanced around the gate, "but four people will lose their lives regardless. Do you want that on your conscience? Four for the price of one. Am I worth it? I'm quite proficient with this gun," she yelled. "I can guarantee I'll get the baby and the *gringa* here before I hit the ground," she yelled.

Connie froze.

"Anna!" Connie pleaded, "I know you love children. Camille's son is a mere child. You don't want to rob him of his family and future. You work hard to make many childless couples happy. Are you sure you want to be responsible for destroying four innocent lives? Their blood will be on your hands alone."

"You mean three innocent lives," glaring at Connie.

Marcello used this distraction to move in closer while Anna's attention was focused on the police and Connie. With the gun still held against the baby's head, every movement or noise caused her to glance in that direction.

Inch by inch, Marcello moved closer to Anna. Occasionally she looked his way, but wasn't worried since he was just an obnoxious do-gooder. He tried to stay on the edge of her field of vision, focused on the gun at the baby's head. He was ready to leap if Anna made a move to pull the trigger. If his timing was off or if she felt threatened by him, the baby and the person he'd come to love would be dead. His emotions did a delicate dance, balancing patience with the adrenaline that was coursing through his body.

"*Señorita* Lopez - Anna." She turned to face an unarmed Guatemalan policeman who walked slowly toward her with his hands up. Marcello wasn't sure what he was saying, but he was obviously a negotiator. As long as Anna didn't focus on him, he was free to inch closer, calculating his next move. Connie was doing a good job keeping Anna focused away from him. With the policeman talking to her and Connie begging to let her and her family go, Anna was overwhelmed. Interestingly, Anna didn't say much other than "Shut up" or "Stop talking!" In the back of the waiting area, Anna spotted several men with long range rifles and machine guns. Guatemala City called out their own SWAT team and the army.

"Tell them to go away or I'll kill the baby and the American," she yelled in English then Spanish.

Marcello motioned with his eyes for the men to back off.

He was now only ten few feet from her. Still out of her peripheral vision. A little closer and he could grab her. His muscles tensed and his arms flinched. His hand steadied, still focused on the gun. He saw Anna's fingers tense, the muscles in her hands and wrist started to bulge. Connie looked at the gun, then eyed Marcello.

Two breaths, then lunged for her just as Anna turned her head to see what Connie was looking at. His hand caught her arm as she pulled the trigger. The gun went off. Anna dropped the baby as Marcello wrestled her to the floor. Connie reached out and grabbed for the baby to break his fall. Two more shots and Marcello was on top of her. He wrenched the gun out of her hand and held it against her forehead. He pulled the blue tooth out of her ear and jerked the cell phone off her belt.

"What's it going to be, Lopez?"

"What? You're a cop?"

"You're finished!" He stood her up and shoved her at Agent Smith. "FBI, Anna Lopez. you're under arrest."

The waiting area was in chaos. People screamed and moaned while police whistles and shouts filled the air. Dozens of uniformed men pushed the waiting passengers and workers toward the opposite end of the terminal.

Marcello looked around for Connie. She was laying face down next to her seat, with the baby crying beside her.

Marcello took a deep breath to make sense of what just happened. He watched the female Guatemalan agent, who'd been so helpful distracting Anna, take the baby from Connie. Two police turned Connie over on her back and dragged her next to the wall, leaving a smear of blood on the floor. Marcello made a dead run to her side. "Connie?" She was out cold, her pulse was still going. A sense of relief came as the paramedics rushed to work on Connie. She squirmed and moaned while the paramedics cut her blood soaked clothing away.

Marcello moved back so the paramedics could work. His arms hung at his sides, Anna's gun still clenched in his hand.

"Hey Amigo." The head of Airport security whispered as he patted Marcello on the shoulder and carefully took the gun out of his hand. "Let me have this, it's evidence. Take care of your woman."

The Guatemalan agents handled Camille's baby with care. Camille was not so fortunate. The Guatemalan agent took her from the FBI and dragged her to their vehicle. "Hey, you're hurting me," she yelled several times, but they kept up the pace. After pushing through several sets of doors and corridors beneath the terminal, they finally stopped and let go of her. Her blouse was torn, leaving her bra exposed. Camille sat on the floor and cried while she tried in vain to rearrange her clothes. The agents stood around discussing something in Spanish and motioned to the double doors ahead. She felt like a trash bag that had been hauled out to the curb and dropped.

With one hand she held her blouse together and looked up at them, "Does anybody speak English here?" They scowled down at her. One agent said, "Be quiet *mujer.*"

"I'm the victim here! I was kidnapped from my country and brought here against my will. I didn't do anything wrong. I only did what I had to do to keep them from killing me. Please, help me."

The agent clamped a handcuff on her wrist and attached the other end to his own.

"What's this for? I thought you came to save me."

"Esave you from what? Baby estealing? I'm taking you to the Guatemala City Police station. There we will decide what to do with you."

Anna's warning to her of how they viewed American blondes and the idea of being in a Guatemalan prison came back like a nightmare.

"You're making a big mistake," she pleaded. "I'm innocent!"

"That remains to be seen," the agent glanced down at her exposed chest. "All criminals claim to be innocent." He rummaged through the diaper bag and came up with a big diaper pin. He handed it to her so she could close her blouse. He also found a cloth diaper and wrapped it around her front like a bib.

"That is the best I can do." He shouted to the other agents and led her outside through the double doors.

§ Chapter Ten

Background Information

Connie had sworn off men a year ago after the mess that forced her to quit the department.

She didn't miss the touch of a man or have a need to be taken care of. At twenty-five she'd done well for herself. She went back to college and finished her MBA.

Her mind often wandered back to the department. She was good, very good. People marveled how she stepped up to each challenge and figured out how to make it work. She always felt focusing on the here and now, disregarding the future was best.

There were lonely times as the lead dog. Once a seminar director said, "When you're the lead dog, you're a prime target from the front and behind." She didn't believe it, but she was so very wrong.

Marcello was her peer at the time and he never once stepped up to support her, not even when she asked for his support. He shrugged and walked away leaving her a lone woman against the system.

Though heartbreaking, she made the right decision to leave. No one attempted to contact her afterward. Everyone kept their distance and made sure they had witnesses when they did talk to her.

She insisted on staying visible through the investigation and the outcome. In the end, Connie was cleared of any wrongdoing and offered a demotion rather than return her old job. She was warned that any "noise" she would make to the public or media would "not be looked at kindly," by the department. But she was vindicated. That was all she really wanted. When she resigned, there was no fanfare. Two Internal Affair reps followed her to her locker, watched as she cleared out her desk. They escorted her to payroll for her final check and then escorted her out the door.

Connie piled her stuff in the car and took one last look at the building she'd made her second home. Her chest tightened. She wiped a tear and drove away.

CHAPTER ELEVEN

Marcello watched the lights above the hospital elevator doors until he reached the third floor. In his hand, he held a bud vase with a single yellow rose. His muscles were still sore from the wrestling match at the airport the day before and his neck was stiff from the four-hour debriefing with the FBI while they compiled their report.

He stepped off the elevator, the long hallway stretched in the distance. Marcello only had to stop at the first room. There were four beds, one in each corner. He peeked at each one until he saw golden hair streaked across the pillow. Connie smiled as her eyes met his. Her small gesture warmed his heart. He knew she was in pain, yet she found enough energy to smile.

"Hey," Marcello asked, "How's the arm?" He set the vase on her side table and rolled it over next to the bed.

"Hurts like hell," her voice was hoarse and dry. "but I'm alive and Bradley and Dolly are both fine." She smelled the rose, set it back on the table. "How are the babies?"

"Couldn't be better." Marcello replied, "The doctor said that other than a bad case of diaper rash, they're fine."

"You surprised us with your courage yesterday," he placed his hand over hers. "Anna had you point blank. I'm proud of you."

"How's my sister doing with the Guatemalan cops?"

"Agent Smith told me that she can't seem to convince them of her innocence. I tried to help by telephone, but they won't listen to me either.

Connie replied, "They told me I'd be out of here tomorrow

morning. I'll go down and see what I can do to help her. Do you think she'll be okay for tonight?"

"Camille made it through the last twenty-four hours. One more night may just humble her enough to make her quit being such a smart ass with the police."

"You know, they now see you as superwoman, so maybe you can help her out. I've already contacted the embassy and they're sending a lawyer tomorrow. I told them Camille had been assisting us at home and managed to obtain diplomatic standing for her. Now she's in a cell by herself, for now anyway."

Connie reached for Marcello's warm, strong hand and cupped her fingers around his while a tear slowly crept down her cheek. "Thank you for all your help."

"My help? I got you into this mess and now you're nursing a gunshot wound."

"Even so, if I didn't come down here, I'd be in back home worried sick. I would've felt completely useless."

Marcello tried to understand what she meant. It sounded awfully clingy. He figured it must've been the medication.

He patted her hand, "We're taking Anna back to L.A. in a couple of hours. Everyone is concerned that someone will try to help her escape. Agent Murray will be here to help you and assist Camille in any way he can." Marcello bent down and kissed the back of her hand, "Murray's a good guy. You heal up and I'll see you soon." He stopped at the door and talked to another man in a suit. Occasionally, he'd point over his shoulder toward her with his thumb.

The next day, with her arm in a dark blue sling, Connie took a taxi directly from the hospital to the prison where Camille was held. Agent Murray was waiting for her in the reception area. Connie was impressed with the building, looking at the art work and high ceilings. "Impressive, isn't it? Brand new building. Kind of interesting that one of the most beautiful buildings in the city is the prison."

A short Guatemalan man in a wrinkled suit strolled up to them and extended his hand, "I'm the interpreter, Señor Padilla."

His big smile and tombstone teeth got bigger when he shook Connie's hand.

"Detective Ramos told me to keep an eye out for a beautiful blonde with her arm in a sling." He chuckled, "Besides that, you look exactly like Camille Brewster."

"How is she? Has anyone in prison hurt her?"

"Are you kidding? With the amount of interest in this case from the FBI, Hacienda Beach Police, Guatemala City Police and Interpol, no one would dare look at her cross-eyed. She's a little worse for wear, but she's fine and..." just then a tall blonde gentleman approached them, Agent Murray stood up. After a short introduction, Connie learned he was her sister's attorney. Mr. Cruz. He sat and immediately laid the file on the table.

"Mrs. Brewster is being held on two counts." He held up one finger, "kidnapping and," he held up a second finger, "armed robbery. I don't think that ..."

"Wait a minute," Connie was confused, "armed robbery? How in the world can they charge her with that? She didn't have a gun."

"Excuse me Miss, but I am speaking of two different crimes." Mr. Cruz looked at his file. "The armed robbery charge is for the ruby ring she had in her possession."

"That's her engagement ring," Connie confirmed. "Her murdered fiancée, Palmer Railton, gave it to her a few days ago."

"Yes." The attorney flipped back a couple of pages. "That agrees with what Mrs. Brewster claimed."

169

"You should know that the ruby ring is made of rare Burmese rubies that were specially cut and set into a ring. Its history dates back to the fourteenth century to the Moorish period in Spain. Historically, rubies were thought to provide a person with the power to live among their enemies in peace. Ironically, the history of these three identical rubies is just the opposite. They seem to bring bad luck and death to those who possess them. They were missing for centuries until they turned up at an estate auction in the 1820's. Again, the set of jewels were stolen and they were never seen together again. The Three Sisters being one of them. When the ring resurfaced, it was almost half a century later in France. It had been stolen with many other items, including firearms. A crime which resulted in the death of its owner. The Spanish and French Police, along with Interpol, searched for years in an effort to recover this priceless ring. It was never seen again until Ms Brewster was arrested yesterday.§

Mr. Cruz closed the folder and crossed his arms. "Do you have any idea how Mr. Railton got a hold of this museum quality ring?"

Connie sat with her mouth agape. There were no words she could say.

"Any idea?" the attorney asked again.

Connie shook her head in disbelief, "I-I knew Palmer traveled to different countries in Central America several times a year. It was part of his job as a lobbyist. He would often bring back trinkets for Camille and the occasional gift for me or my Aunt, but never anything expensive - and nothing like that!"

"Where is Camille's ring now?" Agent Murray asked.

"It is being held as evidence," Cruz replied. "I've seen it. Cleaned up, it would look brilliant. I can see why neither of you second guessed its origin was nothing other than three precious stones. But according to Interpol, it's worth millions because of its history."

"How do they know it's the same ring?" Murray asked making notes.

"There's a stamp on the inside of the ring with a Moorish seal. Interpol verified it and has papers for it. When Interpol gets involved, its big time stuff."

"So it brings bad luck to those who own it." Agent Murray repeated.

Connie refused to believe superstitious, old wives tales or hearsay. "That's a bunch of bull!"

"Think about Mr. Railton and now your sister," Mr. Cruz reminded her.

She realized Camille was in deep trouble not knowing how Palmer got possession of it. She decided to ignore the ring's tainted history and curse. "So what do we do for Camille?"

"I've already talked to the Guatemalan police about Camille's kidnapping. I went through the time line and they agree she didn't have time to be an intricate part of the baby selling syndicate unless she was involved with it on the other end, the US. If that's the case, the US should hold and try her, not the Guatemalan Government. They agreed with that. But because of the ring, they are set on keeping her here until Interpol arrives."

"So what can we do for Camille? I can see a charge of receiving stolen property, but NOT armed robbery."

He shrugged his shoulders, "It was last stolen in Europe, in France to be exact. Interpol has every right to get involved with this case. They will arrive this morning to question Camille."

"I need to see her," Connie held back her tears. "We're never going to get her out of jail are we?"

Agent Murray put his hand over her sling, "We both feel

that you should talk to the powers that be in Guatemala and Interpol. Tell them about Palmer's marriage proposal, the engagement and how you and Camille are innocent of any wrongdoing. Appeal to their best romantic hearts, maybe. It's your best shot at getting Camille out."

"Best romantic what? How the hell am I going to do that?" Connie burst out. "I feel like crap, my arm is killing me and you want me to be romantic?"

Connie sat back and took a deep breath. "Maybe it's not a good thing that I go see her now. I might strangle that girl." She ran her hand through her hair, "I warned her to let the police handle everything. 'Don't get involved,' I said to her, when Palmer was killed. And as usual, she didn't listen and left me to mop up the mess in her wake." She leaned forward on the desk, "Why am I surprised by this situation?" she muttered, "Maybe I should let her take her chances on her own."

"Bad attitude," the attorney warned. "You got to get over yourself if you want to get your sister out. Now I've asked for a private meeting with the police and Interpol as soon as they get here. Camille will be brought up in a few minutes and you can see her. They'll be monitoring everything you say to her, so be careful that nothing is misconstrued. Don't make jokes about anything."

Connie's arm throbbed, she looked at her watch. It was time for something to eat so she could take her pain pill. She went to the bathroom. She combed her hair, put on some lipstick and headed for the hallway. Nothing in the vending machine looked familiar except for a Pay Day chocolate bar. She took a couple of bites and looked at the pill in the palm of her hand. It was then she remembered the codeine they gave her in the hospital made her sleepy. She used her metal nail file to cut the pill in half before swallowing it. At least she got a little relief and remained coherent.

When Connie walked into the visiting room, she found Camille sitting in a chair across a wide table. She didn't look herself. Her hair was matted to her head, her blouse torn with a large diaper pin holding it closed and a black skirt smudged with dust and dried dirt. Two female police stood close to the table to hear every word. They didn't look like the studious types. Probably spoke little English.

Connie sat down and softly asked how she was doing.

"I'm in jail for nothing, how the hell do you think I'm doing?"

"Now, Camille, I'm trying to help."

Camille looked Connie in the eye, "Then get me the hell out of here."

Connie told her the story of her ring and how she will be pitching the police and Interpol to secure her release.

"Interpol? Why the hell are they here?"

"The ring, remember? They say it's a priceless antique stolen in Spain then France." Connie was losing patience with her sister, but knew she had to choose her words carefully.

Camille stared at Connie in silence for a few moments, "I feel ugly," and scrunched her upper lip.

Connie was careful to not say much else other than she was fine, her sling helped with the pain and she was looking forward to going home.

Just then Connie was paged overhead and Agent Murray entered the room.

He nodded toward the door. "I have to meet with Interpol now." She looked back at Camille, "Keep your fingers crossed."

Connie was pacing as they waited down the hall.

"Your sister's going to come out of this all right."

"Oh, I don't doubt that. She always lands on her feet."

"Then what's wrong? Nervous?"

"I get myself shot for her and she didn't even ask what happened to my arm or thank me for coming down here to help her."

All Connie wanted to do right then was lay down. Entertaining a bunch of policeman with an embellished story of romance was the furthest thing from her mind.

In the conference room, she recognized several of the Guatemalan agents and police officers from the shootout in the airport. They sat at a long table, each with a pad of paper. Mr. Cruz escorted her to an empty chair. A short man wearing a black suit and gray tie walked in with three unformed Guatemala City police officers. She felt the pain pill taking effect, her arm hurt less and her headache lessened. She tried to remember the schmaltzy romantic love stories she read in high school and the words of contrived love. That didn't work. It was too many years ago. If she was going to convince the man from Interpol that her sister was a victim, and that Palmer led a secret life, she had to come up with something fast. She then thought of movies that moved her hormones, *Ghost, Casablanca, Roman Holiday.* She thought of all the unrequited love stories she could remember. Lost loves, the moments of love before the tragedy and giving up one's love for the good of mankind or the good of the loved one. Something was making her stomach turn, not one of these movies fit her sister. Maybe Palmer, but not Camille.

The man from Interpol set his briefcase on the table and introduced himself with an alluring French Accent as Monsieur René Du Par or something French like that.

Señor Padilla leaned over to Connie, "I'll translate into Spanish for you," then the three Guatemala City police officers introduced themselves in perfect English.

"Tell us about the ring, Mademoiselle Cane," Monsieur De Par asked with an expressionless face, "and the story behind it."

She took a deep breath, felt the pain in her arm, "My sister, Camille is a single mother who has worked hard to hold a full time position as a court reporter ...er, stenographer for the Los Angeles County courts. She devotes as much time as she can to her son, Bradley. It hasn't been easy for her."

Connie wasn't about to tell them Camille lost custody of Bradley to her husband. "Her entire purpose in life is to keep the bills paid and to give Bradley the things he needs. And on occasion she, tries to give him those little things in life that a boy his age wants. He's a good boy and she doesn't spoil him. I think she does a wonderful job as his mother."

She paused, remembering Brad Pitt and Angelina Joliet, and their off-screen courtships. They'd be good to draw on. Connie took a sip of water, "Then she met and fell in love with Palmer Railton. She told me it was love at first sight,"

She forced a smile and a faraway look, actually holding back the discomfort in her arm. "Palmer loved Bradley and the three of them were very happy. But they were forced to postpone their engagement because of Palmer's constant travels and his work in Washington, DC." She glanced at all the Guatemalan police officers sitting in a row, listening through the interpreter. They were hypnotized by the story as if watching a movie. Connie hoped it was a look of re-membered love.

The interpreter seemed to take longer to translate her words. Maybe he was embellishing?

"The ring, Mademoiselle Cane?" Monsieur De Par repeated.

She turned to Mr. Cruz, the attorney, and asked, "Am I not entertaining or romantic enough?"

"Just keep going."

Connie continued, "They had been talking of marriage for some time. Out of the blue...I mean suddenly, he proposed to her with a dozen roses on bended knee."

"Bended knee?" one of the police asked looking at Mr. Padilla.

A long explanation of the American custom probably followed in Spanish, Monsieur De Par stared at Connie through the entire Spanish rendition of the story. When the interpreter felt he'd made his point with the others, he nodded to Connie.

"He, that is Palmer said, 'Will you make me the happiest man on earth. Will you marry me?'"

She cleared her throat, "My sister accepted his proposal and he slipped the ring onto her finger." Connie wiped a tear from her eye. "That is the way she told me it happened."

"Do you know where Mr. Railton bought the ring?"

"I have no idea. He never said. I doubt Camille knows. She never had a chance to ask." Suddenly, the last scenes of Casablanca and Ghost ran through Connie's mind, "You see, she was so excited to finally be engaged to the man she loved. I think that in her mind, she was already planning the wedding and didn't ask. It's such a tragedy that he was killed that very evening." Connie stole a glance at the policemen by the wall. They seemed as enthralled with her story as ever.

"He was killed? Poof? Like that?" Monsieur De Par snapped his fingers. "They did not celebrate the engagement with a toast or Champagne?" as only a Frenchman would ask. He seemed a bit bewildered.

"Apparently, they didn't have time. Palmer was taking a redeye to D.C that night." The room was silent. Connie looked around. Even Mr. Cruz shrugged. Connie rephrased her statement. "Mr. Railton was taking a very late flight to Washington D.C. that evening, but they planned to have a small engagement party with close friends and family when he returned."

"You don't think that was odd?" Monsieur De Par questioned, "He asks the woman he loves to marry him, then abruptly leaves?"

"You have to understand Palmer," she went on, "he was dedicated to his work. He was a lobbyist and champion of many causes on behalf of children and those in America who cannot help themselves."

Everyone turned to Señor Padilla, "*Qué es un Lobbyist?*" Monsieur De Par also looked at the interpreter. I guess Monsieur De Par understood Spanish, he looked satisfied with Señor Padilla's answer.

"You see, his dedication to his work is what Camille loved about him, and I, as his future sister-in-law respected about him. He loved Camille. That was obvious from the beginning. She understood his dedication to the different causes. But he never, never would have put Camille in any danger by knowingly giving her a stolen ring. He must have bought it not knowing its history. And he wasn't cheap. I'm sure he paid a very good price for it."

The police and Monsieur De Par talked among themselves in Spanish. Mr. Cruz was quietly listening to what he could hear.

"We show from his American travel records that Mr. Railton made frequent trips to Central America, Guatemala being one he frequented most often, followed by Belize. We now know why he was in Guatemala so often, but why Belize?"

Connie shook her head, "I have no idea. I wish I knew so I could help you out with this. Keep in mind, Camille and I have been helping the Hacienda Beach police with the investigation into his murder. Camille was kidnapped and brought here. As far as the ring is concerned, the origin and its history is completely new to me. I doubt Camille knows anything more than I do."

Mr. Cruz then stood and spoke in Spanish. After several minutes of discussion with the local police and airport security, Monsieur De Par said, "I think it is important to have her here so everyone can hear directly from Mademoiselle Camille Brewster."

A few minutes later, Camille was brought in. She looked tired to Connie, but quite alert. It wasn't until she sat down that Connie noticed she was in hand cuffs. She leaned over to Mr. Cruz, "Why the handcuffs?"

"Strictly procedure," he snapped.

Connie was going to say something about his pompousness, instead slumped back in her seat and waited. Señor Padilla changed seats so he could translate for Camille. Agent Murray sat next to Connie, "Don't worry," He whispered. "I know this guy pretty well. When Cruz treats you like shit, it's a good sign."

Camille was brought before the table. She stood quietly while a hushed conversation between the Airport Security, Guatemalan Police and Monsieur De Par took place. Connie couldn't hear much other than Camille's soft voice and her head moving from side to side when they would ask her a question. Her golden hair glistened in the light as it hung down her back. It was matted and unwashed, but still shined. It seemed like an hour before Mr. Cruz and Camille finally sat down. He leaned over to Agent Murray, "They want to speak with Señorita Camille and the Airport Police without you and Señorita Connie. You must leave the room."

Agent Murray and Connie waited on a hard bench in the hallway. She wondered if she was ever going to see her sister or speak with her again. Or was she going to disappear like so many people she's read about in the papers back home? Agent Murray put his hand on her shoulder, "Don't fret. Let Mr. Cruz will do his job."

Connie usually wasn't very religious. Most people aren't when their life is going great. But she truly felt, right then, that praying was all she had left. She squeezed her eyes shut and clasped her hands together so tight that her nails dug into her skin. She didn't know what to say or how to say it, but Connie pleaded with God to get her wayward sister out of this mess. In her heart it seemed that she could just have easily been in Camille's shoes.

After what seemed forever, the double doors swung open and Mr. Cruz stood staring at Connie. He smiled, held his hand out beside him and Camille appeared, no handcuffs. A thousand questions wanted to burst out of Connie's mouth, but all she could do was stand there, smile and wipe away joyous tears. Everyone was smiling except Camille. She rushed past everyone, hugged Connie, "I reek, I need a bath," took Connie's good arm and moved toward the street. Connie resisted and turned to the gentleman who made it all possible.

"Thank you from the bottom of my heart," she looked at Camille, prompting her to say something, anything. But nothing came. Not even eye contact from Camille to her legal team.

"Congratulations, Mr. Cruz" Agent Murray shook his hand.

"No congratulations, it was all her sister's doing." Mr. Cruz looked at Connie, "Your help at the airport and story seemed to have affected them."

Camille turned to the gentleman. "And the ring?"

"It's in Interpol's hands. They will take the issue up with the Guatemalan, Spanish and French governments. It's their job."

Connie nodded as Camille nudged her toward the street.

Marcello finally got his first good night's sleep at home since Palmer's murder. He stopped by the Captain's office as soon as he got in. Anna was under a carefully monitored watch in jail.

"I understand Ms Lopez lawyered up right away." The Captain stood and shook Marcello's hand. "So when is her lawyer getting here and where the hell are the Brewster sisters?"

Marcello explained the situation and dropped his report on the desk. The Captain picked it up and thumbed through the pages, stopping occasionally to read something that caught his interest.

"Very Good, Prado. You trying to impress me, Or are you looking to get promoted to Lieutenant?"

Marcello noticed Agent Smith standing in the corner. "The FBI is planning to be present during Anna Lopez's questioning." Captain explained, "Her lawyer is with her now."

They turned the corner and found a short, fat woman in a wheelchair outside the room.

She put down her notepad and extended her hand to Marcello. "Holly Marks here, I understand you were the officer who illegally arrested my client in Guatemala?"

The Captain rolled his eyes at Marcello.

Holly looked at her notes, "I just spent an hour with my client." She moved her gaze to their faces, "she's ready to give up all the information you need to satisfy the Guatemalan government and some information she has on another case you're working, a murder, I believe."

"Great," the Captain reached for the door knob, "Let's do it."

"Hold on, cowboy," She rolled her chair in front of the door, "My client has some conditions and wants to make a deal."

"No deals. This is an international situation. Once she crossed the U.S. border, this kidnapping also became an issue with Interpol."

"Don't mess with me, boys," she yelled pointing her finger

180

up at them. "I got nine kids at home and I'm not happy
I have to be here at all. You don't want to mess with this
Mexican Jewish Princess." Her voice got louder, probably so
Anna could hear in the next room. "You make a deal worth
my client's information or you are not getting a peep out of
her. Now, what's it going to be?"

"Okay, but you have to prove she's all you say she is."

"There's at least twenty people she can finger that would
bring down the baby stealing ring," Holly nodded. "And
believe me, that will take months of FBI man hours to sift
through."

The Captain nodded, so she went on, "Then you have this
murder you're trying to pin on someone. That would take a
lot of government time also. So don't fuck with me."

She spun her wheelchair around and faced the FBI agents,
"So, what do you boys think? You want to deal or not?"

"No." Agent Smith said.

"So you really are the idiots you look? Make a deal now or I
leave." She looked at her watch, "I gotta feed my kids in half
an hour. What's it gonna be?"

The Captain pulled out his cell and called the District Attorney. In a matter of minutes, Assistant DA, Janet Gleason, a tall, willowy redhead walked down the hall toward
them. She was a far cry from the black greasy haired, Holly
Marks.

Cocking her head to the side, Janet gave her hair a flip,
"Nice to see you again, Marcello. It's been a while."

Marcello swallowed hard.

"Okay, you two," The Captain bellowed, "On your own time.
In my office, this is important."

Captain brought her up to speed on the case. Agent Smith
stood quietly.

"Stay with us, Prado," The Captain reminded him.

Janet said the DA's office would agree to offer Holly Marks a deal for Anna. "Let's face it, Lopez has nothing to lose. We have lots to lose, two cases."

They shook their head as Janet explained the District Attorney's position to them, all the way down the hall.

Holly Marks wheeled her chair toward them with lightning speed.

Janet turned so she wasn't facing Holly and whispered, "I've dealt with Marks before, she's good. She knows police and government law, she'll get her way. Best to eat crow now and get it over and done with. Like I said, Anna Lopez has absolutely nothing to lose and you got everything to gain since you've hit a dead end with the Railton murder. I've seen the evidence you've got on Tony Dillon and it's flimsy at best. No way would it hold up in court. Let the FBI deal with the rest."

"What if her information isn't good enough for the deal?"

"If Marks is willing to spend her time on the case and the deal, believe me it is worth dealing. She wouldn't spend her energy and time on this if it wasn't good stuff." She went on to explain that Marks worked her deals with precision. She probably took her time getting here because she was researching the law for her client before she got here. "She's no fool. She may look and sound uneducated, but she's sharp. My suggestion is to take the deal no matter what she wants. I'll see what I can do."

"Oh, by the way," she turned, "Marks is a single mother of nine kids. She means it when she says she doesn't have time to mess around. She's not above walking out, I mean leaving a meeting and not being available for days. That's her MO and it works every time."

"Well, let's hope for the best," Marcello said straightening his tie.

The Captain pulled Marcello aside, "Is there something I need to know about you two?"

"Nah. She'd like there to be, though." Marcello smiled at the Captain and winked.

By noon, the FBI decided to offer Anna Lopez a reduced sentence and would eliminate any investigation by Interpol or Guatemalan government in exchange for Anna's cooperation. They wanted to shut down the international baby stealing syndicate which stretched to South America and parts of China. Apparently, Anna was the Queen pin. After hours of negotiation, Anna's attorney insisted that her client get a lunch break. "We can continue with the Railton murder case afterward."

The FBI had other ideas. Marathon interrogation sessions were commonplace at the Bureau and they wanted to wrap this up. Holly reminded everyone that if she didn't get a break now, her client would be unavailable for an undetermined amount of time. "Leads can go cold really fast. Do you two want to put the right people in jail or sit around and play with yourselves? Pick one."

At lunch, Assistant DA Gleason explained that in the past, Lopez ordered the kidnapping. She was never in the country when it went down. It would be difficult to prove her seniority in the syndicate. My suggestion is to make the deal. She wants reduced time and a misdemeanor. This on top of the fifteen years for the FBI. With good behavior she'll be out in five. She also demands there be no investigation into her finances. My guess is she has money in an offshore account. Five years of interest in these accounts. She'll be a multi-millionaire, if she has enough in there and I'd bet she does."

Gleason took the offer up the chain to the commissioner and District Attorney during lunch and returned with, "No deal."

Anna's attorney met with Gleason for all of five minutes. Holly Marks wheeled her chair out and muttered, "Just try to find me in a timely fashion."

Gleason and Marcello watched as she skillfully wheeled her chair toward the entrance. "Now what?" Marcello asked.

The Assistant DA put her hand on Marcello's arm, "Looks like you'll have to find the murderer on your own." She tossed the file on his desk. "Call me when you can change the commissioner's mind."

§ Chapter Eleven

Author's note

I was enthralled by the story of the Black Prince's Ruby on my trip to England in 1990. The ruby in the Imperial Crown is huge, the size of a small egg!

Since then I wrestled, played with and enhanced the true story and found a perfect place for this historical account in my book South of the Pier.

The Three Sister's Ruby Ring was taken from the true historical account of the Black Prince's Ruby.

The Black Prince's Ruby is made up of a 170 carat spinel ruby. The full account of the ring will send chills through you as you read the historical account. It has a most bloody trail of conquest beginning in 1366. The trail of this spinel ruby has an astonishing journey full of blood, horror, war and conquest. It's a history of instability, of human greatness and misfortune to those who own or hold it dear.

The ruby was originally owned by the Moorish Prince Mohammad. He was killed by his brother-in-law Abu Said. Abu Said took possession of the ruby and was murdered by Spaniard Lord Don Pedro, the Cruel. This is where the name "The Black Prince's Ruby," got its name in the 14th Century. It even has a speculative history, perhaps from the 1000's. It was thought to have been mined in the Badakhshan Mines in Tajikstan.

The Black Prince's Ruby now sits as the center jewel in the British Imperial State Crown.

I took literary license with the Three Sister's Ruby Ring, but the intrigue and extraordinary gem's history is something people have written about for centuries.

Be sure to visit websites on the Black Prince's Ruby for more information of this amazing true story.

185

Janet Elizabeth Lynn

CHAPTER TWELVE

Marcello and the Captain poured over the crime scene photos and other evidence. Even with a fresh look, they didn't pick up anything new and had to let Tony go. The evidence wasn't strong enough to keep him on a murder charge. The FBI, however, kept in contact with him to discuss his role in the baby stealing ring.

Frustrated, Marcello walked along the beach to clear his head. All he had was an earring, a fiber of a lady's wig, crumpled twenty dollar bill, a velvet ring box, and a transvestite. DNA didn't match. How was that supposed to hold up in court? The transvestite issue alone would probably bring in the ACLU and the whole case would get thrown out.

Marcello felt the familiar vibration of his cell phone from deep in his pocket. He wondered what else could go wrong.

"Hey Prado," the Captain's voice was not what he wanted to hear. "Get back here now. The commissioner is here with the Assistant DA, we may have a break. It seems someone close to the Governor put pressure on the Commissioner to make the deal work and they've agreed to half of what Anna Lopez wanted."

When Marcello arrived at the Police headquarters, Gleason muttered, "Someone must have called in a huge favor." Agent Murray was sitting in the office pouring through some files. "We need Murray here," Gleason added.

She briefed everyone on what would be allowed and would not. She was very straight with them, "Don't blow this," she looked at Prado. "Follow the parameters, and be as flexible as you can with Anna Lopez. The Governor is involved and this is an election year, so this has to go down smoothly."

Demonstrators had already gathered outside the courthouse, the press was alleging that the DA was stalling the investigation into Palmer's murder. Dozens showed up from Foster kids groups and everyone from the minority groups Palmer lobbied for. The largest group was the Gay rights activists. Gleason and Marcello pushed past the mob and hurried to the squad car. They spent the afternoon trying to find Holly Marks. Her house was empty and she didn't answer her pages. The commissioner authorized an APB for her in order to move this along.

At ten o'clock that evening Anna's attorney was finally brought in, accompanied by her own lawyer from the ACLU, Mr. Cruz. Agent Murray's eyes widened, the same attorney Camille had in Guatemala. Murray shook his hand, but no words were exchanged.

In front of the milling crowds outside, Holly Marks threatened to sue the department for harassment and unfair treatment of the handicapped and minorities.

The hastily called press conference didn't go well for the police department. In order to subdue public outrage, the Commissioner announced that they'd make every effort to work with Anna Lopez and her attorney to bring Palmer Railton's murderer to justice.

"She's going to get all she wants." Janet Gleason whispered to Marcello and the Captain, "I told you this bitch was good."

Anna Lopez entered the interrogation room accompanied by Holly Marks and Mr. Cruz.

"Mr. Cruz is an attorney from Central America," Marks introduced him. He nodded.

Calmly, Anna Lopez told her story, "It was the afternoon of Palmer's murder. We'd just completed a successful delivery of two healthy baby girls from Guatemala. My financial person didn't arrive at the prearranged site so I couldn't pay the couriers with cashier's checks as is my normal routine. Out of all the many deliveries Tony and Palmer completed for me. That was the first time I didn't have the money available. I offered to pay them the next afternoon. Tony had played Palmer's wife in the pickup, and I must admit, he was very good at impersonating a woman." Anna shifted her weight and crossed her legs as if she was telling a story at a cocktail party, "Tony became extremely agitated whereas Palmer trusted me and agreed to wait until the next day. But, Tony would have nothing of it and the two of them got into a screaming match. Tony told Palmer, firmly that he would no longer work with him if he didn't agree to hold out for the money right then and there. What could I do? I had no money to reimburse them!"

Anna's facial features changes as she paused and grabbed her arm. "Then Tony grabbed my wrist and threatened to expose the whole operation if I didn't pay them that very instant."

She sat up and straightened the front of her jump suit. "My associates had left, I had no one to protect me. This was the first time I'd seen Tony like this, though I'd noticed a change in his demeanor over the last few weeks. He had been kind of edgy and easily "spooked" as Palmer put it. You see he had noticed it too."

"Do you think Tony was on drugs?" The Captain asked.

"I couldn't speculate. All the years I've known him, he's been clean and sober. I didn't know what to think, and Palmer wasn't sure either what had occurred to cause this shift in his friend's behavior. He mentioned it to me several times." She sat silently, waiting for their next question.

Mr. Cruz and Agent Murray were conspicuously quiet throughout the interview.

"Okay, Ms Lopez, so you were manhandled by Tony," Marcello was frustrated and wanted to finish the interview. He had a feeling the whole story was bullshit. "Then what?"

"Well I did what any business owner would do. I tried to

189

figure out a way of making it a workable situation, you know. What do the infomercial lackeys call it? Oh yes, a 'win-win' situation. I finally offered him my ruby ring as collateral until I could contact my financial person or provide them with a cashier's check from the bank the next morning. Tony reluctantly agreed. Palmer nodded. I handed them the ring. It is an antique, worth several-fold more than the minuscule five thousand I owed them. I had no other contingency. You can imagine the absolute shock I experienced when I learned from the television news that Palmer had been murdered. I was even more stunned to see Camille Brewster wearing a ruby ring." She delicately brushed back a wisp of hair from her face that had come loose from her perfect ponytail. "Camille told me Palmer gave it to her as an engagement ring. For my money, I think Tony found out Palmer gave the ring to Camille and shot him. You must remember, he's been acting edgy for weeks and Palmer was aware of it."

Agent Murray reached in his pocket, "May I ask a question?"

Gleason nodded.

He placed a photo on the table, "Is this the ring you gave Mr. Railton and Mr. Dillon?" He slid the photo toward her.

Anna and Mr. Cruz examined the photo. Anna was about to answer when Mr. Cruz put his hand on her shoulder.

"May I have a conference with my client and Señora Marks, please."

"In the interest of time, I don't think..." Gleason put her hand on Marcello's arm cutting him short.

"Actually, we'll wait in the hallway." The three left the room. "What is wrong with you, Prado?" Captain asked.

Janet forced a whisper, "Do not, and I mean never, refuse a suspect their time with their attorney. Ever!"

190

Mr. Cruz soon opened the door and politely invited them back.

"To answer your question," Anna Lopez began, "This is not the ring I gave Palmer."

"What do you mean, not the ring you gave him." Captain was confused.

"It is not the ring."

"But before you said it was the ring you gave them."

"No," Marks repeated. "That is not what she said," pointing to the recorder.

"I said," Anna cajoled, "Camille was wearing a ruby ring when I saw her in my office. This is not the ring I gave Palmer and Tony."

"Who gave you the ring?" Jane asked.

"A friend in Belize, José Verde. He asked me to hold it for him. I assumed Palmer would give it back to me."

"And where can we find this José Verde?" Marcello asked.

"I have no clue."

Janet Gleason made a few notes and looked into Anna's eyes, "You have proof of all this?"

"I keep a security video system going in my office all day to record my business transactions, in the event of a disagreement just like this." She sat back, "You need evidence? Tony is on it taking the ring and making his threats to me and Palmer. If you want it, let me know. I can have the DVD here in less than twelve hours," she looked at Holly and nodded.

"I'll bring it personally." Holly Marks added.

"Twelve hours, " Janet repeated, "no more."

191

"You mean twelve hours from when I leave the building don't you."

Gleason stared Holly down.

Marcello spoke up, "We're also missing the weapon that killed Mr. Railton. You wouldn't by some odd twist, happen to know where it is. Would you? It's a Beretta .32 Tomcat."

"Watch the attitude detective." Holly scolded.

Anna Lopez smiled and nodded. "I own two Ruger .38 Specials. I loaned one to Tony Dillon for his trip to Guatemala. He was always afraid of being robbed like some gringo tourist, so I loaned him the gun before each trip and he returned it in exchange for his check. Since I didn't pay him, he kept it. And we all know what happened with the second one."

"Cute. A nice little lady's gun," Marcello was trying to be insulting.

"We didn't find any evidence of a gun in his car, or gun powder on his hands," the Captain interrupted. "His checking account doesn't show large sums being deposited. In fact, he doesn't have much in there at all. Any idea where he keeps his money?"

"Like any self respecting crook," Holly Marks stated, "Someplace else. We done here?"

Marcello ignored Holly and looked at Anna square in the eyes, "Do you have any idea where he keeps his stash?"

"Try the Fitness Club in Hacienda Beach. He probably has a locker there. He has a Post office box. He never uses a street address, as far as I know."

Marks piped up, "God, do we have to do all the work for you people? You seriously didn't think of that with all your intelligent detectives working on it?" She motioned to Anna and wheeled her chair to the door.

The Captain ordered Tony picked up again along with a warrant for his Post office box and gym locker.

Marcello reached to turn off the tape recorder but Anna blocked his arm. "I hope this helps, I'd like to see Palmer's murderer put away for a long time. He was a dear, long time friend who really wanted to change the world. He helped a lot of laws get passed for Hispanic aliens in this country." She lowered her eyes, "He deserves to rest peacefully and with dignity."

Marcello switched off the recorder. He knew the last part of the Anna's confession was for the jury.

"I expect a copy of the entire tape as evidence of my client's cooperation and a signed agreement to be delivered to my office within twelve working hours," Mr. Cruz insisted.

Marcello accompanied the uniformed officers taking Anna down the hallway to her cell, "I meant everything I said at the end. Palmer really was a good guy."

Marcello felt like he was being played, "You call ripping the babies out of the arms of their mothers to be raised by strangers in a foreign land, and killing the babies when they don't meet your needs being a good guy?" His heart hurt when he remembered the infant that washed up on shore, that tiny little body just beginning life. It had to be connected someplace.

Anna stopped. "These children will have much healthier and better lives here than where they came from. And Palmer would never kill a child, ever." When the uniformed officers pulled her along, she shouted over her shoulder, "I wouldn't put it past Tony to hurt a child, but Palmer?... never.

"Do you know how hard it is going to be to find a Joe Verde in Southern and Central America?" Gleason said to Marcello.

"If that's his name!" Captain nodded to Marcello.

"In my book, I think Lopez denied ownership of the ring she gave Railton since no one can prove it was hers." Gleason added, "Very smart move."

"All we have is Anna and Tony's word."

While Tony waited for his attorney to arrive, he watched the security tape from Anna's office. He saw himself arguing with Palmer, grab Anna's wrist, tease her with the gun and take the ring from her.

Marcello shut off the tape while Gleason stood between Tony and the monitor. "Well, what do you have to say?"

"I'm not saying a word without my attorney."

Accompanied by the aroma of baby wipes, Tony's friend and attorney twittered into the room with remnants of make up on his chin. Unlike the obsessively punctual Holly Marks, Duane Abernathy was half an hour late. He insisted on speaking with Tony and seeing the security DVD that allegedly showed his client threatening Anna and Palmer.

Janet Gleason walked down the hall to meet him. But before doing that, she went into the adjoining observation room where Marcello was watching.

"What do you think?" she crossed her arms and nodded toward the room, "Full blown sex change or just make believe?" Marcello shrugged. Abernathy turned his attention away from Tony long enough to wave at the two way glass. He'd been through this routine many times and knew they were watching him and his client.

"Where in God's name are they getting these lawyers?"

"Takes all kinds," Marcello muttered while checking his cell phone for messages. Connie and Camille were back in town and he was waiting to hear from them. A faint smile crept across his lips.

Abernathy stepped into the hall and gently closed the interview room door behind him, "Okay boys and girls." He knocked on the observation room door and waited of someone to emerge. "My client, as you can see, is ready to make a statement, but he wants to deal."

Marcello nodded and waited.

"Reduced sentence. What do you think?"

"Absolutely not. We have him on DVD," Gleason insisted as Marcello opened his mouth to protest. "If he wants to give more information, that's fine. Then we'll see what we can do. No guarantees."

"Oh really. Come now, Ms Gleason, you know you're compelled to share all the information you have with me. I want to know where you got that DVD. Was it Ms Anna Lopez?"

"Yes, she is our source and we plan to use this disk to convince your client to cooperate. Looks like we're one step ahead of you." Gleason didn't flinch, "You work with us and we'll try. But understand, I'm not promising anything - no promises- Nada."

Abernathy bowed to the pair, "I'll advise my client to carefully choose all of his words." He returned to the interview room with Marcello and Janet Gleason right behind him.

Tony had watched the tape for the third time and slumped back in the chair. "When Palmer and I went to the parking lot, I was pretty happy about the way things went with the two babies we'd just delivered. But I was still pissed off at Anna for not having my money ready. I was willing to work with her. I just wanted to scare her. That's all."

Tony rubbed his palms together with resignation. "We got back around one. Palmer and I went our separate ways and planned to meet at his place at five o'clock. When I arrived, I was still in my wig and make up. He met me in the street.

I showed him the outfit I bought for the next trip. We laughed all the way to his door. We sat on the sofa. Palmer examined the ring in the box. We were sure it was real but if not, it still had to be worth something. Then the door bell rang. I hurried into the back room to change. I hate wearing all that makeup. It makes my face itch, especially when you're, you know growing a beard."

Abernathy rolled his eyes and nodded in agreement, then looked at Gleason. "Anything else you want to know?"

Gleason ignored him, "Then what happened?"

"I'd finished washing my face, removing my wig and was putting on some moisturizer when I heard the doorbell again. Then I heard two very loud pops. I thought it was kids playing outside in the courtyard. They like to do that because of the acoustics," he looked up at Marcello and Janet. "It amplifies the sound, you know echoes."

"Okay we got it, it was loud."

"That's when I heard a crash." Tony's face scrunched in horror. "I ran to the front room and there was Palmer, laying on his back, staring up at me from under the glass table. His yellow shirt was full of blood. He just stared up at me. I bent down and tried to rouse him, then I felt his neck. Blood came trickling out of his mouth. I'll never get that picture out of my mind." He cupped his head in his hands. "There was nothing I could do. He was gone. Calling 911 wouldn't have helped. I saw the ring box on the floor. I picked it up, opened it and the ring was gone. So I dropped it where I found it. I couldn't figure out who knew what was in the box besides Anna Lopez and me? Oh God, that sounded bad didn't it?" He looked at his attorney. "I shouldn't've said that, should I?"

Abernathy patted his shoulder, "You're doing just fine, Tony, go on."

He took a big drink from his water bottle. "I assumed Anna sent her boys to take care of Palmer and me. Only I wasn't in the room, thank heavens. So they probably thought I went home."

"About how long were you in the back room?" Marcello asked.

Tony straightened up - eyes swollen and red. He shook his head, "As long as it takes to remove a wig, makeup and lacy blouse. I then washed my face and put on a t-shirt. Maybe 30 minutes."

"It took you half an hour to wash your face and change?" Marcello asked in disbelief.

His attorney chimed in, "Cut him a little slack, please. It takes a lot of time to get all that foundation out of your beard stubble."

"Oh, and I also removed my fake nails. Sometimes that takes a few minutes." Tony looked around. "I ran to the back room, threw all my stuff in my duffel bag and split. But I didn't kill him," He dropped his head, "I cared for him deeply. He was my dear friend."

"What was Railton's relationship with Camille Brewster?"

"I told you in the hospital, he loved me not her. He only needed her as an occasional arm decoration for public appearances. That's all."

"Yet he proposed to her and gave her the ring."

"No." He leaned toward Marcello, "How many times do I have to say this?" pounding his chest, "He loved ME, not her!"

"So you disagree that he gave her the engagement ring?"

"Why in the world would he give her an engagement ring if he wasn't going to marry her. He disliked the entire family, 'dumb blondes," he called her and her sister. And he hated that spoiled little brat of hers, B-r-a-d-l-e-y. He hated kids. As soon as we got our money that ring was going back to Anna. And if we didn't get paid, we were going to sell it. But after we talked, Palmer suggested we use the money for a trip to Paris for just the two of us. They don't mind people being real over there". He sat quietly for a few minutes, "So you tell me, what motive would I have to kill him?"

"Oh I don't know, maybe because he proposed to Camille Brewster or maybe because you disagreed with him about what to do with the ring. You know, stuff like that." Janet was beginning to lose patience with everyone.

"I didn't kill him," he screamed, and slammed both hands on the table. "I wouldn't kill him any more than you would kill that Brewster bitch. I see the way you look at her. You're pathetic."

Marcello moved to stand up but Gleason put her hand on his knee, "Did Palmer want to sell the ring?"

"Don't answer that Tony," Abernathy put his hand on Tony's shoulder ever so tenderly, "That's pure speculation and I won't have my client subjected to hearsay. We don't know what Mr. Railton would've done."

Marcello pulled out a photo, "Is this the ring Anna Lopez gave you and Mr. Railton?"

Tony glanced at the picture, "Looks like it."

Marcello repeated the question, "Is this the ring Anna Lopez gave you?"

Tony did a double take of the picture. He picked put the photo, "Maybe. It had three stones, I thought they were square... maybe not. He brought the picture closer. "The band, it looks different."

"Yes or No?"

Tony looked at his lawyer, he nodded. "I didn't really look that closely at it. It was in the box the entire time we had it. I never took it out."

"You're saying you're not sure then?"

Abernathy took offense, "There is a fine line between questioning a suspect and coercion Detective. You're beginning to cross that line."

Marcello recoiled, "What did you do after you left Lopez's place that afternoon?"

"I went shopping for a new dress. I told you."

"And Palmer?"

"I have no idea. I met him at his place later that afternoon."

"Can you prove it?"

"I have my credit card receipts. I got a pink and white dress for our next trip for Anna."

"Where is Anna's gun?"

Tony sat back, "You'll find it with your warrant."

Gleason and Marcello were silent.

"You'll find it," he smirked. "And you'll find it was never fired, at least not recently."

"The make?"

"I had Anna's Ruger."

"Hold that thought." Gleason took Marcello into the hall. "We have a pretty good chance here. I would like more evidence than this, but I think it's good enough to stick Tony with the crime. The evidence is marginal, but with Anna's statement and the DVD we have a good chance of convicting him." She scanned Marcello's face of some trace of reaction, "I say we book him and see what happens. Seems with opportunity, motive and means, it's a shoe in! Let me know what you find with the warrant."

Marcello said nothing.

"For what it's worth, I knew Palmer Railton. He worked with

me a few times on some foster children's cases. His heart always seemed to be in the right place and we did manage to get several good laws protecting some of the kids that fall through the cracks. His own grandmother took him in when he was abandoned by his mother. He knew the plight of several kids in his school in the South and it bothered him greatly. I was abandoned but I was taken in by a wonderful Mormon family. I was one of the lucky ones and I know that too. So we teamed up and went to Sacramento. A year later we got what we wanted. Whether or not he was gay, I don't know. We had a strictly professional relationship. I don't think he was, but I can't say for sure. This was pre-Brewster from what I understand and he was a good guy.§

"We have a four-hour window that's not been accounted for. What do you think?" the Captain added.

Gleason shrugged, "Ask his fiancée, see what she has to say. And verify that was the ring he gave her."

Marcello headed to Connie's place. On the way, he called her to let her know he was on his way and they had found the murderer. Camille answered instead.

"It's about time." Camille snipped, "I was really beginning to wonder about you people. I'll tell Connie you're coming."

"Good," he muttered, "At least Connie will be happy to hear the news." He wasn't surprised when Camille slammed the receiver down.

After arriving at Connie's beach cottage, Marcello looked out the back and saw Camille sitting outside on the concrete garden wall, finishing a tall glass of ice tea. Connie pointed her thumb, "She's been like that since we got back, very closed and quiet. I think she's depressed."

"Hmm." Marcello snorted, "You don't think she's taking advantage of your compassionate nature?"

"How would you feel if you lost your fiancé, your engagement ring and spent time in a Guatemalan Jail?"

He showed her the picture of the ring, "I need to ask Camille to identify the ring. Something has come to light that doesn't add up."

Connie looked at her picture, "That's the ring, but don't show it to her. It will only upset her even more. You know it's the one she had. Please don't do this."

"There is a four hour window for Palmer we can't account for the afternoon of his murder. Any idea where he may have gone?"

"Maybe to get some roses? You think?" Connie meant to be sarcastic.

"Or maybe buy a ring." He told her about Tony and Anna's uncertainty about the ring.

"So where did he get the ring?"

He looked again at Camille, "So, she's been weird since the prison stint?"

She nodded.

Marcello opened the screen door and walked over to Camille. "I thought you'd like to know that a friend of Palmer has been arrested. All the evidence points to him. We're gathering more evidence as we speak, but I'm sure he's our guy."

Camille looked straight ahead and said nothing. Marcello put his hand on her arm. "It's over."

"Is it going to stick or will he get off on some technicality? I'm a court reporter remember? I've seen a lot of people walk who were obviously guilty."

"You and I both know you can never tell what a jury will say or do. All we can do is present the best evidence."

"What time did you see him that afternoon?"

"I guess it was about three or three-thirty, somewhere around there."

"What did you do from three-thirty until midnight?"

"Oh, looked at wedding dresses, went to borders and browsed through wedding magazines. I went home and made some tea like Aunt Dolly always did when we had something to think about. Then I poured through the magazines and nodded off I guess."

"I need to ask you, is this the ring Railton gave you?"

She nodded as she moved her fingers around the picture of the ring.

Marcello reviewed the ring issue.

"So it wasn't Anna's ring? He didn't know it was hot?" Camille was surprised.

"This is a recent development. We're still trying to figure it out." Marcello said.

Connie leaned out the door, "Camille, honey, I think we need to get away from all of this. Let's go see Aunt Dolly. I know it's only an hour boat ride over there, but it always feels like we're a thousand miles away. If the police need us, we can be back at a moment's notice."

Marcello added, "I think it will do you good."

Camille stood and stared at them, "To set the record straight, no one assaulted me, sexually or otherwise while I was in Guatemala. But I was raped of my dignity every minute I had to stay in that filthy, rat infested dump while you and my lovely sister her were fucking around down there."

"Camille! What are you saying?" Connie yelled.

Camille poked Marcello in the chest with her finger, "You left me there to rot while you went on to get what

202

you chased after, Anna Lopez." She threw her arms in the air, "And you, my loving sister, lounging around in a comfortable bed with nurses waiting on you hand and foot, feeding you and helping you with your itch..."

Connie shot back, "I had a bullet in my arm, you ungrateful bitch. And all because of your stupidity I had to undergo painful surgery in a Guatemalan hospital."

"Now girls," Marcello stepped between them.

"Get out, Detective!" Camille pointed at the door. "A lot of good you are." She stormed into the bedroom and slammed the door, causing a framed photograph of her and her sister to crash to the floor, breaking the glass.

Tears washed down Connie's cheeks when she saw the photo fall. She instinctively reached for the bedroom door, but Marcello held her back.

"She's been through a lot, let her be for a while. Go to Catalina the change will do you both good."

"I've had it with her." Connie held her injured arm, remembering the pain of the bullet tearing into her flesh. "I can't take this anymore," she moaned. "I am so tired of her screwing up my life. And me like a fool, always picking up after her. I'm done."

Marcello put his arm on her shoulder, "You need to get away, both of you."

He pulled out his cell phone and booked both of them on the first boat to Avalon in the morning. He then called Dolly and told her they were coming early and they needed some "motherly advice."

Before he left he took Connie's chin in his hand, "You know we did all we could in Guatemala to get you and Camille home safely. And you realize the department put the apprehension of Railton's killer ahead of everything else. You know that, don't you?"

Connie put her hand on his chest. "I know you did Marcello and I hope Camille will come to realize that, soon." He stood close and ran his fingers through her hair. She closed her eyes, lingering in his touch.

Marcello took the long way home on surface streets. Camille's accusations hurt him deeply while he struggled to understand her insensitivity to Connie. This was not a time he wanted to go home to a cold, empty house.

As Connie watched Hacienda Beach fade into the distance, she couldn't remember a trip to Aunt Dolly's that seemed to take so long. Camille stayed below, having drinks with the guys on the crew. She always was a sucker for a man in a clean shirt. When Dolly met them at the landing, she knew something was different. She'd seen spats between her nieces before, but nothing like this. Not even when they fought over boyfriends in high school. Camille sat down in the front seat of Dolly's golf cart leaving Connie to sit in the rear, facing backwards. Everyone was silent until they reached the house. Camille ran up the stairs to her room.

"Stop right there, young lady," she stopped on the seventh step."Get down here and stop acting like some fifteen year-old drama queen." Connie crossed her arms and smirked at her sister who'd been reduced to an obedient child. Dolly saw Connie out of the corner of her eye, "Don't you think you're pure as the driven snow in all this, Constance Lynne Cane." Dolly pointed to the living room, "Both of you in here, right now. I'm going to make us all some tea."

She walked to the kitchen shaking her head. She glanced over her shoulder with a withering look that the twins remembered all too well from their childhood. She returned with the tray of tea and cookies, "I am not happy with you. The both of you are going to sit here until you work out whatever it is that's eating at you. You can get up to use the bathroom, but that's it. I want no yelling or shouting, no swearing. And above all nothing physical. I'll be right here to enforce the rules."

Dolly was sure Camille was depressed and the sooner she got over this the better. Carefully, she asked, "What happen to you in Guatemala?"

"I was arrested," Camille sneered. "And thrown into a smelly prison."

"She won't talk about it." Connie looked at Dolly, "I tried to find out, but she won't talk to me. I don't know why."

"Were you taken advantage of? Did someone touch you-rape you?" Dolly asked.

Camille didn't respond. She stared out over the harbor, rocking in the chair and rubbing her wrist.

"I think it's odd," Connie noted. "She never did that before."

"Yes, she did," Dolly reminded her. "You were too little to remember. She did that when you two first came here, after your parent's funeral. She spent days rubbing her wrist and rocking in that exact spot.

"I wish she'd talk to me," Connie said, "This is weird. Camille is sitting right in front of us and she won't even react when we talk about her. It's like she isn't even here."

Three hours later, nothing had changed. They were still in the same clothes. Not a word had been uttered. While Dolly made dinner, Marcello called. "I need to talk to Connie, is she available?"

Dolly hesitated while she looked back into the living room. Her two nieces sat in separate chairs facing each other, but their faces were turned toward the window. Dolly walked into the living room. "There's a call for you Connie. BUT - This isn't over yet. When you're done, you go right back in there."

"The gun used to kill Palmer was not the gun we found on Tony, so we don't have all the evidence." This wasn't the

205

news Marcello wanted to share, "It looks like someone else killed him or Tony used a different gun and got rid of it."

Connie sighed, "I was hoping the evidence would give Camille closure on all this. I guess we'll have to wait longer." There was no response from Marcello. Connie continued, "Listen, I know you're doing all you can to find the killer. I appreciate all you've risked to help Camille in Guatemala. If she went to Georgia and visited with Palmer's grandmother, I think she might break out of this depression. Earlene is a lovely lady and it may help Camille. Can she leave the state for a few days maybe?"

He agreed to pull some strings so Camille could travel. "You'll be legally responsible for her. Do you understand?"

"Haven't I always been?"

"You'll need to be on standby should the FBI want to talk to your sister again or need to take a statement from her."

Connie accepted the responsibility, "After all," she said with complete defeat, "Who else in this world is going to keep Camille on a short leash?"

Suddenly, Connie remembered. She and Camille sent a picture of the ring to Aunt Dolly through their cell phones. She looked through her cell phone and there was the picture. She sent it to Marcello texting, "I hope this helps." As she pushed SEND she remembered that innocent night just eight days ago.

Connie asked Dolly to speak with Earlene.

"Oh mercy, I have plenty of room and the weather is great now." Earlene was quiet for a moment, "You know Dolly, I'm sorry. May I call you Dolly? I didn't have much contact with Palmer. It would surely be nice to hear about this last days and how much he loved your dear Camille."

Dolly knew it was going to be a hard sell to get Camille there. She didn't even want to think about the chore it would be to get Camille to talk.

"Camille has been in a major funk and I am praying that going out to see you would bring her closer to Palmer and perhaps help her to let go. It might mean some closure for her."

"Well, I would love to have all of you."

Dolly graciously declined the invitation, "I'll send them right to you."

When Dolly returned to the living room, she announced the trip to Georgia. "I don't care to see any more squabbles between you two. I'm getting too old to put up with that foolishness. You two are getting on a plane tomorrow and flying out to visit Earlene. Connie was excited about going to Georgia. She'd always wanted to see the South and Georgia was the heart of it.

"I remember, she is a very nice lady," Dolly turned to Camille, "Well, that's one person who'll enjoy themselves. Now what about you, Camille Elizabeth?"

"Why are you meddling in my affairs? Palmer was MY fiancée. I don't need anyone's help, especially yours." She'd never yelled at Dolly before. Her aunt didn't allow yelling from her late husband or the girls when they were younger. "You are going. No discussion. Palmer was the only family Earlene had and you, Missy, are the only connection she has left. It's your obligation and duty to see her at this time in her life."

Camille knew better than to cross her aunt. She reluctantly agreed to go. Dolly didn't just send them off on the plane, instead she accompanied them to the security check at the airport to be sure they got on the plane.

While waiting in the security line, Camille sulked, and Connie went through the work Dolly needed to do to deliver food to her customers tomorrow. "Honey, I'll get into your computer, follow your directions and I'll be all set. I'll even

use an on-line map to route me. I'll start the cooking tonight. My lands, sweetie. I haven't cooked like this in years
and am looking forward to it, too."

That statement worried Connie. Aunt Dolly hasn't cooked
in decades and when she did, it wasn't anything to write
home about. She almost decided not to go to Georgia, but
her sister was more important than food. Connie began to
script the phone message, in her head, she would leave for
her customers when she returns. She would apologize for
whatever it is that went wrong.

§ Chapter Twelve

Background Information

Janet Gleason was abandoned when she was eight and remembered a baby sister before she was left on church steps. She grew up in a few foster homes until she was placed with a large Mormon family.

Janet was one of thirteen foster children who lived with the Bleacher family. They were poor. They worked hard to grow a vegetable garden to supplement meals. Mrs. Beecher made bread every day for the family of fifteen. Mr. Bleacher was an insurance agent who played piano for all the churches in the town. Each foster child was given a crack at piano lessons. Janet tried but was pronounced tone deaf. But then she always thought his teaching methods were a bit off.

When she was eighteen, she decided to find her mother and sister. She got a job waiting tables and selling Avon cosmetics in her spare time. Eventually, she found her sister, Amy Long, who had been adopted by a loving family. They forged a nice relationship. They decided to go to law school. They roomed and took classes together in law school. After graduation, they set out to find their mother. They have been searching for four years and nothing so far. At least she had her sister in a neighboring city to call family.

Janet Elizabeth Lynn

CHAPTER THIRTEEN

Camille's spirits seemed lifted as she snagged an empty seat in the row ahead of Connie and checked out the man sitting next to her. He wasn't bad looking and she didn't see a wedding ring, but then she couldn't see his hand under his coat. She relied on her tried and true flirting techniques to break the ice.

Connie leaned in and whispered, "Lighten up, Camille. Do you think he's going to screw you the minute we arrive in Savannah? His wife is probably waiting for him with a kid hanging onto her skirt."

"Don't get in my way sister or you'll regret it."

Just as Connie predicted, as soon as they hit the baggage claim, the hunky guy hugged his waiting wife and picked up his two little kids.

As they passed by the young family, Camille mumbled, "That's just pathetic."

"Girls, Girls. Over here." Earlene called while waving her thin, short arms.

Connie had to bend at the waist to hug her around the neck, "Now which one are you, Connie or Camille?"

"I'm Connie," she smiled.

Camille stood off to the side staring out the window. "I'm sorry Earlene, but she's not been herself. I need to apologize for her," she explained the situation on the way to the parking lot. Camille followed a few paces behind them.

"A Hummer?" Camille exclaimed when she saw Earlene's vehicle. This was the first sign of excitement she'd displayed since Guatemala.

"This baby gets me where I want to go and then some." Earlene pulled out her remote and pressed a button. Suddenly the big silver SUV came alive. The doors clicked open a few inches followed by small, lighted steps that appeared from underneath the doors. The tailgate swung up and the interior lights came on. Earlene hoisted herself up into the driver's seat, "This thing is pure power on the road. No one messes with me," Connie and Camille watched with amazement at the finesse she used to maneuver through the parking lot. The top of Earlene's head just barely appeared above the dashboard, so she drove by peering through the spokes of the steering wheel. Earlene was fearless, "Ain't nobody gonna get in my way." She inserted herself into the traffic.

"I think she's gone a little loopy." Camille whispered from the back seat.

After an uneventful hour of rolling green hills and pastoral shady tree-lined landscapes, Earlene slowed and turned left onto a gravel road. Connie and Camille hung on as the road dipped and wound through the countryside. Just as the dust cloud was about to overtake them, a rooftop appeared above the foliage, and then several windows.

"People call it the face," Earlene pointed to her house, "Folks say it kinda looks like two eyes staring up over the crest, wouldn't you say?" She swung the Hummer around the corner at the end of the tree line. Before them stood a lovely two story house, painted pink and white, bedecked with fussy gingerbread decorations peeking through the overgrown vegetation.

Earlene swept her arm across to the field next to the house, "The color goes with my flowers in the spring. See?" The house matched most of the pink roses. The occasional bush of tiny white roses looked like the house's gingerbread shutters dispersed throughout the field. While they were admiring the view, Earlene skidded to a stop in the gravel, throwing her guests forward. Luckily, their seatbelts held them in place.

She was out the door and on the ground before everyone caught their breath, "Okay girls," She called as she dusted herself off, "I got some cold lemonade waitin' in the icebox. Hop on out."

"I really think someday she's going to kill someone with that monster." Camille complained.

"Or seriously injure herself just getting out of that thing," Connie added as she followed behind dragging her wheeled carry-on through the gravel to the house.

Camille set her cart on the porch step, when the screen door flew open. Earlene stood there holding a small pitcher of lemonade with ice floating on top. "Well, what are you two doing, dawdling around? Get up here on the porch and have something cold." Camille took both hands and flung her wheeled cart up on the wood floor of the porch. Connie took a different approach, backing up the steps while bumping her cart up each one.

Looking around, Connie was reminded of one of Tennessee William's stories. The wrap-around screened porch was populated with rattan chairs, tables painted white and gaily decorated with pink and white flowered upholstery. On the floor, a lemon yellow shag throw rug. It was the perfect porch for eating and anything else you wanted to do.

Earlene plopped the tray into Camille's hands, "You take care of this, I'll get the muffins," From inside the house, she yelled, "Just put it down anywhere, Sweetie."

Camille chose the large, low table in front of the settee. Connie pulled their luggage carts to the side and joined her. Just in time for Earlene to come barreling out of the house with another tray in one hand, her cane in the other. "Here's some hot, fresh, good old-fashioned carrot muffins. I baked them just for you two. They were Palmer's favorite." Earlene gave Camille a wink, "Of course you know that." Camille made a disgusting face that Connie picked up and kicked her under the table. "Be nice," she whispered, "Remember that Hummer is our only way out of here and she's got the key in her pocket."

Earlene came back with some napkins and poured the lemonade, "Okay girls, eat up." As much as Camille wanted to hate everything about Earlene and Georgia, she had to admit the carrot muffins were heavenly, putting every pastry she ever had in Beverly Hills to shame. She split a second one, "You have got to try these. They are killer muffins and I'm not exaggerating."

"I'm glad you girls are hungry. You both look pretty skinny. I've got a pig roasting in the oven for dinner, but won't be ready 'til later. I also invited a couple over who knew Palmer many years ago. They're anxious to meet you."

"Tell me Earlene," Camille asked with her mouth full of muffin, "how far is your nearest neighbor?"

"Oh," Earlene took a big swallow of lemonade, "maybe five miles. Look," She pointed straight out from her house, "you can see the roof of the Masson family over there. You'll like 'em. They'll be here about seven for dinner and visitin'."

The rose scented breeze wafted through the porch. "It's going to be a warm evening."

When the girls finished their drinks, they divvied up the trays and glasses, and followed Earlene into the house.

As they arrived at the kitchen, Camille commented, "Wow, this is like a museum."

"I'm sorry, where are my manners? You must be tired. Let me show you to your room."

"Connie looked at her watch and deducted three hours. She realized it was close to lunch time in California.

Her cell phone buzzed. It was Dolly, "Why didn't you call to tell me you were there? I was worried!"

Camille grabbed the phone from Connie, "Yes we're fine.

214

We're just getting settled, sorry about that," she said in one breath, then immediately said good-bye and hung up. Connie was sure she just hung up on their aunt. Connie redialed Dolly. She apologized for Camille, then told her aunt all about the rose garden, the house and the carrot muffins. The twins followed Earlene to an intriguing crescent stairway with black iron railing. Earlene climbed the stairs with no problem, but the girls struggled with their carts as they pulled and wrestled the wheels up the carpeted steps.

"You okay?" Earlene asked when she noticed Connie leaning against the wall.

"I just feel a little odd."

"That's just the house. It's a bit crooked on account of it bein' so old. The floors are a little off. The whole upstairs slants just a bit."

"Oh good," Camille replied, rolling her eyes, "I was beginning to think the lemonade was spiked."

"I opened the window to air it out. It might get a tad breezy, but you can close it whenever you want." Earlene looked around to see if she needed to do anything else to help them. "Y'all get settled and I'll come fetch you in a couple of hours." Connie gave her a hug before she hobbled out and closed the door behind her ignoring Camille.

"God..." Camille sighed while she walked around the room. "This place looks like Barbie threw up in here." Then she whined, "I'm gonna need something stiffer than lemonade to get me through tonight."

Connie pulled back the rose quilt on her bed, "This is inviting," she bounced on the mattress and laid down.

A loud knock on the bedroom door startled Connie from her nap. She looked over at Camille's bed. Her sister was sprawled across her bed, the purple sheet draped across her naked butt.

215

Earlene knocked again and yelled, "You two going to sleep all afternoon? Don't y'all want dinner?" She poked her head in the room. Camille stirred.

"Glad to see you made yourself comfortable. Come on you two, get up. I need help getting dinner ready." She rolled in a blue and white cart with two towels and bowls. "You can wash up in this. We don't have any plumbin' up here. Oh, and dress cool. It'll still be around eighty degrees tonight."

"Did you say, there's no plumbing up here?" Camille repeated. Connie scratched her head and looked at Earlene, "Why?"

"I never had a need for it, nor any of my guests. Now hurry along."

The girls made it down the stairs in matching beige cotton dresses, Camille's in eyelet and Connie's in soft cotton. The table was already set with lovely tea rose China, a tall vase of pink and white roses and pink basket weave placemats nestled on a pure white table cloth. All the silverware was piled in the middle of the table. "You want me to finish setting the table?" Connie yelled to Earlene.

"Sure, one of you finish that and the other come help me in here."

Camille grabbed the silverware from Connie, "Oh no you don't. You go help her in there. I can't deal being alone with her more than ten minutes."

"Fine." Connie trotted in to the kitchen and came face to face with the biggest ham she ever saw. For some reason when Earlene said the pig, she didn't realize it wasn't a roast pork but a ham. She got closer and saw the head with an apple in it. "Is this..." pointing to the head.

"The head is plastic, I just use it to look authentic,. The ham is from my neighbor's farm. They sugar cured it. It's really good."

Connie smiled when she noticed wine glasses lined up on a tray next to an ice bucket holding two bottles of white wine. "Camille will be glad to see that."

The counters of the steamy kitchen were covered with dishes full of vegetables, bowls of rice and baskets of corn. They were all standing in perfect order, ready to march into the dining room.

"Here," Earlene handed Connie a huge butcher's knife and a large fork, "Carve."

Having never carved anything, Connie quickly put down the knife, she explained that she was a city girl and couldn't possibly cut the ham in style.

"What style?" Earlene said, as she picked up the knife and fork, and began hacking the ham into chunks. "I never could get the feel for thin slices either."

The sound of a car crunching along the gravel road got Connie's attention. Camille looked out the window and watched a couple get out carrying a large box.

After a few minutes of muffled conversation, Camille and guests came into the kitchen. It was the guy they met on the plane with his wife! Connie recognized him immediately and Camille was already flirting with him with her eyes, all the while shooting knowing glances at Connie.

"Hello, Auntie Earlene," the woman drawled. "Here's your dessert, just like you asked."

"Oh," Earlene peeked into the box. "Just you wait until you taste Carlota's Lemon Velvet Cake,"

"Sorry," the woman said extending her hand to Connie, "Hello, I'm Carlota. Just call me Lotty. And this handsome creature is my brother, Beau." Connie glanced his way, he and Camille couldn't keep their eyes off of each other.

"Beau," she whined, "Where are your manners."

Suddenly, Beau broke his eye lock with Camille and headed to Connie, "I do apologize Ma'am," he took Connie's hand. "You were the lovely ladies on the plane. Weren't you?"

Connie had a feeling she was in for a long and tortuous night. Once Camille got a little wine in her, she was going to have to keep close tabs on her.

Beau and Lotty were a fun couple, a very close brother and sister relationship that complemented each other. Their stories about their early days at school with Palmer were adventurous. Earlene didn't know half the mischief the three of them got into. Stunts like stealing Palmer's grandfather's underwear were genius. Then he'd yell at his wife for losing them. Those kids concocted mischief that neither she nor Camille would have thought to do in fourth grade. Camille turned to Beau, "You three must have been rather bright to come up with half that stuff."

After dinner, Beau led Connie and Camille to the back porch while Earlene and Lotty prepared dessert. Nothing prepared them for the amazing show, the large screened in porch led to backyard that glistened in the sunset. It was lined with roses, forming a stunning path through an eight foot tall rose arch. As they strolled through the arch, an outdoor dining area was set for four.

"My goodness, Earlene did all this?"

"You betcha," Beau took both ladies by the arm and guided them down the path. The grass was soft, the tea roses fragrant with a warm breeze swaying by them. "Aunt Earlene and my father worked on this together. Her family inherited this farm from my great grandfather after the war, the Civil War. A soon as they were emancipated, they got all this."

"Her family were our family's slaves?"

"Yep, her family and two others. He gave it to all three families to divide it up the way they wanted. Earlene's family bought out the other two and ended up owning all of this."

218

The lawn extended almost a mile ahead. As they strolled, the path lights came on with approaching night fall. Earlene and Lotty carried trays of cake and iced tea.

"You'll love my sister's cake. The most lemony cake and filling you'll ever taste." He was right. The velvety lemon cake was just that, smooth.

Connie was surprised how the evening turned out to be a real kick. After Beau and Lotty left and the dishes were washed, Connie slipped on her soft cotton nightgown and laid in bed. She watched the gentle breeze move the curtains like the waves on the sea. Camille was in the other bed, snoring. She'd downed enough wine that evening to put a sailor to shame. Connie pulled the curtains aside to look out at the star-filled sky.

Her sleep pattern was already screwed up from jet lag. She deliberately drank only one glass of wine so she could be sure to keep her eye on Camille and Beau. Since she couldn't sleep, Connie took her pillow and crept downstairs. She went out onto the screened porch where she listened to the crickets and katydids talking to each other. She took a deep breath of the fragrant magnolias and roses that filled the night air, fluffed her pillow and stretched out on the settee.

"Well, here you are Miss Sleeping Beauty," Connie slowly opened one eye. It was daylight and Earlene was standing over her in a lavender sundress. "You going to sleep all day, girl? It'll be noon in a couple of hours, it's way past gettin' up time. We's havin' breakfast in the rose garden. Come along now."

Connie sat up, still in her nightgown. Bewildered, she remembered laying on the settee, cuddling up on the soft cushions and watching the stars. Suddenly it was daylight. She stood up, stretched and felt the shag rug between her toes. Camille appeared on the porch, balancing a cold cloth

219

on her head and a glass of orange juice in the other. She reached into her pocket and handed Connie the cell phone. "Here, you better call Aunt Dolly. My head hurts too much to think." The phone showed three calls from Dolly."

Connie stepped into the kitchen and asked where the faucet was. Earlene was glad to show her the pump mounted on the counter.

"You take this little cup of water here and pour it in the top of the pump like so." Earlene grabbed the long curved handle and gave it a couple of pumps up and down. Clear water began to gush forth into the sink. "There ya go, that's how you get water round these parts." Connie splashed water on her face then gave Earlene a kiss on the cheek before heading up the stairs to her room. She looked at herself in the mirror. Her nightgown looked like a summer dress. So rather than change, and since it was only the girls, she put on her slaps. She picked up the glass of orange juice Earlene has left on the vanity and called Dolly on her cell before she headed back down the stairs.

She followed the brick path through the rose arch. When Aunt Dolly finally picked up, Connie told her about Beau and dinner the night before. "We're fine, it's only jet lag. You don't need to come out here, we'll be leaving soon." Connie hesitated, "How are things going with my food deliveries?"

"Oh, I almost forgot. It went fine, and I made a few changes I think your people will like. I'll tell you when you get back."

Now Connie was worried!

The warm sun felt good on her face as she strolled to a spot surrounded by pink and white roses where Earlene had set a bistro table with chairs amid the wonderful fragrance of the roses.

"Howdie-doo you two. I hope you're hungry." Connie noticed a side table laid out with food. She noticed a fourth place setting at the table.

Earlene clapped her hands, "Well, look what the cat

dragged by," It was Beau. Camille quickly came to life and put on her biggest smile. Good thing she was wearing her sunglasses.

"Ladies," Beau did a slight bow then bent down to hug Earlene. He quickly went to Camille and kissed her hand. He then went to a completely embarrassed Connie who now wished she had changed clothes. She had no idea Earlene had invited a guest.

Beau sat across from Camille, "Y'all look beautiful in the morning light."

Camille peeked over the top of her sunglasses, batted her eyes and said softly, "I could arrange it to happen more often." Connie was already uncomfortable sitting in the middle of all this flirtatiousness when she felt something on her leg. She took a quick glance under the table and quickly snapped, "Before you get to excited, sister, you should know that's MY leg...Come on you guys, it's too early for this."

The night before, Beau was the perfect gentleman, paying equal attention to all the women, including his own sister. Connie remembered how comfortable she felt with the conversation and attention she got while remaining on guard for Camille's benefit. And this morning wasn't any different. He paid constant complements and included everyone in the conversation. It was Camille who turned the discussion sexual.

Before he left, Beau added an invitation for dinner that night at his place for all of them. Earlene declined graciously, as she had a meeting with her rose club, but insisted that they go. Camille pouted. She obviously wanted Beau to herself.

"He seems like a nice guy, a real southern gentleman. I like his sister, too. Neither one is bad looking. Honestly, Camille, you really need to tone it down with Beau. You're way too obvious."

Camille put her feet on the rattan coffee table. Connie was

ready for a huge argument. But Camille asked, "You think he's getting any?"

Stunned, Connie took a moment to refocus. "For God's sake, you just met the man!"

"Yeah, but he'd be a good one, especially since he's not married."

"Hold on. Anyone that good looking has to have a girlfriend in the woodwork someplace."

"Or," Camille pulled the cold cloth from forehead and turned to Connie, "he's getting some from his sister. I think those two are way too chummy for comfort. But then again, we are in the South." She gave Connie a little wink.

"Are you sure you're my biological sister? Sometimes I think you are just plain twisted."

Earlene dropped them by Beau's front gate on her way to the meeting, "It's just a short walk past the gate, girls." She pointed toward what looked like a forest. They looked back over their shoulders at her like they'd been dumped on the edge of nowhere.

Earlene handed Camille a covered plate. "Now, you tell them they're my famous spiced, nut corn fritters."

"Oh, good. We can use these for breadcrumbs." Camille quipped.

"Whatever would you do that for?" Earlene questioned.

"In case we get lost, y'know, like Hansel and Gretel."

Earlene let out a laugh, "Heaven's sake, the walk will do you two good after lying around all day.

Camille took Connie's arm and sang, "Oh, we're off to see the wizard..."

"Camille, grow up."

"Are you scared?"

"No, I'm just not used to being left by the side of the road a thousand miles from home. I guess you felt like that when Anna Lopez hauled you off to Guatemala."

"You're damn straight I did."

They walked for a few minutes through the tall willows until they came to a clearing and a huge mansion. "My word," Camille said with a bad southern accent and fanning herself with her hand. "I had no inkling they were so wealthy."

"Well, you have the vocabulary down but you're dripping way too much sugar."

Connie brushed away a cloud of gnats and continued until they came to a small white gate flanked by rose hedges. "Oh God, more roses." Two boys in shorts were riding their bikes in circles, laughing and screaming to hurry up. When one stopped, the other smashed into him. They looked about six and eight years old, little toe heads with freckles. They stood up, brushed themselves off and walked to Connie and Camille.

The older boy reached for Connie's hand, "My daddy said we are supposed to estort you to the house when y'all come."

Camille giggled and replied, "Of course, you may estort us."

"Come dith way, please."

The younger one took Camille's free hand. In the bay window of the house, Connie saw Lotty wave as the boys led them to the front door. Beau appeared on the porch and stood by the steps among the tall pillars. "Well, looks like you fine, young gentlemen found yourselves some lovely ladies."

"Ahem," Beau motioned toward the ground with his hand. Awkwardly, each bowed. "That was pretty good boys." Lotty looked at the two little guys and smiled, "We may just make gentlemen out of you yet. Now, go play but don't get all dirty. I'll call you for dinner real soon." The boys bolted

223

down the stairs and around the house.

Lotty took the plate of Earlene's well known spiced nut corn fritters and placed it on the table. Beau escorted them to the parlor where Mimosas were set out.

The house didn't look like it had changed since the 1920's. The wrought iron stairway looked like Earlene's. They had pressed tin ceiling decorations and fans turning lazily above their heads. Connie wondered if her place had been modernized or was a dinosaur like Earlene.

"I tell you," Lottie grinned, "my nephews are the greatest thing that ever happened to me."

Camille's revelation about the two of them made Connie stop and wonder.

"Look at her." Beau said, described his sister. "The glow in her eyes puts the sun to shame. When my wife died of cancer I thought it was the end of my life. I didn't know what to do with two wonderful little guys or how to begin to raise them. Jill was an amazing mother and wife," he explained with pain in his voice. "Then my beautiful sister stepped in, took us in and we were able to move on and still remain a family."

"So Lotty," Camille asked, "are you married?" shocking Connie with her bluntness.

Lotty froze and looked at Camille for a moment before putting her drink down, "I've been in several relationships," she confessed, "but none of them beats the satisfaction I receive being a full time Aunt to the boys."

A short lady with copper skin and large hazel eyes stepped into the room and announced that dinner was ready.

"Thank you, Suzette. Would you please call in the boys?"

Beau offered his arm to each one of the twins while Lotty showed them into the dining room, a long narrow room in apple green carpet and white walls. The boys ran into the room and stopped as soon as they saw the stern look of their father. They suddenly remembered how to act when they had company and they took their places by their chairs.

Camille spent much of dinner stealing flirty glances with Beau, although she managed to behave herself in front of the boys. Beau discussed his work as principal of the local high school, "I'm so thankful we don't have the problems you have in California, or even Savannah. But I'm sure it'll be coming to our little corner of the world soon enough."

"Now, let's not insult our guests, Beau." Lotty chided "They're from Los Angeles and I'm sure they love their city as we love ours."

"Always the diplomat," Beau toasted Lotty. "My apologies ladies, I didn't mean it the way it sounded. Large cities have their good points, what with exposure to different cultures and life styles. After all, we are a country of many mixtures. Unfortunately, the kids here don't get a wide variety of ethnic experiences." He paused, "I'm sorry for getting on my soapbox."

Suzette brought out a plate of something that smelled wonderful, "Hot Pickled Beef," Lotty announced. The plate had slivers of beef surrounded with spicy apple slices. Connie and Camille were picky eaters, but they decided to be polite and taste it. It was delightfully refreshing and tangy for a hot evening, and so were Earlene's spiced, nut corn fritters.

"Perhaps you can show me the property when we're finished." Camille leaned in Beau's direction. "I always like a stroll after dinner, don't you?"

His shy smile brought out dimples that caused Camille to grin broadly.

"I'm sure the boys would like a walk too," Lotty suggested. "They love going for walks with their daddy," she added. Camille smiled at the boys. Connie could tell Camille wasn't happy at all with Lotty's idea.

Lotty and Connie sat on the porch and enjoyed a glass of apricot brandy under the scented magnolia trees. "Do you know," Lotty mentioned, "that my grandfather owned a still and made this very brandy out back of the barn for years before he made it big in real estate?" Connie shook her head and took another sip, "We still enjoy this apricot brandy year round." As the sun dropped lower in the sky, the two women watched the strolling foursome shrink in the distance as they walked west.

"Beau was a broken man when he came here." Lotty wasn't holding her liquor well. "Jill was the love of his life. Those two little boys were confused and lonely, they missed their momma terribly. It's been two years and the three of them are just now getting back to normal." She then turned and looked Connie in the eye with an intensity she only saw in horror movies. "I don't want him to get hurt. Not now." Her voice was flat and chilly. "You better watch your sister or I may have to take care of her myself."§

"I can't control what my sister does." Connie answered. "And your brother is a grown man. He can take care of himself."

Without flinching a facial muscle she repeated, "Watch your sister. That's all I'm sayin'."

After Connie and Camille returned from dinner, the three women sat on the porch quietly, listening to the night sounds and watching the stars.

"See that haze?" Earlene pointed toward the valley. "It don't come often, but when it does it usually means a scorcher the next day."

Connie just blurted out, "You know we need to discuss Palmer's funeral." It needed to be said and avoiding it would do nothing to help. "Now that the murder investigation is over they'll release the body soon. You two need to make the decisions."

Camille shouted, "It's barely been a week. It's not over until it's over. How can you even think about that at a time like this?" She threw open the screen door and ran to the rose garden.

Earlene put her hand up, "Let her go, Connie. Your sister needs time to work through all of this. Just let her go and we'll discuss this in the morning. I'll make the decision on my own if I have to. He is my grandson, my blood."

Camille didn't come back in the house for some time. Connie had gone to bed. Rather than waiting and lecturing, she turned over and closed her eyes.

In the middle of the night, Connie was awakened by rustling noises from Camille's bed. "What happened?" A half asleep Connie rolled over and anchored herself on her elbows.

"Go back to sleep. Really, that woman needs to do something about the plumbing situation in this rattletrap of a house."

———

"Get up, get up you two." Earlene sprinkled water on their faces.

Camille moaned and swatted at the air.

Still in their nightgowns, Connie and Camille staggered down the stairs to the back porch and collapsed into the chairs half asleep.

Camille lifted her head, took a gulp of iced tea and munched on a biscuit. With one eye partially open, she stuck her finger in a bowl of warm goo beside her plate and put it in her mouth. "That's gravy!" she complained. "Shouldn't it be oatmeal or grits or something?

"You're supposed to put the gravy on the biscuits." Connie said.

"Yeah right." Camille was her old morning cranky self.

227

Connie sat up straight, put a biscuit on her plate and ladled some creamy country style sausage gravy over the top. "So you still think Beau is messing with his sister?"

Camille stared out the screen, "Not anymore," she turned her arm around and displayed two scratches on her shoulder.

Connie distinctly remembered her climbing into bed and covering herself up in the middle of the night. "Where did you go?"

Camille pointed out the window.

"Honestly, in Earlene's rose garden?"

Camille dragged her biscuit through the gravy and took a bite. "The guy's an animal. Hey, this biscuit and gravy thing tastes pretty good."

Connie couldn't keep her eyes open and napped on the porch. She looked out the screen at Earlene and Camille sitting in the rose garden. She strolled to the garden. "You slept late," Earlene looked at her watch, "Come sit, I saved you some lunch."

Camille told Connie that she wanted to leave for home that afternoon and had changed the tickets to the four o'clock flight. "Earlene helped me set it up." She winked at Connie. "I'm going for a walk, then I'll pack. You two enjoy the roses."

Earlene watched Camille walk briskly toward the back gate. "Your sister is anxious for the trial to get underway and move on. I can't blame her."

But Connie knew her sister. Like a teenager sneaking out of the house, she'd gone off to meet Beau for a roll in the grass or maybe the backseat of his car.

Earlene broke Connie's train of thought, "Come, let me show you my latest hybrid rose," Connie followed the little lady through her rose garden until they came to the most exquisitely formed rose she had ever seen.

"I've named it after Palmer," Earlene cupped a blossom in her hand and gently stroked the petals, "because it's pale pink color matches the sorrow in my heart. "I'm calling it, the My Son rose." She looked up from the flower, tears glistened on her dark cheeks, "Camille agreed we should have a service in Los Angeles as well as one here. Then we'll bury him in our family plot over in Savannah."

"I'll bet Palmer loved these roses. Why don't you bury him here?" Connie asked.

"Palmer? No not my Palmer. Roses are the only flower he couldn't smell, touch or even get near. When he was a child we found out he was violently allergic to roses. The doctors said he would never grow out of it either. Oh no, he wouldn't want to be anywhere near a rose, not even in death. I wouldn't even consider it."

"Really?" Connie was confused. "I had no idea he was so violently allergic. What would these beautiful flowers do to him if he touched one?

"Oh, he'd get a violent asthma attack from the pollen if he smelled the flower, and hives and red splotches on his skin if he even touched them. I couldn't have any of these around when he was here. "We almost lost him when he was ten. Nobody knew what was wrong until I finally took him to an allergist. I had to dig up all my prize winning roses. It tore me up but what could I do? I gave them to friends. Thank God they took good care and cultivated my lovely babies." Earlene squinted up at her in the midday sun, "Why are you so interested?"

"Just curious. I've known people with hay fever, but never a violent reaction like that to any one flower. It must be very rare."

Earlene answered, "That's exactly what those doctors told me. It was very rare, but my Palmer was stricken by it as surely as a toad will eat a bug. What a shame, and they smell so sweet."

Connie couldn't concentrate, folding and unfolding several shirts over and over again as she packed. Good thing Camille wasn't here. She didn't know what to think. She remembered Camille got many bouquets of flowers from Palmer, but never roses. She also remembered visiting his condo with Camille and his place was full of colorful artificial roses. She distinctly remembers him saying, "I like to have roses around, they were my grandmother's favorite flower." She didn't think much about it then but now, why would Palmer run the chance of a major asthma attack, hives or even worse by giving Camille a dozen roses when he proposed?

It didn't make sense, things weren't adding up. Connie looked out the window and saw Camille strolling toward the house. She had to ride next to her on the flight home, five hours, and wondered how she would bring this up.

Connie could still see the lovely red roses sitting in a vase on Camille's windowsill. The color of the rose did match the red in the rubies. How could Palmer have stood at the florist, looking at roses to find the perfect color to match the stones?

"You seem chipper this afternoon," Connie asked. "What's going on?"

"I miss Bradley and my friends at work. Earlene was right. The best thing for me is to move on and live my life."

On the way to the airport Camille was humming some song to herself while Earlene prattled on about the funeral plans. Connie committed to help with the L.A. funeral and promised to attend the service in Savannah. But when Earlene asked what Camille thought about her plans, she just shrugged.

At the airport, they exchanged hugs and kisses before leaving for home. Connie watched her sister the whole time they waited in the security line and at the gate wondering what she was thinking. Camille talked on the phone with her boss, reviewing something to do with work. Connie kept running Camille's story of the proposal through her mind, bended knee, a dozen red roses, ruby ring that may have been stolen centuries ago.

Camille was way too preoccupied planning her new life with Bradley and her work to notice Connie's confusion.

Connie tried every scenario to explain the roses and the ring but it all dead ended.

It seemed too macabre to even consider that her own sister could have had something to do with Palmer's death, but she needed to know the truth. The pieces of the story her sister told her didn't fit. Eerily, she found herself rubbing her wrist like Camille did. The things Camille said to her in the Guatemalan jail reminded her that her sister maybe capable of doing anything.

Their flight was finally called and Camille pushed through the crowd to her seat while Connie stayed in line and boarded when it was her turn.

"What took you so long? Did you go pee or what?" Camille already belted in the window seat reading a magazine, even though it was assigned to Connie. Connie ignored it and sat in the middle seat. Camille was quiet for the first hour, looking out the window while Connie rehearsed the details of the murder in her mind. Camille turned her head from the clouds, "I need to make a life for me and Bradley. That's going to be my priority... and I'm not going to get involved with anyone. I'm done with men. I need to be with Bradley and help him through this. I've been an absentee mother too long."

"How can you say that? You see him every week."

Camille shrugged.

231

"Tell me, what really happened to you in Guatemala? When we got you out, you were a totally different person. Were you raped?"

"Almost, but not by men. The women in prison were all smelly, short, black haired witches. They saw me and began to touch my hair. I didn't speak enough Spanish or whatever they were speaking, but I knew when a couple of them were making passes at me. That's why I made a scene and they put me in solitary confinement to get away from those Dikes." She looked blankly at the seat in front of her. "Not one male guard even gave me a second look. Just women. I couldn't believe I was not attractive to men... just women.

"So, how did screwing Beau help you?"

"You're smart," she laughed. "I needed to know that men found me attractive again. And Beau was just the one to do it." She smiled a big grin, closed her eyes and leaned her seat back. "You have no idea what you missed. He was good. I mean, this guy had stamina. You wouldn't..."

"Camille, that's enough. Everyone can hear you." Connie glanced at the elderly woman in the seat next to her. She must've heard everything, because she stiffened up and wouldn't make eye contact.

Camille looked over, "She probably can't hear well. I mean look at her, she's old." Connie peeked at the lady again and to her surprise saw a hearing aid in her ear.

"Sorry about my sister," Connie whispered, "a little too much pre-flight celebrating.

Camille hit Connie on the arm, "I'm not drunk."

"She doesn't know that!"

§ Chapter Thirteen

Background Information

Lotty was always told how pretty she was, not very smart, but pretty. Her mother focused her on looking perfect with make-up, hair and clothes.

She fell in love with a young boy two years older than her. He told her he loved her. At fourteen she was sent away for eight months so not to bring embarrassment upon the family. She gave birth to a little boy. Her parents made her give him up for adoption.

She came home riddled with shame. Again, her mother focused on her beauty rather on her inner strength. She swore off men, filled her loneliness with typing classes and volunteering at the Children's Clinic. Mother refused to allow her daughter to work in an office. It was beneath her.

Lotty was sent to finishing school in Atlanta where she learned to sit, walk and stand with grace and poise. When the class ended, she stayed in Atlanta against her mother's wishes and worked as a typist for the Children's Clinic she loved.

She met Jasper Smith when she was thirty-three. He was working as a registered nurse at the clinic where she volunteered. He was young, but mature. She was older and young at heart. He taught her how to play golf and tennis. She took him to bridge parties. They were best of friends and that slowly turned into love. He already had a small house ready for a wife and family, and she always wanted the traditional family life with a home, children and gardens.

Jasper and Lotty broke the news of their engagement to her delighted parents. Next was to meet his family and let them know of their engagement.

The Smith family was excited to meet Lotty anticipating

their engagement. They flew to Jacksonville for the weekend to meet the clan. The family gathering included dozens of people complete with aunts, uncles and cousins. It was perfect. The next morning...bad news. Jasper was the son Lotty gave up for adoption twenty years earlier. Horrified the man she fell in love with, and planned to marry, was her son.

Devastated, she returned home an emotional mess. A few months later she got the news her sister-in-law was dying of cancer. Lotty combated her depression by focusing on helping her brother and two young nephews deal with their dying mother and wife.

CHAPTER FOURTEEN

Connie's cell phone rang as she stepped off the plane. It was Marcello. She didn't want to see him now. "Connie, I need to see you tonight."

She let out a long sigh.

"Don't get your hopes up," he joked, "It's not a booty call."

"Hey!"

"We compared the Interpol picture and your cell phone picture." He was matter of fact, "it's the same ruby ring."

"Okay. Nine tonight, my place." Connie pushed the End button on her cell phone, but didn't feel relieved.

Camille and Connie found Dolly deep in thought standing by the airport curb. Once she saw them, she smiled.

The sisters got their luggage. With Dolly caught in the middle, they left arm in arm. "So how did the meal deliveries go?" Connie asked.

"Oh, just fine," Dolly light up. "I made a few changes I think your customer will like."

"Changes?"

"I made a banana loaf, put some extra spices in the mix and set their table for dinner. I think their house smelled and looked very inviting."

"Why?" Connie confused. "Why did you change what I told you?"

"I think a change would be good for them. Besides, it's important to keep them happy."

"But they were happy the way things were!"

"Well, they are even happier now."

Connie immediately checked her voice mail. Two of her customers thanked her for the bonus goodies and offered to pay an extra ten dollars for more loaves each week. She shook her head as she put her cell phone back in her purse. Leave it to Dolly to make it better.

They finally got to the parking garage when Dolly stopped in her tracks.

"I think we turn left here," after a few moments of silence. "Yes, here." She pulled the girls in a dead run, "Come on," she chided.

They walked the entire length of the aisle. "Now where did I put the car?" Dolly mumbled.

The girls waited patiently, leaning on one foot, then the other.

"We must have missed it." She pushed the lock button on her keychain remote as she meandered down each aisle... nothing. The girls followed patiently. Finally, after the third pass by, they flagged down a security vehicle.

"I think someone stole my car," Dolly said worried. Connie crunched her face. It was her work car.

"Are you sure you parked it here? There's a..." the security person began.

"She knows where she parked her car, Sir. She's not a mental case," Camille blurted out. "Help her find her car!"

"As I was trying to say, before I was so rudely interrupted..."

"I want your name," Camille insisted whipping out a pad and pencil, "What is it?"

"My name is Michael Morales. Be sure you spell it correctly

in your complaint letter," and then carefully spelled it for her, letter by letter.

Infuriated, Camille's face reddened.

Connie pushed her out of the way, "I'm sorry, sir. What were you about to say?"

"As I started twice already, we have two garages on opposite sides of the building exactly alike. Many people get confused with which one they parked at."

Dolly's eyes widened, "Of course, I remember a blue duck on the walls. This has an orange giraffe."

Connie apologized profusely, grabbed Camille's arm and darted after Dolly.

"Well, he didn't have to be so rude," Camille complained.

They dropped Camille off at her condo, first promising to get together for dinner the next night. With Dolly in the passenger's seat, Connie headed home, telling her all about the trip. "Earlene's roses were beautiful and the food was great. We met a nice brother and sister who are her neighbors".

Dolly didn't respond. She just looked straight ahead.

"Aunt Dolly, is something wrong?"

"I don't know. I think I may have done something stupid and I don't know what to do now." Connie got off the freeway and stopped at a park. She put her arm around Dolly's small shoulders, "Tell me, what happened?"

"I'm afraid I blew it for Camille and... maybe everyone."

Connie waited patiently for the dear old lady to catch her breath.

"That young man, Ricky, came to see me the day you two left for..."

"Oh, my God." Connie yelled "Did he hit you up for money while we were away?"

"He said he had proof that our Camille killed Palmer and if I didn't give him fifty-thousand dollars he would turn the video over to the police. Connie, could this be true? Could she have killed Palmer? How? She loved him, he proposed to her, she has a ring."

"Did you pay him?"

"I could only scrape together five-thousand dollars yesterday. I promised him the rest today. What if he doesn't come by to collect the rest? What if he lied to me and doesn't have a tape? What am I going to do?"

Connie assured her that she could take care of it and headed to her beach house. "What should we do?" Dolly continued, "Should we go to the police? Why would that Ricky say such a thing? If he tells the police his lies, Camille could get arrested and sent to the chair." Dolly was shaking. "What will happen to Bradley?"

"They don't use the chair anymore."Connie held her close. "Bradley can't think that his mother is a murderer. I can't let that happen to him."

Now Connie wondered if they should let Tony go down for Palmer's murder. The police had a pretty strong circumstantial case against him. If, in fact, her sister did this awful thing, should they let her think she got away with it? Connie couldn't focus. There was way too much going on in her head.

They found a note taped to Connie's front door, "Be back for the rest. R."

Tears filled Dolly's eyes, "I need to get the rest of the money or else..."

"Did you see this video?" Connie asked.

"No. But I can't take the chance he doesn't have it."

"So, how do you know he won't blackmail you again a year from now when he runs out of money? This could go on forever."

"I know, but I'll be dead and someone else can deal with it. I know, I'll start a trust fund…"

"You'll do no such thing. If we don't stop this now, an innocent person will get life in prison. Can you live with that on your conscience? And if the real killer gets away, they could do it again and again. How many more lives are you willing to gamble?"

Connie left a voice mail for Marcello to confirm he was coming at nine, "Sooner if you can. Something has come up."

With one hand on the phone and an eye on Dolly, she watched her aunt walk through the French doors and outside to practice her Tai Chi. She always said once she centers herself, she can focus better. Connie kept her in visual contact the entire time. Ricky was probably watching the house, like a weasel.

During her wait, Connie wrestled with the possibility of having to turn in her twin sister. "We can always change our minds," Dolly broke her meditation and turned to Connie. "And tell him something else."

Dolly was tearless and hardened. "Don't do this Connie, I beg you, don't do this. If the shoe was on the other foot, Camille wouldn't do this to you. I know she wouldn't."

Who knows what Camille would do, especially if there was a reward? Tony, after all. wasn't innocent. He was part of the baby stealing ring, too. But he didn't commit murder.

"If you do this for me I'll be sure she never does it again." Dolly insisted.

"How will you do that? And what will prevent her from killing us to shut us up?"

239

"Never," Dolly shouted at Connie, "She'd never kill me or you. What kind of a monster do you think I raised?"

Connie heard a car door close. "That's probably Marcello."

As Connie went to the door, "The kind of monster that kills for no reason," she muttered, "who lies and is willing to perjure me and you to save her own neck." She looked straight at her aunt, "You've got to either support what I tell Marcello or I'll do it alone."

Connie opened the front door. A man pushed her out of the way and slammed the door. It was Ricky. He had a gun.

He motioned to Dolly to move out of the way to separate the two of them. "You called Marcello. Stupid bitch."

He grabbed Dolly by the neck, his arm covering her face. He pulled her out the back door. "If you want to see her alive, change your story."

"You can't do this Ricky - Marcello will be here any minute."

"That may be too late," he snapped. "If you follow me, I'll kill her." He disappeared down the alley with Dolly.

Connie ran to the back gate in time to see a car speeding down the alley. She knew that by the time she could get her own car out of the garage, they'd be miles away.

Connie slumped down against the garage door with her head in her hands and wept, "Damn it, Camille, look what you did."

Ronnie, her neighbor, helped her up, "What is going on? Cars screeching down the alley and the police banging on your front door."

"Did you say the Police?" Her neighbor nodded. Connie ran through the house.

"Ricky got Aunt Dolly," she screamed, "He's going to kill her." She grabbed Marcello's arm. "Do something quick!"

A few moments later, Marcello returned with her neighbor.

Ronnie recounted he was lifting the garage door open when he had to step out of the way to let a car get by. "I thought it was odd that the car waited by Connie's garage. So I made a mental note of the license number, put my car in the garage and took out my trash. That's when I saw a man push an older woman into the back seat and get in. The driver threw a cigarette butt out the window, then raced down the alley." Marcello was taking notes as fast as he could. "I was about to check and see if everything was okay when I saw a police car drive up. I figured something was up. Then I heard Connie crying in the alley."

Ronnie smiled ear to ear and handed Marcello a small manila envelope. "One of them dropped a cigarette butt. I watch CSI, thought you'd want this."

"Any idea who the other man was or why Ricky would want Dolly?"

Connie shook her head.

After Ronnie left, two CSIs showed up and fingerprinted the door, then went back to the alley. They made a mess of the door jam and the back gate with the fingerprinting dust. Her house looked like a greasy auto repair shop.

Marcello pulled up a chair by Connie, "You want to tell me what this is all about?"

"Where do I begin? Everything's all screwed up."

"Start from the beginning, Connie. What happened leading up to this?"

Connie broke down and told him about the video Ricky said he had, the payoff Dolly gave him, the rest of the blackmail and how Dolly was afraid to call the police. "Believe me Marcello, I didn't know about the video until Aunt Dolly told me." She threw her arms up, "And I have no idea how Ricky knew I called you."

"What's with Camille's involvement with the murder? Do

241

you know what's on the video?"

"No, only that Ricky told Dolly it would prove Camille killed Palmer."

"Connie, if you want me to find Dolly. I need to know what happened. All of it."

"All I know is what she told me."

Marcello maintained eye contact and waited.

"Ricky says Camille killed Palmer."

Marcello waited.

"According to Palmer's Grandmother, the proposal didn't make any sense to me." Connie rubbed her wrist. "Earlene said Palmer was literally deathly allergic to roses, but Camille claims that Palmer gave her a bouquet of roses when he proposed. According the Earlene, his allergy has been a lifelong thing."

Connie watched the other police officers moving around the house and noticed them poking into all her drawers and cabinets, "Ricky didn't touch anything except Dolly and the doors." She commented to Marcello, "Besides, he was wearing canvas work gloves."

"Come down to headquarters. You'll be safe there while we track down the car Ricky was in."

"I'm exhausted. I just got back from the east coast today. It was a five-hour flight from Georgia, and I've got jet lag. All I want to do is sleep."

"Where's Camille? She's in danger, too."

Connie shook her head. "We took her home first."

"Her son and babysitter are in danger as well."

Connie listed all of Bradley's favorite restaurants and places he liked to go, as well as where Camille and Lisa take him.

242

Marcello took Connie to his house, "Stay here, you'll
be safe. The guest room has a lock. Call me on my cell
if anything comes up. I'll call you the minute we find
something. We have an APB out on Camille for her safety."

"What about what I told you about her...?" she stammered.

"Until I get proof, it's all BS from that Ricky character. As
far as I know, we have the killer locked up."

"And the roses?"

Marcello tossed a handgun on the dining table and left the
house.

Connie found the guest room. She flopped on the bed, put
the gun under her pillow and passed out. She didn't dream.
No twilight sleep. Just darkness.

———— —————

A female guard escorted Anna Lopez from her cell to an
interrogation room where Marcello and a uniformed policeman were waiting. Her bright orange jumpsuit reflected off
the dull cement walls when she entered.

"Gentlemen, to what do I owe this visit from such distin-
guished members of the police department? It's a bit late to
ask me for a date is it not, Detective Prado?"

Marcello ignored the comment and thanked her for meeting with them. It was past midnight and it was her choice to
accept the meeting. His mood changed to business. "Who is
Pico Moran?"

A smile slowly appeared on her lips, "Oh yes, Pico. Good
man. He never questioned anything that I requested of him.
He just did as he was instructed. He was in Guatemala with
me, but I suppose you weren't properly introduced. You
have my apologies for that breach of protocol. Why? Is he
here now?"

Marcello read from his note pad, "He's part of a kidnapping

earlier this evening, driving a car registered to you, Ms Lopez. A dark blue Mercedes, license number 5JOOAL. Can you think of any reason he would be driving your car?"

"Are you sure it is him?"

"I have DNA that says it's him"

"I've been incarcerated and without visitors since I got here, except for my dear attorney. That reminds me, she should be present for this. Would you please have someone contact her? You see," she swept her hand down her jumpsuit, "I am not in the position to give instructions to anyone. He must be taking orders from someone else."

"Like who, for instance?"

"Questions? Do I need my attorney?"

"I'll put in a good word for you and let your attorney know."

Anna shrugged.

"Who was Pico Moran taking orders from?"

"I haven't a clue. I know he doesn't possess the creative or abstract abilities to initiate an operation of this kind on his own. He's a good man, though."

Marcello's face didn't change, "Tell me about a young man named Ricky Row."

"Now there's a sweet young person, and rather attractive as well. He'd make a great male escort, if I was into that kind of business. But I don't engage in that. Never have." She squirmed around on the seat of her chair for a more comfortable position, never breaking eye contact with Marcello.

"Do you know Dolly Moorhead?"

"Oh yes, she's the aunt of those twins, Camille and her sister... what's her name, oh, Connie.. Palmer mentioned

244

them to me several times. He really liked Camille."

"Why was she taken?"

"Who, Camille? I would have no idea."

"Their aunt, Dolly Moorhead." Marcello was getting impatient.

"Really? What a shame. She seemed like a nice old lady according to Palmer. And you think Pico is doing it on his own? That would never occur."

"You're being very cooperative, Ms Lopez. Is there any reason why I should believe what you're telling me?"

Her smile turned seductive with an invitation that glowed from her eyes. That made him uncomfortable.

"He might be hiding out in a warehouse I used to own. It's empty now, or I think it's empty. I remember leasing it to a man, but I don't remember his name."

Marcello slid his note pad across the table. "Write the address to the place."

"If that's all you need," she winked jotting down the address. "I'm going back to my exquisitely appointed cell for some beauty sleep," she stood and left the room without once looking back or ending the conversation with her usual grace.

Marcello glanced up, the uniformed officer muttered, "Whew!"

"You got that right."

Marcello called the captain with the address Anna had given him, "I just talked with the Lopez woman. We need SWAT down there."

Marcello and a black and white pulled up to the warehouse. The sky was getting light. SWAT was already in position.

On Marcello's order, they slowly crept toward the big sliding doors and rushed in.

"Damn it!" Marcello threw his arms up as he looked around the huge empty space. It was absolutely clean except for an opaque black plastic tarp hanging from the ceiling across one corner. An officer of the SWAT team waved to Marcello and pointed toward the bottom of the tarp. A sliver of light peeked under the black plastic. Three of the SWAT team leveled their weapons at the corner while a fourth inched along the wall.

"HBPD, come out with your hands up."

Silence. No movement, nothing. The SWAT member by the wall slowly pulled back the plastic. Two dark skinned men in brown suits lay dead in a pool of blood. One was face down with a scalpel sticking out of his neck, eyes bulged from his head like hard boiled eggs. The other was on his back. A medical examining table jutted diagonally from the corner. Blood pooled beneath them.

A crime scene unit examined the bodies before they were sent to the Coroner. "The bodies are still warm. They both died less than four hours ago." Pointing at the one with the scalpel in his neck, "This one bled out maybe half his body weight." He stepped around the blood pool, "Looks like this one suffered massive blunt force to the back of his head. No matter how many times I've seen that," Jim continued, "I still get grossed out. How about you Detective?"

Marcello turned away from the gruesome corpse, "I believe the one with the scalpel in his neck is Pico Moran. I don't know who the other poor slob is."

Marcello was saved by his cell phone. It was the captain calling, "You'll never guess what just happened."

"Don't mess with me Sir, what's up?"

"Ricky and Dolly turned themselves in at a precinct down by the docks. I'm having them transported here. And don't worry, I'll go easy on the old lady."

"Nah, you don't have to, she's a tough old bird."

Marcello decided to let Connie sleep until he had more to tell her.

He returned to the interrogation room and observed how it was going.

The Captain pointed at the one-way glass, "Ricky gave a statement that he was coerced into kidnapping the Morehead woman. He said that it was better if he did the kidnapping than the two dead guys". Captain looked at Marcello, "Personally, I don't trust the little weasel."

The Captain continued, "He says that when they got to the warehouse it was pretty obvious your dead friends had torture or worse on the menu."

Marcello asked about Dolly, in the room next door. They looked through the glass at her, sitting alone, staring at her hands. She'd look around the room as if she was expecting Connie or Camille to walk in and take her home. The interrogator was writing. Captain recapped, "She said that when the opportunity presented itself, Ricky attacked the two goons and took them down. Afterward they went to the closest police station and turned themselves in."

Marcello turned up the volume so he could hear the exchange with the interrogating officer. Dolly explained, "I wanted to be sure it is clearly documented that we turned ourselves in and were not arrested or had to be found."

In the other room, the interrogator was pretty rough on Ricky but he held up and would not admit to murder. He claimed self-defense because he felt his and Dolly's lives were in imminent danger. He insisted that he was forced into the kidnapping. Then, he demanded to see a lawyer.

Marcello looked on as Ricky's questioning continued, "This interrogator is new, isn't he?"

"Yeah," The captain replied, "How'd you know?"

"Well, aside from the fact I don't recognize him, he's trying too hard to force a first-degree murder and kidnapping admission out of him."

Ricky looked at his questioner and relaxed with one arm over the chair back, "I just ate and peed, so I can last a couple of hours of this. And my story won't change. That's because this is the God's honest truth. Now I want a lawyer. I'm finished talking to you."

Ricky knew his rights and Marcello needed the DVD of Palmer's murder. He yanked the door open and stormed into the interview room.

"So it's you again," Ricky folded his arms. "I suppose you're the bad cop and you're here to break me? I want my lawyer."

"We're not calling your lawyer until you tell us where the DVD is."

"DVD? What kind of DVD?"

"Don't play with me, the video of Palmer Railton's murder. We know you have it. Where is it?"

"I have no idea what you are talking about."

"Dolly Moorhead and Connie Cane both told us you claim to have a video of the murder and tried to blackmail them with it. Where is it?" §

"You have been misinformed. I have no such DVD. Go ahead, search my place-search me."

"We are and we will." Marcello replied. "My people are at your place right now."

"One more thing so that I may get some brownie points," Ricky stared back at Marcello.

Ricky said, "I speak pretty good Spanish so I listened to those goons when they had me handcuffed," showing them his bruised wrists.

"They spoke about a ship or boat, I believe it was in Guatemala and about a baby," Ricky started.

"That's not news, we took care of that days ago. Don't waste my time."

"Oh, don't forget to call my damned lawyer." Ricky yelled after him and chuckled.

Marcello knew Ricky wouldn't cave, so he consulted with the Captain and called Ricky's attorney.

"Nice to see you again and so soon!" Janet Gleason had a tone of sarcasm.

Both of them reviewed the case against Ricky for Janet.

"Sounds like coercion to me." She shut the folder. "It screams self-defense all the way down the line. Especially if the old lady backs his story." She winked at Marcello, "He'll probably use the video as a bargaining tool to reduce his sentence. That is, if he has it. Maybe we can do it without his lawyer. Want me to talk to him first?"

She strolled into Ricky's room and took a seat across from him. His head was on the table. A glimpse of her legs as she walked by and a whiff of her subtle scent prompted him to sit up. But after ten minutes of getting nowhere, she left the room.

"Get his lawyer. I see this all the time. He's street-wise and he's playing us. If he says he doesn't have the DVD, you won't find it until he is ready to give it up. In the meantime, you may lose valuable time. He got the other kidnap victim to verify he was an innocent victim. Without her testimony against him, you'll get nothing and… no conviction."

§ Chapter Fourteen

Background Information

Camille always knew how to manipulate people. Her biggest asset was how to read people and figure out what they wanted.

She had her father and mother wrapped around her finger, Uncle Harold did anything she wanted.

In school she knew how to work the classroom and teacher. Her principals, male or female, liked her and made her a priority when planning events.

"She has no shame," as one of their scout leaders put it. She saw right through Camille and made her toe the line. It was a rough scout year for Camille since Connie out shined her in all of the activities.

Connie always thought Camille was cheating on tests and sleeping with, or blackmailing the professors in college. She never studied, partied constantly, but made straight A's.

Aunt Dolly tried to be fair with both girls, yet Camille was always a handful. Uncle Harold and Aunt Dolly fought constantly over her, giving Camille the upper hand with her Uncle Harold. After all, Uncle had a mind of his own and saw fit to make his own decisions.

CHAPTER FIFTEEN

"Who are you supposed to be?" Ricky asked when a young, pregnant woman eased herself down in the chair next to him and fanned herself with his file folder.

"I'm Tiffany Smythe, your attorney."

Where's Mike?"

"He refused to work with you any further. He called the public defender's office and they sent me."

"What, are you right out of high school?" He shouted at the glass, "This is my life, can't I get a real lawyer?"

She kept rubbing her large tummy hidden under a billowing brown maternity dress. "Hey wise guy, I'm all you got, so be nice to me. Oooh, jeez, it's warm in here."

Ricky folded his arms and looked at the ceiling.

"I've looked at your file, Mr. Row, and I'd advise you to stick to your story of self defense."

"I didn't do anything wrong. That's why I turned myself in."

"What's this about a missing DVD purporting to show the commission of a murder?"

Ricky was silent for a moment. He knew Mrs. Smythe and the DVD were his only chance to stay out of jail. He explained that he had the video hidden, and he knew what was on it. He also insisted that he only be charged with withholding evidence. That was all he'd agree to.

Tiffany told the police and Janet, "Withholding evidence is the only thing he will agree to."

251

"Listen Tiffany..." Janet stopped abruptly, "Mrs. Smythe," she immediately corrected.

"Are you sure he has the DVD?" Captain asked.

She nodded.

"And are they accessible?" Janet added.

"He says he does and you can get your hands on them in less than thirty minutes. I believe him. Why would he lie when the stakes are so high?"

Janet Gleason was about to push for jail time, when Tiffany's cell phone rang, "Excuse me, I have to take this," and walked a couple steps away to answer the call. "It's under the sink," she mumbled, "where it always is. I'm in a meeting. I told you I'll get the tacos on the way home."

Her face turned beet red. "I'm sorry. My husband is home alone with the kids and doesn't know where anything is. Men!"

Janet chuckled, "How many kids do you have?"

"This is my fourth." She patted her tummy again, "I'm sure he's going to be a football player. He'll have to be with three sisters bugging him. You know..."

The Captain interrupted, "May we get back to the issues at hand ladies?"

"Sorry," Janet turned to Marcello "Do you feel you can get him the deal he wants?"

"No way," The captain insisted, "We are making too many concessions with this case as it is. Absolutely not."

"Call me when you want the DVD bad enough," Mrs. Smythe insisted, "I'll be waiting. By the way," caressing her rounded tummy, "I'm due next month, I wouldn't wait too long."

She slowly lifted herself off the chair and waddled to the door. Marcello blocked her way with his large frame.

"Mrs. Smythe, can you please talk to him? We have a woman who is key to this case. She's missing and in danger. We need to find her and the DVD."

"He's a sharp boy, he knows you're desperate and he's not happy about the way you blew him off. He won't budge. Meet his demands or you get nothing. Quite frankly," she stared at the Captain, "he can hold out longer than you can."

"Please," Marcello added. "We're just trying to get to the truth."

"Give him something or I'm going home."

Janet walked her out, signaling for the men to stay put. Then she poked her head in, "Do you know the closest place she can get a bag of tacos?"

Now it was Dolly's turn. She verified Ricky's story about the kidnappers and a baby being thrown off the ship a week ago or so. "I know a little Spanish," but Dolly was badly shaken. "I never had children of my own. How can someone willingly toss a defenseless child overboard? Even if it is to keep from being arrested? How?"

Marcello ran to catch Ricky and his attorney in the hallway. "We need to talk," and pushed him back in the room.

"Tell me what those goons said about the baby."

"And waste your time? Why should I?" Ricky folded his arms.

Marcello grabbed Ricky by the collar and threw him against the wall. "Start spilling it."

His lawyer screamed down the hall, "Emergency, 911,"

while aiming her cell phone at them. Officers rushed in to see Marcello holding Ricky against the wall and pulled him off.

"You are all witnesses to his incident and can be ordered to testify." She pushed several buttons before the phone was grabbed form her hand. "Too late, it's already been sent to the ACLU." She smiled at Marcello and the Captain, "Ball's in your court."

After several hours of heavy duty negotiations and the Captain yelling at Marcello, Mrs. Smythe poked her head in the office. "He's ready to talk but only if he gets community service for withholding information. All the other charges get dropped." Gleason and the Captain agreed only if Ricky dropped any charges of police brutality.

Ricky refused to talk with Marcello in the room. He repeated what he heard from the kidnappers, "The baby was taken out of Guatemala by ship. A Coast Guard cutter approached the ship to inspect it. One of the men threw the baby off the ship with all its bags. If it's worth anything, the two men felt badly about it." He looked at the two way mirror. "You may want to inform that Prado idiot of that. It might make him feel better."

In the other room, Dolly turned to the two-way window, tapped on the glass and called out, "Hello? Anybody? Can I go now? She opened the door and peeked out just in time to see Marcello walk by. "My legs hurt from sitting in this hard chair."

Marcello took her out and walked her up and down the hallway, holding her arm as they went. "I wish I could help you with Camille," Dolly couldn't hide the disquiet in her voice. "But I don't know where she is and I'm worried harm has come to her again."

They walked in silence for two lengths of the corridor.

"Dolly, we are trying to find Camille. If you know anything you have to tell us."

"That's the problem, I don't know anything. Just about the DVD Ricky says he has. I don't know what's what."

After they returned to the interview room, Dolly verified that Ricky was forced to kidnap her. His gun wasn't loaded, the guy in the front seat had a knife and held a loaded gun on Ricky the whole time.

"I was so scared at that warehouse." Dolly waved her hand, "I managed to distract those two hooligans for just a second, but it was long enough for Ricky to grab a scalpel off the table and jab it in one guy's neck. Oooh, it was awful. The blood spurted all over like a fountain. I jumped the other from behind. I hugged his neck, wrapped my legs around him and held on for dear life. He tried to shake me off, but Ricky hit him in the head with a pipe. I stayed on top of him until his knees buckled." She pulled her sleeve up and showed Marcello the bruises she had on her arms. "I'd show you the ones on my back, but it wouldn't be proper."

Marcello smiled and patted her hand.

"It was wild, really wild. It was just like in the movies, everything went so fast."

Marcello sat her back in the chair. "Then Ricky hustled me out of there to a restaurant down the street. But it was my idea to go to a police station and turn ourselves in."

She sat up proudly, "I saw it on a talk show, how police are mean to suspects when they have to chase them and I wanted everything to be above board. Ricky was an innocent victim in this whole kidnap thing, like I was."

Marcello called Connie, but no answer. He zoomed to his house hoping she had stayed put.

Marcello snuck into his own place and stood outside the guest room not sure how to break the news to Connie. He tapped on the door. "Connie," he called then tapped again. Suddenly dread overwhelmed him. Did they find her too?

He slowly opened the door and saw her outline from the hall light. He walked to the bed and clicked the light on the nightstand.

"Connie," he nudged the bed. She propped herself up on her elbows.

"Any news?"

Her golden hair crisscrossed her forehead and cascaded down her neck.

"We've got Dolly, she's fine. Come, I'll take you to her," and held out his hand. She sat on the side of the bed to get her bearings, as he sat beside her.

"I'm so tired of this mess. When will it end?"

"Soon, hon..., soon." He almost called her honey. It had been a long time since he called a woman by that name. It almost slipped out.

The Captain and DA agreed to Ricky's terms.

Ricky wrote down the address to a twenty-four hour workout place. "And the locker?" Marcello pressed for more.

Ricky looked at Ms Smythe.

"Can I insist on showing them or should I let them spend hours looking for the locker.

"Well gentlemen," Ms Smythe asked, "you want to take him for a ride? No pun intended."

They escorted him without handcuffs to the workout place and into the locker room. Ricky reached on top of the lockers and pulled down a magnet. Then he got on his knees, held the magnet on the cement floor and waved it.

Out came a metal key and attached itself to the magnet.

"Okay, here's the key to the locker 22A. Have at it," and tossed it to a uniformed cop avoiding Marcello

"Okay, we got it," the officer held up the DVD.

Connie waited with Dolly to hear if they had any news of Camille.

Marcello walked in, "We have new evidence. It seems Tony is indeed innocent of the murder. Do you know where Camille is?"

Both were silent, "You mean, you think she killed Palmer?" Dolly asked

"I have no idea. She doesn't confide in me every minute of the day," Connie irritated with Marcello said. "You find her. It's your job."

"Don't look at me," Dolly insisted. "Besides, I know Camille wouldn't kill anyone, especially someone she loved so deeply. She and Palmer were very happy."

Marcello ushered them into his office and turned his laptop so the screen faced Dolly, "No one should have to see something like this. I'm sorry." Marcello pressed the space bar and an image went into motion.

Dolly watched Palmer open the door as Camille entered. She immediately pulled out a gun, pointed it directly at Palmer's chest and shot him twice. Palmer fell backward onto the floor like a rag doll. Tears poured from Dolly's eyes as Camille picked the ring box up from the table, opened it and put the ring on her finger before tossing the empty box on the floor.

A red spot on Palmer's chest quickly grew to cover his shirt.

"I don't understand." Dolly cried, "This can't be real."

Camille paused for a moment and looked down at Palmer's body, then turned and walked out the front door. The video continued to run.

"Who is that?" Dolly asked.

A man crouched down and touched Palmer's chest. Marcello paused the video.

"That, Ms Moorhead, is Tony Dillon. We have him in custody for Palmer's murder." When Marcello started the video again, Tony went to the front door and looked around. He then went back inside the house, and ran out of the apartment with a large bag.

Marcello paused the video.

Dolly was speechless. She pulled several tissues out of the box on the desk and wept.

Connie slammed her hand on the table, making the stilled video image shake. "God damn it Camille! We trusted you."

"Have you been in contact with Camille?" Marcello asked. "Either of you?"

Dolly sat back with her arms folded, "You know where I've been."

Marcello looked at Connie. She couldn't tell him the truth in front of Dolly and shook her head.

"The longer you two prolong this, the worse it will be for both of you. We need to find her before anyone else does. For her own safety, where is she?"

"Connie, honey, if you know where she is, tell him," Dolly pleaded, "I'm sure there's an explanation for this. We need to hear it from her."

Connie bit her lip and looked at Dolly for some kind of support. Dolly's red eyes said it all.

"I never thought I'd be put in a position like this. Did you Aunt Dolly?"

Her aunt slowly shook her head and stroked Connie's cheek, "I feel so foolish."

After a couple of deep breaths, Connie stared at the floor, "She told me she planned to work for a few hours with her boss at his place after she had dinner with Bradley and Lisa. Camille has a close work relationship with her boss."

Dolly proudly added, "She has always been dedicated to her work. That's why she is so much in demand at the court-house."

"Auntie," Connie couldn't hold it back anymore. "How in the world can you be so proud of Camille when it's obvious she killed Palmer and was willing to blame an innocent man?"

Marcello picked up his laptop. "You two are free to go," leaving Dolly and Connie to argue.

"Let's go home, it's been too long a day and night," Dolly looked at her watch and did a quick calculation in her head, "We can make the next boat to Catalina. I've been such an old fool!"

They stared off toward the horizon and were silent most of the way to Avalon. Dolly felt like a spider that has lost her web, the only web she ever knew.

The day had finally come when Connie couldn't pull Camille's ass out of the fire. All the reasons that flooded Connie's mind of how she shouldn't have been suspicious of her sister faded into the word "betrayal."

As they walked the hill to Dolly's house, Connie looked up at the sky. To her, even the palm trees seemed sad with their fronds drooping toward the earth. Nothing would ever be the same. For decades to come, Connie knew she and Dolly were in uncharted waters of change.

"You know," Dolly said, as she opened the front door, "Camille couldn't have killed Palmer, there has to be a simple explanation to all this. Maybe Ricky spliced the video to make it appear she killed him. I mean Palmer must have recorded hours and hours of Camille. No, I wouldn't put it past him. After all, he did try to blackmail me."

"Remember, he also saved your life at the warehouse, unless what you told the police happened to you there was wrong."

"Everything happened as I said. I wouldn't lie about that." Dolly sat on the couch. "He rescued me from those thugs."

"It's nice of you two to join me," Camille leaned in the doorway from the dining room. "It sure took you guys long enough to get here."

Connie jumped to her feet, "What the hell are you doing here? The police are looking for you and you told me you were going to work late tonight."

"So? And why would the police be looking for me?"

"Girls stop it. We have bigger problems. You two don't need to squabble." Dolly rose slowly from the couch and pointed a finger at Camille.

"Cut the bullshit, Camille. We've both seen the video from Palmer's condo. We know what you did. Did you know about the video?"

Camille took Dolly's hand, "Please help me. My boss said that if I can get to Mexico, he'd help me start over there. Please help me. I promise I'll never bug you again. I had dinner with Lisa and Bradley. I tried moving money from my account, but it's frozen."

Connie and Dolly were numb. They couldn't believe what she was saying.

"I suspected they eventually would find the video. I only found out about it when Marcello told me. That's why I stayed so close to the case."

"And what about Bradley, your son? Remember him?" Dolly interrupted, "How do you think he will handle this, knowing his mother was a murderer who skipped out on him without saying good-bye?"

"I promise I'll send for him once I get settled. I promise. I don't want him to think I abandoned him, but right now I have no choice. The police are watching Lisa, Dale and Bradley. I had no place else to go."

"I don't think much of your promises anymore," Connie added, "Everything has been a big lie...everything."

"Don't do this to Bradley," Dolly cried, "He loves you, honey."

"I already feel awful, Auntie. Don't guilt me into turning myself in, please. Just get me to Tijuana. I'll take it from there. You won't have to worry about me ever again." She looked at Connie.

"I'm not helping you this time, sister. Help yourself, turn yourself in. You killed Palmer and were ready to let someone else pay for what you did."

"Tony was stealing babies!

"He wasn't innocent of that, but he didn't kill anyone in cold blood."

"Don't you understand? Palmer was with another woman and he flaunted it in front of me," Camille cried. "He told me he loved me. He asked me to marry him for God's sake." She wiped the tears that flooded her eyes. "I was to meet him at his place... or that's what he told me. All the while she was in the apartment."

Dolly looked at her with disbelief on her face, "So you killed him for two timing you?"

"No!" Camille sat on the couch, rubbing her wrist.

"I killed him for lying to me. For giving me a dream to look forward to, of finally having my own family, Palmer, Bradley and me. One family all together as one. That's why I killed him. He stole my dream."

Connie wanted to throw her arms around Camille. She felt the pain that chopped her heart into hamburger. Palmer should not have promised her the moon. Having someone break your heart and step on your dreams would throw any woman over the edge. But killing him in cold blood?

Dolly sat down, put her arms around Camille and rocked her. It was a scene Connie wanted to be a part of it. Instead, she left the room.

Within a few minutes, two LA County Sheriff's deputies were at the door. They found Camille curled up in Dolly's arms. "Camille Brewster, you're under arrest for the murder of Palmer Railton. Stand up."

Tearfully, Dolly looked up at them, "Gregory," Dolly exclaimed. "How can you do this to Camille?" She looked at the other deputy, "And Peter, you've known Camille since third grade. Put those handcuffs away. You two used to play in the mud together."

"Sorry, Ms Dolly. We have to put the handcuffs on her, it's procedure."

Camille stood without a word and stared at the floor as her two childhood friends pulled her arms around her back and handcuffed her. When they asked her if she had weapons on her she just shook her head without looking up. As the deputies led her toward the front door, she glared at Connie standing in the hallway, cell phone still clutched in her hand. It hurt Connie not to be able to put her arm around her aunt and tell her everything would be all right, like she'd done countless times before when Camille was in trouble. Connie couldn't say those words. Not this time.

Marcello scheduled Ricky's community service for one month, "Probation is a lot easier than jail time," Marcello closed his folder.

"You don't like me and I don't much care for you," Ricky immediately added, "I screwed you out of a conviction. That only proves who's more cunning."

"So how did you get the DVD?"

Ms Smythe put her hand on his shoulder, "Off the record?"

Marcello nodded.

"I said off the record. Affirmative?" Ms Smythe insisted.

"Off the record," he put his pen down and sat back.

"I was in the upstairs bedroom when I heard Palmer and Tony talking about the ring. Tony went into the back room. I went to the top of the stairs about to tell Palmer I was there and the door bell rang. It was Mickey, wanting him to play catch. Palmer declined.

"Then the door bell rang again. He answered it and it was Camille." He was quiet for a few moments, his eyes lowered. "I saw her shoot Palmer, point blank. I couldn't believe it. "

"Then Tony came in and checked out his body. He went back into the back room and ran out the front door." He put his face in his hands.

"I got my bearings and decided the video would be worth something to someone. So I turned off the camera and took out the DVD."

"I went down the stairs and saw Palmer. He looked so confused and lost. I said 'Palmer?' and nudged him. He was gone. I made the sign of the cross, tossed a twenty-dollar bill I owed him and left. I always pay my debts."

Marcello stood, "We're done here."

Just outside the door, Ricky stopped, "How's Ms Dolly?"

"Yeah, like you care, duping her out of five thousand dollars."

"Surprisingly enough, I do care about her..."

"A bit old for you buddy, don't you think.?"

"Your heads been in the gutter way too long," Ricky smirked, "No wonder you're a lonely SOB."

"Leave that nice lady and her family alone. You've done enough damage to them."

Ricky leaned forward for a comeback but stopped before he could formulate his words.

Camille slouched in her chair as Marcello watched her from the observation room. He was heartbroken. He knew now that she'd used him to avoid suspicion.

"Shame," he said softly to the glass, "I really did care for you."

The Captain pushed the door open, "Prado, what you're doing in here? You're supposed to go in and talk to her. You ready?"

Marcello put his hands in his pockets, "I'll get right to it," and headed to his office for his laptop. Part of him wished he'd never found the incriminating DVD.

Camille's familiar smile sparkled when he stepped into the interview room. "Marcello, I was hoping you'd be here. Thank you for making them take the handcuffs off me."

"Sure, whatever." He sat across from her and opened his computer. "I don't get it Camille - you? Why?"

She shifted in her chair, undid the top two buttons of her blouse and leaned forward, "He was cheating on me with some tall, redheaded bitch. He asked me to marry him and I guess I just freaked. But to be perfectly honest, I don't really remember the incident. It was like an out-of-body experience. When I saw the ring, I knew it had to be my engagement ring. It was mine, so I took it. There was no way he knew it was hot. He'd never do that to me. A stolen engagement ring? Gimme a break."

Marcello showed her a picture of the ruby ring, "Is this the ring you took?"

She glanced at the picture, "You know it is."

"So you shot him over the ring?"

"Don't you understand? I loved Palmer."

Marcello opened his laptop and pushed the buttons.

She watched, emotionless, at the images on the screen.

Afterward she sat up, letting a smug grin escape her lips. "Ricky, he set this whole thing up. I'll bet he edited the video to make it look like I was alone in this."

"Why would Ricky want Palmer Railton dead?"

"Jealousy." She waved her arm in the air, "Ricky realized that Palmer wanted me, not him. He knew about my relationship with Palmer and he couldn't stand the fact I was getting all Palmer's attention. Ricky's the one who told me that Palmer was cheating on me. I went there to have it out with him when I saw the redhead. Ricky set it up so I would be there when big red was there. I guess he knew I'd lose it. But kill him? No way. Ricky did it and made it look like I did it."

"I understand he gave you roses?"

Camille closed her eyes and took a deep breath. "I made that part up. I stopped at a flower shop and bought the roses myself.

She wiped her eyes, but there were no tears. "Ricky did something to the DVD. I wasn't alone."

The Captain came into the room with a uniformed female officer, "We've already checked out the DVD. It's the original - unedited right down to the time coding at the bottom. There is no evidence that the DVD was tampered with. We've even matched the video serial codes to Palmer's video camera. It's definitely an original," He tossed a folder on the table.

Marcello turned his laptop around and explained again how Palmer had a security camera in his condo. Camille frowned and hunched against the table. Marcello pressed the key that set the image moving again as he'd already done half a dozen times.

Camille watched again, massaging her wrist through the scene. She pushed the key herself to stop it.

"Camille, that redhead was Tony Dillon dressed as a woman. He and Palmer were about to celebrate a successful baby theft transaction. That ruby ring was collateral until Anna Lopez could get them the cash she promised them. There was no other woman and the ring wasn't yours. Railton was planning to return it to Lopez."

He fast-forwarded to show a wigless Tony passing in front of the camera. "Palmer Railton died from a gunshot wound to the heart. He probably never felt it. Death was instantaneous."

Camille's eyes turned stone cold. "You can't believe I was the only one in on this. Connie encouraged me and even helped me plan this. She didn't like Palmer. She was jealous I was getting married for the second time, and she couldn't even find one guy to propose... and Aunt Dolly was planning to get me out of the country, to Mexico until those deputies showed up. It wasn't all me."

Marcello could hear the desperation in her voice, like an animal backed into a corner. He saw that she was ready to do whatever it took to get out from under this charge.

"You'll give up anyone to save your sorry ass. Won't you?"

"If I go down for this," she said slowly, articulating every word. "I'm going to take the rest of them down with me."

Marcello opened the folder and examined the report and pictures. "See these lines," Marcello pulled out the pictures. "They match exactly to the lines from a sample of video taken from the camera."

Camille stared at the pictures with lines across the page. There was no doubt.

"You want to book her or shall I have her do it?" The Captain pointed his thumb to the female officer.

"I don't know about Palmer, but your sister and aunt love you. In all my years in law enforcement, I've never seen anyone put themselves in the danger that they did just to help you. That was the closest I've ever seen unconditional love between family members, and you try to implicate them? The sister who literally took a bullet for you?"

Marcello asked, "Where did you get the gun?"

She shook her head.

The Captain leaned over her, "Where did you get the gun?"

"Palmer gave it to me. He was concerned that I would have problems with some of his fans or those against his special interest groups."

"And where did he get the gun?"

"Central America, I guess."

"Where is it now?" The Captain hovered over her.

She folded her arms and leaned back. "I put it in a brown paper bag and threw it in a dumpster behind a grocery store."

Marcello stood up and left the room.

Camille twisted around in her chair and yelled after him, "I didn't do this alone."

He stopped at the door, "I'm afraid you did," and left.§

"You know, this is just like Guatemala," she told the Captain. "They left me to the wolves down there and they're doing it again to me here."

After the interview was over, the female officer handcuffed Camille and took her to her cell.

Marcello watched the entire thing from the observation room with Janet Gleason by his side, "She hasn't a clue, does she?" Janet looked at Marcello. He shook his head.

"Well, I'm done here. Call me if you need me." Janet said with a light touch on his shoulder. He nodded and stared at the floor.

When Marcello finally left the dark stuffy room, he bumped into Connie and Dolly with their arms around each other, crying. He sat next to them explained, "She'll be held until arraignment, probably for forty-eight hours. Then she will appear in front of a judge." He didn't have the heart to tell them she tried to sell them out for her sake.

The officer escorted Camille past Ricky, standing next to his expectant lawyer. They stared at each other as she walked by. Then she came across Dolly and Connie. Both stood, not sure what to say or do. Marcello stood by.

"I'll get you someday, sister. You will pay for setting me up like this."

§ Chapter Fifteen

Background Information

Camille had parked her car down the street and walked around the park to Palmer's place, anticipating what Palmer wanted to talk to her about. She was early and planned to make dinner ahead of time to surprise him and celebrate.

Her dream would finally come true.

She stopped short, just around the corner. She saw Palmer hugging a tall red head then walked arm in arm to his apartment.

She crouched behind a tree devastated...heartbroken. Betrayed! "How could he do this to me?" All of her dreams of a complete family, raising Bradley with Palmer, burst. "Why?" she asked over and over.

She looked up at a park scene. Parents were running after their kids and playing Frisbee. That is what she planned... all of it!

She slowly and deliberately walked to her car, took the Beretta 32 out of the glove box and slipped it into her purse. She got out of the car and closed the door. She locked it and walked, in a trance. taking short steps along the way. She found herself at Palmer's door staring at the little window. She hesitated, then her hand slowly moved to the doorbell. Once she started, the universe was set in motion and nothing could stop it.

As soon as the door cracked, Palmer smiled, "Well this is a ..." she pulled out the gun. Her finger pulled the trigger twice. The universe came to a screeching halt.

She put the gun away and looked at him as he stared at her through the glass table. The ring box was sitting on the table. She opened the box, took the ring and tossed the box.

269

She ran through the plant filled patio, down the street, around the corner and into her car.

She rolled the gun in a brown paper bag and tossed it into a dumpster behind a market.

The End

Made in the USA
Lexington, KY
25 April 2017